Praise for
The Losers' Club

"Reading Richard Perez's THE LOSERS' CLUB was a revelation to me. It is a novel by turns funny, poignant, and illuminating, perfect in its portraits of both the East Village scene of the mid '90s and the often desperate personal ads subculture in New York City. Yet it is much more than a fictionalized social document. Beneath Perez's dead-on descriptions of downtown clubs and bars and of the people who patronized them is a sense of deep longing for what has been lost—and for what may never be had. Perez's is an exciting talent and his work goes far beyond most of what is published today."

—Henry Flesh,
Lambda Literary Award-winning author of *Michael* and *Massage*

"Richard Perez is a clear-eyed chronicler of the New York club scene and a compassionate observer of the lives lived in the carnival at the center of the world.
He is a sociologist and a historian, telling the truth about the way we live now.
He's funny, honest, and compassionate.
We can only hope that *The Losers' Club* is but the first act in Richard Perez's Human Comedy."

—John Dufresne,
Louisiana Power & Light, Love Warps the Mind a Little

"Each year brings new and talented young writers to the literary scene. This year Rich Perez is one of them."

—Shirley Ann Grau,
The Keepers of the House
Pulitzer Prize Winner

"Richard Perez has the ears of the angels—lend him yours."

—Barry Gifford,
Wild At Heart

"*The Losers' Club* evokes a real and genuine sense of place—the world of the East Village—and people—single, young and desperate—written with zest, energy and enthusiasm."

—Tama Janowitz,
Slaves of New York, A Certain Age

"I couldn't put it down. It's a brave book with a great deal of heart."

—Poppy Z. Brite,
Lost Souls, Drawing Blood

"An interesting and affecting first novel."

—Oscar Hijuelos,
The Mambo Kings Play Songs of Love
Pulitzer Prize Winner

"*The Losers' Club* is a fine novel.
Richard Perez has a wonderful eye for details
and the humor to be found in urban decay.
It is a book to be savored."

—Tim Sandlin,
Sorrow Floats, Social Blunders

"This is a story of youth, very well told, and it dwells in the mind long after a reader finishes it."

—Joanne Greenberg,
I Never Promised You a Rose Garden

"*The Losers' Club* gives a complete panoramic view of the downtown New York scene, and along with all its flamboyant extremes... this novel has an appealingly old fashioned love story at its core."

—Madison Smartt Bell,
All Souls' Rising, Ten Indians

"Every generation must describe for itself what it means to be a young writer or artist struggling with anonymity and a mountain of rejection slips in a city like New York. Richard Perez's *The Losers' Club* tracks the poet Martin Sierra's melancholy and yet somehow humorous and hopeful life with an acid, yet not unsympathetic, pen. Perez has written a sharp, quick-paced satire of the personal ads subculture and the generally doomed semi-relationships it leads to, the bizarre and manic club life, where slam-dancing and other dangerous sports fail to mask the chronic—one might say terminal—loneliness of the participants. I especially like how the kaleidoscopic whirl of people and objects energizes the author and delights the reader with an almost photographic sense of time and place."

—Robert Siegel,
Best-selling author of *The Whalesong Trilogy*

"A fast, fun read."

—Richard Rhodes,
A Hole in the World, The Making of the Atomic Bomb
Pulitzer Prize Winner

"Rich Perez is a rare writer who moves with ease through the blasted lyric pain of childhood, the mysterious and sensuous and powerless world of being a kid, into the spotty drastic charm of '90s downtown flashy and downtrodden New York ... having arrived at adulthood so that he can taste it with pleasure...."

—Eileen Myles,
Chelsea Girls, Cool For You

"Mr. Perez has written a kind of contemporary fable of his generation's life in Manhattan, a fable at once humorous and poignant."

—Alan Lelchuk,
Brooklyn Boy, American Mischief

Breakthrough

Original Fiction

Acknowledgments:

A very special thanks to **Ron Kolm**
writer, poet, esteemed
East Village archivist—
for his editorial contributions
to the manuscript in progress.

The author would also
like to express
gratitude to **David Long**
for his
"writing intensive" and
his many, many
insightful suggestions
regarding the
The Losers' Club

~ Most of all ~
thanks to: **Jane Watson, R.E. Gessner, Mary Perez**

Portions of *The Losers' Club,* in slightly different form, first
appeared in *Papyrus*, Vol. 7. No. 2, *Papyrus* Vol. 7 No.3,
and *Small Pond Magazine* V. 38, No. 2.

For permission to reproduce selections from this book
write to:
Ludlow Press
P.O. Box 2651 New York, NY 10009-9998

The Losers' Club

complete restored edition!

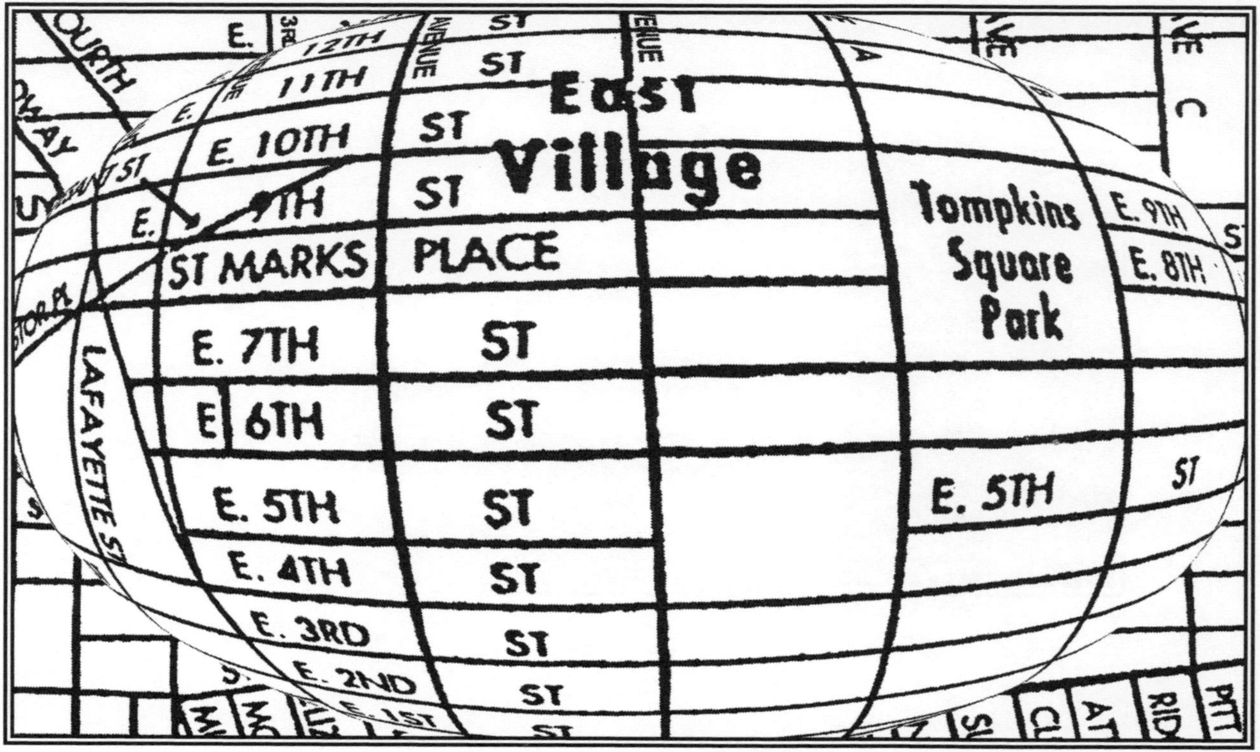
East Village
Tompkins Square Park
E. 12TH
E. 11TH
E. 10TH ST
E. 9TH ST
ST MARKS PLACE
E. 7TH ST
E 6TH ST
E. 5TH ST
E. 4TH ST
E. 3RD ST
E. 2ND ST
E. 1ST
E. 9TH
E. 8TH
E. 5TH ST
LAFAYETTE ST
AVENUE
AVE C

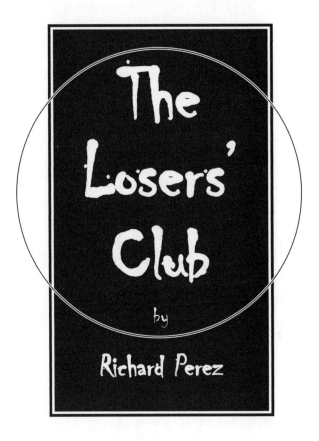

The
Losers'
Club

by

Richard Perez

Ludlow Press
New York
2005

Ludlow Press
P.O. Box 2651
New York, NY 10009-9998

Distributed by:
Biblio
(National Book Network)
To place an order and/or contact
Phone (toll free): 1-800-462-6420
FAX (toll free): 1-800-338-4550
Email: custserv@nbnbooks.com
THE LOSERS' CLUB:
ISBN-10: 0-9713415-5-9
ISBN-13: 978-0-9713415-5-5
"Complete Restored Edition!"
Library of Congress Control Number: 2004092887

Cover Design by Scott Idleman for *Blink! Design*

Publisher's Cataloging-in-Publication Data

Perez, Richard.
    The Losers' Club
/ Richard Perez. — 1st American ed., restored — New York :
Ludlow Press, 2005
        p.   cm.

ISBN 0-9713415-5-9
    1. United States—New York City—Fiction. 2. United States—
social conditions—Fiction. 3. United States—East Village—Fiction. 4.
Personal ads subculture—Fiction. 5. Love Story—Fiction. 6. Club culture—Fiction. 7. American poets/writers/dreamers—Fiction. I. Title

PS3616.E474 L67 2005
813'.6—dc21   CIP

*"People say that what we are all seeking
is a meaning for life. I don't think that's
what we are really seeking...
I think what we are seeking is an experience
of being alive."*
—**Joseph Campbell**

"We are here to laugh at the odds...."
—**Charles Bukowski**

A young, clear-eyed woman emerged from the dark.

"Disappointed? Sad? Need someone to talk to? A person who'll understand?" Her voice was soothing, her manner strangely sincere. "I know how you feel."

She smiled. "Hi. I'm Sophia. And I'll be that special person, the one you've been searching for."

Her image doubled: "Reliable. Caring. Always waiting, always here…"

Now there were four identical faces (the chorus of voices beginning to warp): "Here, waiting—just for you!"

Again the image splintered: to eighths, then sixteenths. "So, tell me. Tell me."—laughing—"What are you waiting for?"

Again and again, her face continued to fragment, to diminish until it was pixilated and remote, like a reflection caught inside the eye of an insect.

1.

Eyes flicking open, Martin tipped forward in his office swivel chair. At last, when he realized he could no longer postpone the inevitable—his time nearly done—he issued a long sigh, straightened up, and returned to scribbling on the latest creased manuscript: unfinished work from the previous morning.

Only minutes later, sure enough, he heard cursing outside the door as a key jammed in the lock.

"*WAA-AATCH-out!*" swelled the loud, unmistakable voice as the door burst open.

Martin turned to see *who else?* but the only other inmate of this box trap office.

"*WHAT-CHA' doin'*, bro?" (That was the actual term he used: "bro.") And striding up, craning his neck, tried to catch a peek at what Martin was working on.

"Revisions, Chaz," explained Martin, covering up. "*Revisions.*"

"Ha! *Ree-visions.* Revisions, my ass! Beatin' off again, eh?"

"Yeah yeah. Ya got me. I'm so embarrassed," Martin said flatly.

"*Noooo*," he intoned, breaking into a broad imitation of their Japanese boss. "*Literature? Poetry?* On the *clock*, no less!—Martin-san, that is *no goo-ood!*"

Martin opened the bottom drawer of his desk and tossed in the marked pages, lightly kicking the drawer shut. "Yeah yeah, I know. No good."

"Some people never learn." Chaz laughed again. Then slamming down a folded copy of the day's *New York Post* in Martin's lap: "Now *that's* literature. Wise up, *pendejo!*"

"Right."

Straightening up at last, turning serious: "Any word from the gimp upstairs?"

"Haven't gone up."

Chaz stretched a bit, loudly smacked his belly through his gray NY Knicks sweatshirt, then sauntered back out through the door and into the warehouse to check on the arrival of new freight. Calling out to Martin: "Late again, my man? *¿Si, amigo?*"

Martin hung silent.

"Won't get into that, *eh?*" His voice echoing.

Martin again opened the drawer and neatly rearranged

his pages of writing, which he then placed in a folder inside his knapsack.

A moment later Chaz re-entered the office as if for the first time. "It looks like shit, so far. We got shit. Am I right?"

"Shit," Martin concurred. "When you're right, you're right."

Chaz finally removed his coat, a gray western-style duster. "There was something else I had to tell you." He scratched his neck. "What was it?"

"Another phone call?"

"Shit, did I mention that?"

"What?"

"That chick-pal of yours—Rikki—called?"

"Nikki?"

"That's the one."

"When?"

"Yesterday."—yawning—"After you popped over to customs."

A light blinked on Martin's phone, a Japanese woman's voice crying over the open speaker: "Maaartee-san!"

"—Thanks for not telling me."

"Sorry. Them drugs, y'know."

"Maaartee-san!" the voice interrupted again. "New boss want to talk to you!"

"*New* boss." Martin sighed. "New boss *want* to talk."

"You're in the shit now, my brother," said Chaz, smiling. "Listen, I'll ditty-bop upstairs first."

"Put in a good word for me."

"Will do," he said, already out the door. "Right after I go—uh, y'know—*drop a brick.*"

2.

Martin had worked at Japan World Transport [USA] Inc. for four years, currently earning about a dollar more than when he started. How did Martin end up in the export /import business when he had absolutely no interest in that field, when it had *nothing* to do with what he felt passionate about, namely books and art? Easy.

He ended up as an "export assistant," just as he ended up in all his other jobs: by accident. A chance ad in a newspaper had brought him to this place and it seemed no worse than any other job he had held until then. Taking a quick look at his résumé—

Martin Sierra
34-48 78th Street
Jackson Heights, NY 11372
(718) 555-6577

EDUCATION:
Queensborough Community College. The Arnold Smithline/Simon Trefman Award for Outstanding Achievement in English. Frequented Dean's List. Queens College, B.A., English. The John Golden Annual Award for Creative Writing; The Tobin-Kreuzer Award for Poetry

SKILLS:
Good phone voice, persuasive, self-motivated.
Fluent in Spanish.
Write clearly and concisely.
Dedicated and creative. Well organized.

EXPERIENCE:
DELI CLERK, Plain & Fancy Deli, Flushing, NY. General deli clerk. Operated register, occasionally took inventory.

FILE CLERK (Temp), Greenpoint Savings, Flushing, NY. Filing, copying reports, etc.

> TUTOR (Private), of a learning-disabled child, Elmhurst, NY. Clarified abstract concepts and increased child's understanding of and interest in his school work.
>
> GARAGE ATTENDANT, Queens Garage Corp., Astoria, NY. Parked cars. General garage duties.
>
> PHONE OPERATOR, Playorena, Hollis, NY. Heavy phone work, answered inquiries, obtained addresses for mailers, addressed and stamped brochures, took registrations, obtained credit card approvals; kept office records, filed, stuffed envelopes, pieced together Teachers Manuals, tallied advertising results, tied day's mail and performed other general duties.
>
> BINDERY, Pennysaver Press, Inc. Long Island City, NY. General duties in the Pressman section of Pennysaver plant. Operated standard "cutter," as well as assisted in the operation of "saddle stitcher."

There were other jobs, of course. And now this job seemed no worse than the rest. So that's why, after four years, he was still here. Why not?

"—Put in a good word for me, Chaz!" Martin called out again, to be sure.

"Said I would, *cabrón!*" Chaz shot back through the door. And he faintly reiterated: "Right after I—uh, y'know—*bust a dook.*"

3.

Quitting time. *Oh yes.*

That night, fresh from a Brooklyn-bound F train, Martin breezed up 6th Avenue to a run-down bodega where he could cop a cheap forty. "*¿Es todo?*" the clerk asked. He gave the nod.

Sack in hand—looking flat-out the lowlife (but hardly caring)—Martin stepped out to the sidewalk to take his first deep swig of the night—"*Ahhhh!*"—then headed south, aiming to lose himself on the ranging streets.

All around? the jazzy unending flow of traffic, floating and shifting headlights, scores of yellow cabs, mesh of traffic noise: the bumping and pounding tires, the blaring horns: *New Yawk' City.*

He meandered—half-dreamed plans drifting in and out of his mind—until reaching W. Houston Street where he hooked a left, east, and, quite naturally, headed down past Sullivan, Thompson, La Guardia Place....

Along the way, playing at The Angelika? One French, one Hong Kong midnight film with potential. *Keep it in mind.* He walked forward, past overlapping graffiti flyers posted on traffic signs (*Whipping boy COST, Gotcha! REVS*) ... thinking of work, trying to explain to his boss why lately it seemed he was feeling less than inspired:

"Work hours," Martin said. "You know, Chaz and I—always having to *wait.*"

His boss looked confused.

Martin explained that not having a strict "cutoff time" was a definite problem. "Salespeople make promises we try to meet," stated Martin. "We arrange the truck pickup, end up waiting to ship the freight—and it never seems ... I dunno—*good enough* somehow." His emotion getting the best of him: "Speaking for myself, Mr. Haizu, sometimes... sometimes, I feel like a rat on a wheel."

"*Uh?*"

Martin tried to clarify: "You know, one of those hamster things?"

Haizu didn't seem to get the picture.

Again Martin tried to explain. Maybe it *was* a language thing.

"So—*anyway.*" Haizu broke in now, eager to speed this up, cut this discussion short. "Martin-san, *heh*, please, must try … harder."

Martin frowned.

"Harder."

"'Hard-er.'"

"Must try."

"'Must try.'"

"Must try *harder*," nodded Haizu.

Yeah. As if *he* had the language problem, needed the practice.

The looming, darkened facades of century-old cast-iron buildings rolling past, Martin continued to sneak pulls of the bottle, the paper sack concealing it soaked and dissolving under his hand.

"Try … must … harder…."

Martin swung past the gauntlet of street merchants on Broadway, selling clothing, hats, craft jewelry, and exotic oils.

¡Malparido*!…

Some bossa nova music off in the distance, until that open-windowed car whizzed past….

Recalling work again, Chaz: "Shit, did I mention that?"

"What?"

"That chick-pal of yours—Rikki—called?"

"Nikki?"

At last, tracking past a deranged beggar performing slow-motion karate moves, Martin took a final belt of the sack and, on the corner of Astor Place, abruptly stuffed it, nose-down, into an overflowing city trashcan.

Just up the block was a new Barnes and Noble, and soon, ghostlike, he found himself penetrating it—floating

---

*See a glossary of this and other Spanish insults in the back of the book.

past pyramid displays of new arrivals, the usual assortment of celebrity author and true-crime bestsellers—arriving at "no man's land": the meager poetry rack. Not a living soul in sight.

A volume of selected verse by Pablo Neruda lay on the shelf. He opened it. *Bilingual.*

On page 275 was a section entitled, "Sonnets Of Dark Love."

He grew absorbed in the Spanish language text until a bespectacled hep-chick drifted into his field of vision. Urgently scanning the rack, she finally turned to him. "You work here?"

"Ah, no," he replied. "But maybe I can help you with something?"

She frowned. "Doubt that."

Martin frowned back. "If it's that book by Jewel*," he said. "I think it's by the counter."

That did it. Face flushed, the girl looked at him narrowly, then huffed away.

Unsettled himself—his peace broken—Martin closed the book and returned it to the shelf, soon mindlessly lingering before a special hipster rack, constructed with the needs of this particular neighborhood in mind. Books by Henry Miller, Jean Genet, and Jim Carroll (no Charles Bukowski?) were piled high.

In the end, uneasy, he trailed past the restroom, which was locked. Then, he found himself back on the street, feet hitting the pavement, now past Astor Square and the giant cube sculpture—a huge, cast-iron block tipped and suspended on end—and the young, mostly white, hip-hoppy skaters or "yo-boys" jerk-popping their boards and leaping overturned city trashcans.

---

*adorable '90s pop/folk star turned "bestselling" hardcover/audiotape poet

Past Cooper Union, Martin paused at the light. *What to do, what to do….*

St. Marks Place, in all its glory, lay just across the street.

He regretted not calling Nikki. What was he thinking? He meant to. Meant to call her. But the day seemed to speed past, and now here he was. What would she be up to?

Que tonto, he thought. *Always fuckin' up….*

His gaze drifted to the dark rock-'n'-roll bar, *The Continental,* up the block. Then he was sauntering up to the front of the club and a drove of people, the usual cluster of freaks and hooligans, loitering outside. A quick sweep of the eyes: scraggly hair, tattoos, motorcycle boots, dirty leather; sops, strays in black and gray, like Martin; some smoking roll-your-owns with a studied disregard, others talking at each other lackadaisically, eyes wearily averted.

Martin recognized some faces from "around" (other local bars and clubs), without knowing any names.

He eyed several attractive, solitary *chicas* but, as usual, his own shyness prevented him from stepping up and striking a conversation.

He skulked, eavesdropping a bit, trying hard not to look out of place.

At last, spying a lone, blue-eyed brunette (and fortified by the beer buzz), he sidled up to her. " 'Ey, what's up?" Indicating the club: "Who's wailin', tonight?"

" 'Wailin'?' "

"Playing."

She glared at him morosely and muttered, "*I* ain't ya mother. See for *yourself!*"

Martin's face went blank.

Oh.

-Kay...

"Thanks anyhow."

Jesus Christ.

Stepping back a bit—collecting the dashed pieces of his ego—he tried again, this time spotting a waif-like neo-hippy, who seemed at least half-friendly.

He nodded, trying to think of something light and funny: not to appear so sorry-assed. Several bits of slapstick wafted through his mind but hardly anything substantial enough to lessen his gloom.

" Hi," Martin started weakly.

She turned to him, frowning, as if to say: *Do I fucking know you?*

After a moment's hesitation, Martin motioned toward the club: "Any idea who's—?"

"—No."

That's as far as it went.

The next moment, Martin-the-lady-killer was at the corner grocery payphone, plugging his other ear against the street noise. The phone rang twice before someone picked up.

"Nikki?"

"Marty," replied the voice. "I was just thinking about you!"

His spirits were lifted. "No kidding?"

"No, I was," she insisted. "Where are you?"

"The East Village," he said. "By *The Continental.*"

"Oh yeah? Who's playing tonight?"

"Don't know yet, but I thought I'd check it out. Listen," he got straight to the point. "Didn't get the message that you called."

"Figured that," she said.

"You know where I work, how it is."

"I know," she said. "Things any better?"

"Oh, *you know*..."

"I do." And she did.

"Anyway." Getting back on track. "Whatcha' up to?"

"Huh?" she asked. "Why?"

"Well, I was just thinkin'—I mean, it kinda crossed my mind—if like, you'd wanna come down, maybe hang out?"

"When?"

Er. "Y'know..."

"You mean, *now*?" Sounding vaguely confused.

"Well ... maybe, sometime *tonight*?"

He cleared his throat to cover an awkward pause.

"Marty, really," she said gently. "I wish I could. But, you know, those shows usually end so late."

"Uh-huh."

"And I have work tomorrow."

"Right."

"Sorry," she admitted. "Can't."

Martin shouted over a passing ambulance siren: "Hey, it's good *somebody* cares enough about their job to wanna get to bed at a decent hour!"

She mumbled something sounding like: "I dunno."

"No," he forced a laugh. "I'm just saying: it's a *good* thing."

"This Saturday, Marty? Okay?"

Right then he could imagine her smiling on her end of the line.

"At the park?"

She laughed. "Of course. Provided you're still in one piece."

11

"Come again?"

"I mean, don't get too smashed. Try not to fall face down in the gutter this time!"

"Callin' me what, a *borracho?*"

"That Spanish for 'poet'?"

Martin laughed. "Good one."

Not so far off, either.

"*Hasta luego,* buddy."

"Yeah. Bye, Nik." He hung up.

Feeling somewhat lighter, Martin checked his watch: considered entering the club. Some pretty gals still outside.

Still seemed a bit early, though.

Lemme see, he weighed. What were his options? What did he want?

Unable to decide, by default he ended up inside the grocery, where he brown-bagged not one Red Dog but two, killing both just outside. So, sure enough, Martin was nursing a good head by the time he entered the murky interior of the club, parked his ass on a stool, and in a snap ordered his third consecutive—this time ("for a change") a draft of "ole' dark."

The barmaid, a slender attractive redhead in her late twenties, glanced away and casually informed him: "No draft, tonight. Just bottles."

"A Red Stripe is fine."

Again eyes averted, the barkeep shook her head, murmuring something.

"Hah?" He leaned forward on his stool.

"We're out," she clearly imparted this time, leaning forward herself.

("*Reality is a juiceless /*

orange," wrote Charles Bukowski.

Yes, indeed ...)

He looked at her. Then, straight-faced, he spit it out: "How about a Bud Light?" *Jesus Christ.*

"Right," she said, suddenly chuckling over something else Martin didn't understand, then strutted away.

Yeah whatever, Martin registered. He was just starting to get uptight again, if not downright paranoid.

Swiveling on his stool, he felt compelled to survey the room. *Shit, where were the ladies?...*

Apparently the gals outside hadn't entered. And, typically, the ratio of guys to gals in this smoky dive was 8:1.

It came to him suddenly, this *other* dispiriting fact: in all his years of hanging out around town, in bars and clubs, Martin could count all the people he had genuinely spoken to on one hand. Never mind, *women.* In fact, despite his constant, often manic efforts to "get out" and make contact, despite what seemed like his endless attempts to hook up, he hardly seemed to make the acquaintance of anyone, really. A handful of laggards and misfits, was all....

He mused then, half-seriously, was it a curse or just plain bad luck?

The barkeep at last returned and placed the bottle on the bar, popping the cap.

Turning, Martin eyed her and raised a crooked finger. She leaned in, smelling faintly of clove.

"Let me ask you something," Martin said quietly, looking into her eyes. "Do I ... do I look *okay* to you?"

At first the barkeep backed off.

In spite of himself Martin could almost read her mind: what kind of dumb question was *this?*

She said apprehensively, "Whaddaya' mean?"

Martin wanted to ask: Am I too *short?* Too *ethnic?* Too *uncool?* What was it? *What was wrong with me?*

Instead he asked, "I mean, y'know ... do I *look* all right?"

She stared at Martin as she might've eyed Hannibal Lecter.

She shrugged. "Sure. You look fine."

Laying down a five, hardly appeased. "Just checkin'."

4.

Martin was on his fifth—a Corona—when part of the first band—introduced as "Useless-Nameless"—took the stage, several of the male members, as was the latest trend, wearing ladies frocks.

"You *SUCK!*" screamed one drunken patron before they even got started.

"Keep it down, *Ma,*" one member muttered into the microphone, cigarette dangling. "You *promised.*"

After five minutes of mistuning their instruments, amid a rising veil of cigarette smoke ... the lead singer, a towering clown-faced transvestite—complete with emerald pre-styled wig and crown of thorns—took the stage, approaching the microphone, heels clopping, to an avalanche of whistles and catcalls.

"Pipe down, girls," he/she said calmly. "We can't all be the queen of the ball."

The transvestite turned to look at the members of the band. They seemed ready.

"This first little ditty," he/she grinned, "is a tune I wrote on the occasion of my first suicide attempt two years ago, right here in the loo of the famous *Continental Divide.*"

"Better luck next time!" someone yowled.

He/she smirked. "Yeah. Maybe I'll take *you* with me."

Snickers, scattered applause.

"The name of this first song," he/she continued, "actually, it has two titles," turning back to acknowledge the female drummer with a nod, "'Loneliness Has Followed Me All My Life' or 'God's Lonely Woe-man.'"

Another lout contributed, "Yeah, whatever! Just *sing*, ya heifer!"

"*Sing*," he/she replied, "right." And then, with a wave of the arm, it began:

There was a clash of cymbals, followed by a surge of guitar fuzz inside a crackling electronic hum. Then, spitting and shrieking—*noize* music erupted from the PA.

"HA! "

One frenzied minute, then an unexpected halt: everyone froze—musicians, music, lead singer.

Suddenly the transvestite stood poised, smiling wickedly through a gauze of smoke, gingerly cradling the microphone on its stand: a mutant Marilyn Monroe about to coyly sing "Happy Birthday" to The President.

"—FIVE SIX SEVEN EIGHT!" Another ferocious jolt and then a screeching sonic roar.

Reeling across the stage, the lead singer broke into a spastic war dance; distended guitar licks shredding and hacking, thrashing and wailing, flaring and surging with ecstatic life! The audience now electrified, hooting and howling: a pulsating roar sweeping through them.

"Crank it, *Ese!*" The lead guitarist went into full swing hunched over his lurching, shrieking instrument.

"—Rip it up!" And, here, contrapuntal to the relentless doomsday drumming—plucking a thumping groove—the bass player stood with jackboots so wide apart that if someone had tapped his back, he would have fallen flat on his forehead.

The strident, ragged-edged guitar riffs continued, churning and wrenching, throbbing and crunching … now abruptly ascending, reverberating, wheeling steeply, onwards and up—rapturously!

Yet, at that point, closing his eyes, Martin couldn't help but think—no, not of the music—not of the club—no, not of the hour—he couldn't help but think of one person:

Nikki.

Where was she? he thought.—Where was she, *right now*?…

5.

Later that night, outside his door, Martin dropped his keys for the second time. Despite his wooziness, he managed to locate the cylinder.

Inside his studio, he hovered unsteadily over the answering machine. No blinking light, nothing.

"Crap."

Clothes still on, eyes wide open, Martin lay on his stretched sofa bed, staring at the cracks along the ceiling.

Just then, if he listened closely enough, he could hear the squeaking bedsprings of the neighbors upstairs.

"It's so big!" He thought he heard someone say.

¡Mierda!…

He reached for the phone beside the sofa. Then, placing it on his chest, weighed his decision to use it.

—*Aah, why not.*

"1," then, "900…" He could dial the number in the dark.

As always, the cheerful recorded message began: "Hello and thank you for calling—"

Martin stabbed another digit and the recording skipped forward: "Thank you. Please enter your four number extension."

He entered it.

"Now your five digit security code."

Martin did so. There followed an excruciatingly long pause.

"You have," the recorded operator informed him at last, "*zero* messages!... To continue or to browse other ads, please press—"

Click.

Again his attention drifted to the neighbors upstairs.

The light still on, eyes hazy with sleep, Martin unzipped his pants and tried to masturbate. Half-heartedly, he imagined an Olympian duo—two toned, tanned, yes perfect naked bodies—going at it, coupling as vigorously as feral animals.

"Yes! Yes! Keep going!" urged the goddess-like half, legs locked around his waist.

"I intend to!" asserted her masculine mirror-image, boundlessly pouring into her.

On and on, it went, the couples' raw ecstasy reaching outlandish heights ... the pair emerging, on some warped esoteric level, as one: two glorious, fornicating, self-medicating halves of Martin's own psyche: the anima and animus. Ying and yang. Angel and devil.

"Now, up my ass!" she cried.

Already anticipating it, he'd moved into place. No mess, no awkward moves ... all smooth and effortless.

Martin's attention drifted beyond the flood of sunlight,

the wild flowers in bloom, hovering butterflies....

He made out a small figure—a boy—standing by a large pond, watching while other children his age laughed and played, taking turns easily skipping stones across the still water.

Martin watched the boy try one: reach down, delicately pick up a piece of dry shale, feel it in his hand.

At last he hurled it. Waiting for it to skip.

The stone splashed once—*plop!*

Sank.

6.

That Saturday, as often before, Martin met Nikki at a park not far from where she lived. In Queens, New York.

This park, "Oakland Lake," as it was known officially, consisted of a small, roughly peanut-shaped lake surrounded almost entirely by steep, sloping hills covered with tall, gangling trees. And, obscure as it was, in a remote corner of Bayside, both Nikki and Martin shared a history with the place.

It was Nikki's favorite hangout since moving from Philly after her mom's final divorce and subsequent departure for Miami. And it was *here* coincidentally, this same place, where years earlier Martin would skip from community college—cut school—with the sole purpose of finding a comfortable tree stump or rock to sit on and spending some time alone. It was *here*, before ever knowing Nikki, in these quiet woods, where Martin would come to read and write and dream about his future, hoping for that day when he could at last, somehow, get his life "together." *Fulfill his promise.* Then, too, he had fabricated an elaborate, dream-sustaining fantasy in which he imagined himself an

American expatriate living in the Paris of the 1920s—only he was living in his own country. He convinced himself he was destined for vast prosperity and fame.

Quite naturally, his *writing* would take him there.

Now, walking along the narrow path skirting the brambles, Nikki asked him for an update. Martin's face was a blank.

"—The *news*. Any luck with those magazines? Placing your work this week?"

Nikki wore khaki shorts that morning, her long chestnut hair loosely tied up in back so that a few long curling strands escaped, partly framing her lovely face.

"Any luck?" he finally answered back. "Nah. Just more of the same. Zip."

"And how about the other?"

Did she mean the ads?

She smiled faintly.

At last he confessed: "Even worse. If you can imagine."

Nikki seemed more disturbed by this than Martin. She tugged at him and sighed. "I wish I could set you up, Marty, I really do. Just, I can't think of anyone. And, you know, all of Mariella's friends are either attached or spoken for or"—frowning—"not exactly conducive right now to a relationship with any *guy*."

Martin stifled a big laugh.

"—What? Why that look?"

"Nothing."

"Really, Marty. I ask around all the time."

"I believe you, I believe you." Martin broke a smile. "And thanks." *Jesus*. He bumped her affectionately. And she bumped him back, harder.

At that point a heavyset female jogger appeared from

19

the opposite direction. They stopped horsing around and trailed along the path.

"Listen," Nikki spoke up. "If it's any consolation, it's not easy for *anyone*. Despite what you may think."

Glad for this entrance into her side of things, he asked, "So now that you've mentioned it—what's going on?"

She looked away, uneasy. "What's *'goin' on'*?"

"What"—he asked—"is the score between you?"

It was her turn to look blank.

Martin smirked. "Between you and Mariella." He finally laughed. "What are we talking about here?"

Nikki frowned, gazing down.

Whenever the discussion turned to her girlfriend, Mariella, she grew fuzzy. Distant.

"I mean right now," Martin said. "Are we talking 'hiatus,' at this point?"

"Maybe."

"'Maybe'?"

"I don't know," she said.

"You mentioned something like that to me, last time."

"Yeah, I know."

"That you were taking a short break. Thinking about it, at least."

"I know."

"Well?"

"It's the truth. If you can believe it," said Nikki. "Only now it's gotten more complicated. She's proposing a 'reunion' date, too." She forced a smile. "So, I guess, *that's* the 'score.'"

Martin sighed wearily.

"What's the matter?"

"I don't know."

She prodded him.

"Just ... it's, I don't know ... "

She turned to him. "*What?*"

"Don't you ever get the feeling that *everything* is just so temporary?"

They walked along the gently winding trail.

"Keeps me up at night," Martin said. "Doesn't it scare you?"

"Should it?"

Martin shrugged. "I think so."

"Okay, *Jean-Paul Sartre* ... Mr. *'Nausea....'*"

Finally he broke a smile.

Nikki bumped him again, laughing. "Lighten up. Things'll improve."

"You sure?"

Holding his gaze, she smiled. "*Trust me.*"

Martin took a fresh look at her. Wearing her Village silversmith earrings, partly concealed by the loose wavy strands of hair, munachi amulet around her neck, she looked as jaunty, as endearing as ever.

No one could make him smile like Nikki.

"You need to look on the bright side, babe," she said.

"It's easy for some people."

"Oh, shut-up!" she laughed.

Finally the path opened into a clearing. Martin and Nikki lingered to look across the lake. A breeze was lightly ruffling the surface, and in the distance, geese and ducks spotted the water.

Impulsively, Martin reached down and grabbed a piece of dry shale.

Felt it tightly in his hand.

"Should I?"

"Go ahead," she grinned. "Tempt fate!"

It sailed. Splashed once.

Plop!

7.

"—*Aah*," Martin had said. "Fuckit!"

It was nearly a year and a half earlier that he had spotted the ad in the "Seeking Friends" column of the *Vox* personals:

> SWF, into writing, seeks thoughtful, inspired, down-to-earth 'intimate' for parks, cafes, films, E. Village bar hopping, long cynical phone conversations, and general understanding in a chaotic world. Platonic.

As usual, Martin's love life at the time was lousy and his luck with meeting people and making new friends seemed nearly as bad. The ad hadn't specified whether the person should be male or female, so Martin reckoned, "Why-the-hell not?…"

In the mood to flex his writerly muscles, this time he actually sat down and composed a letter that he sent to the newspaper PO Box.

Usually when he did that—especially if the letter was gushingly sincere and earnest—he got no response.

This time, it was different.

She left him a message, some phone tag followed, then two nights later, she called him back and, after a conversation that easily lasted two hours, during which they touched on personal histories, selected likes and dislikes, they lastly arranged for a simple get-together downtown.

"Why don't we, y'know, go for some coffee?" she suggested.

"Sure," he replied, treating it casually.

And that was the start of it.

8.

At the time of the first meeting, as she revealed to him by degrees, Nikki had just broken off with someone and was in that numb, limbo stage of recovery: unable to hook up emotionally or psychologically with anyone new—although, in fear, desperately wanting to.

"So you're free, now?" he'd asked. "I mean, *technically?*"

"Not quite," she said, somewhat embarrassed. "Actually, I'm having an affair."

When asked how she could be having an "affair," when in effect she was not currently *in* a relationship, she haltingly tried to explain: "Well … in my mind, on some level, I'm still *involved*. No, not *technically*. And not on paper either. I guess you can say it's still in the 'phantom' stage."

When Martin asked what she meant, she went on, "You know, when you hear stories of people in war losing an arm or a leg and for a long while afterward still feeling it's there?"

Martin understood.

"Well, less dramatically," she nodded, "that's where I'm at right now." She smiled weakly. "The body may be willing but the spirit is numb."

Then the affair was just a distraction?

She assured him, "It won't last."

His attention lingering on her full, soft lips, her bright green eyes, in time Martin felt compelled to ask: "This new guy—how did you meet him?"

"Who?"

"The one you're having the affair with," Martin said naively.

This made her smile.

"How did I meet this person?" she reiterated.

Martin nodded.

"Through the personals."

"Really?" This gave him hope.

She nodded, "I've used them before. Tried other ways of meeting people. But, lately, I don't know. It just wasn't working for me. It's possible that in a bar or club I might be attracted to someone—think, 'now *that's* a person I'd like to get to know'—on the basis of looks. But, lately, it's been my experience that I keep meeting people that I have nothing in common with. I mean, *nil.*"

"See," she explained. "For me there needs to be a basic commonality. Even as friends, we'd need to come from the same place. Otherwise, there would be no understanding. No context to share things."

"No place to start from," Martin added.

Good one: he was on the ball that day.

She smiled. "Right."

What was she interested in, then? What were some of her likes?

Films: *Bicycle Thief, Breathless, Umberto D., My Life As a Dog, Harold and Maude, Housekeeping, Breaking The Waves, Sunset Boulevard.*

Books: *Eleven Kinds of Loneliness, Revolutionary Road, Lolita, Orlando, My Antonia, Catcher, Love in The Time of Cholera.*

Favorite Poets: Elizabeth Bishop, Rainer Maria Rilke,

Mary Oliver, T. S. Eliot ("The Love Song of J. Alfred Prufrock"), H.D.

Music: tastes changed weekly, although Ani DiFranco, Elliot Smith, The Velvets, and Meat Beat Manifesto were constant favorites.

Favorite Booze: Absolut, Cuervo Gold, Maker's Mark— whatever else was on sale at the local Liquor Mart.

Just the tip of the iceberg.

After coffee that day, Martin arranged to "hang out" again the following week. And Nikki was willing, made time; able to do so, in part, because her "fling," her rebound lover, Mariella, as it turned out, was a famous filmmaker, always busy, flying to the west coast as frequently, it seemed, as Martin hopped the F train.

After the second time, seeing her in Bayside ("There's this little park we could go to, very private ... "), meetings with Nikki increased to at least twice a week, interspersed with phone calls every few days, finally nearly *every* day.

He thought of her constantly, compulsively, and in his insecurity wondered what the bejesus she saw in him, although she hinted that he somehow managed to put her at ease, being, as she once put it, the "least intimidating" person in the world.

To that he said, "Gee thanks. No, really."

Another time, while hanging out at her apartment in Bayside, she called him her "little boy lost," and alluded, teasingly, to the fact that he wasn't the most "masculine guy, okay," (by which he assumed she meant comment "a") but instead of being insulted by this remark (aware, by then, of her general preference) he actually felt flattered, felt it a compliment.

That night she even kissed him.

While watching a video of *Henry and June,* smiling, she'd leaned over and pressed her lips against his ear.

When he faced her, she put her tongue in his mouth.

No sex, though.

He understood she was in a relationship.

He understood, right?

Sometimes he wasn't sure what to think.

Martin was grateful for her company though; comforted by her affection for him, which often turned demonstrative: she was the type of woman who loved to touch, kiss and hold hands, evidently comfortable with her own body and sharing it in a way that was rare with women—at least in Martin's experience.

Certainly Martin never complained.

Yet, since he had known her, she'd always remained, just barely, barely, out of reach.

Times when he felt their friendship was on the verge of blossoming into something more were squelched by the reappearance of Mariella, fresh from the west coast, confident and triumphant with news of some fabulous upcoming project.

And, in his mind, he thought Nikki still preferred women.

How could he compete? He couldn't.

Still, he tried to keep an open heart: as long as she was with him, on his mind, he was filled with hope.

She remained someone to bolster him against life's many disappointments. Someone to discuss art with, and books, and poetry, and films (without embarrassment). Someone to enjoy a simple stroll with in the park.

Share a box of Jujubees with. Or Dots.

Celebrate life with.

She was his best friend, his *mija*.

And, of course, of course, he always kept his fingers crossed.

9.

> *"The world is full of shipping clerks
> who have read
> the Harvard Classics"*
> —Charles Bukowski

Martin thought of that quote the third time he met with Nikki.

The East Village this time, they were strolling along Avenue A, laughing, when Martin ventured to discuss his job. Trying somehow to put it into perspective (perhaps without being entirely honest with himself), he said, "See, to me, it's just a paycheck. A way of paying the rent. As I see it: if it wasn't this silly job, it would just be some other piece of crap. I mean, okay, what I *want* to do is write. Poems, stories, maybe a novel down the line. But right now I can't even get published. And, even if I did, there's no guarantee I'd earn any money at it. Any real money, any-how."

Nikki kept quiet, reserving judgment.

"In the meantime," Martin continued, "I've got to stay above water. Y'know pay the bills, buy groceries—all of that." After a while he added, "I know people say: 'You *are* what you *do*,' but I don't necessary agree with that."

"No?"

"Nuh-uh. 'Cause right now that would make me an export assistant, a shipping clerk."

"But you'd also be a writer," she pointed out.

"Not in the eyes of most people," Martin said.

He thought of a story to underscore his point: "There was this one guy I knew. Lived on 11th Street, on the west side actually. He was a painter. An artist. Oils and mixed media. Worked nights as a janitor. He was an artist, y'see—a good one—but just couldn't earn money from it."

Nikki seemed with him so far.

"Now, at get-togethers, social functions and the like, people would sometimes rush to pop the question, "So, what is it that you 'do'? 'Well,' he'd say, 'I'm an artist, but right now I'm also a janitor.' And, of course, that never went over too well."

"Why not?"

"Hell, the moment he said 'janitor,' that was the *last* thing they heard. And, right away, they'd move along, scan the room for better prospects. Point is: y'see, he might've been a *genius*. But, to these people, once he said 'janitor,' that was it. That was *all* they saw him as. And what's worse—even sadder, I think—they assumed it was all he'd ever be."

"That sucks," Nikki admitted.

He turned to look at her. "I mean, I hardly have to say this, right? That's just the society we live in, where people pass easy judgments, sum you right up, based on surface things, what you do, or have to do, right now, just to get by."

Martin asserted, "*He* hadn't 'sold out,' right? because he was still an artist. If anything, it was them—these other dips—they'd made the concessions, settled a long time ago."

Nikki agreed "—He was just trying to hang in."

"Right. And, this guy owed it to himself to survive.

28

Why?—Because as every flea-bitten mutt believes, every scroungy mongrel—even down in skid row—*'cada perra tiene su día'!:*'every bitch has its day'!"

She faced him, smiling.

"And the point is, the point is, to stay *alive*. Maintain yourself. Hang in, creatively. *To keep your head!* And still *be there* when that big day finally rolls around!"

Nikki laughed.

They walked a while in silence.

She said finally, "So what happened?"

He turned to her. "Uh?"

"What happened? To your friend, the artist?"

Martin shrugged. "Oh him. He died."

She almost stopped in her tracks.

"Yeah," he muttered. "Later moved to Bayonne. Shot himself. He was a big alky too. Forgot to mention that."

"That's a sad story, Marty!"

"Yeah." He thought a moment. "Guess it is."

10.

```
┌─────────────────────────────────────────┐
│   JAPAN WORLD TRANSPORT (USA) INC.       │
│              { EXPORT }                   │
└─────────────────────────────────────────┘
```

As usual, the key jammed in the office door cylinder. *¡Coño!*

9:13, read the JAL wall clock.

Wasting no time after dumping his knapsack, Martin flicked on the copier machine, warming it up. Returning to his desk then, reaching into his bag, he withdrew a stack of badly creased poems and stories.

"*Okay* then," he said aloud.

Today, he needed to copy no less than a hundred forty-eight pages six times.

Surely it would only take a moment.

He was halfway done when he noticed the blinking red light on his telephone. Bouncing over, he hit "Intercom."

"Maartee-san," rang Tani's voice. "Boss want to see you!"

Oh, Jesus Christ! Martin snatched the receiver: "Five minutes, tell him. *Five minutes!*"

With that, he went back to making copies, the stench of toner already turning his stomach. The fresh, warm pages he lovingly arranged in a new office folder—discreetly appropriated.

Ten minutes later, Martin was seated at his desk (his precious copies stowed away) when he eyed the phone.

What's another minute?...

Picking up the receiver, he dialed the usual number.

"Hello," began the cheerful prerecorded voice, "and thank you for calling *The Vox Personals* line!"

Leaning back in his seat, Martin poked a digit, skipping ahead.

"Thank you," continued the message. "Please enter your four number extension."

He entered it.

"Now your five digit security code."

Martin did so. Waited. Was about to hang up, when:

"You have," said the recorded operator, "*one* new message!"

He stiffened in his chair.

"To hear your message," the operator reminded him, "please key '*eight*' on your touch-tone phone."

Martin keyed "8."

Finally: *Beep!* "Hiiii!" began a bright female voice. "My name is Monserrat. Really loved your ad. Thought it was the coolest. You sound *really* special. It's hard to meet someone who's, um, bright but not *mmm,* y' know, really *boring?* Um, I can see by your ad that you're interested in writing and books, the arts. Hmm, well. Me? I guess you can say I'm into film, right now. I'm *hot* on Italian movies. Early Bertolucci, especially. Um, I went to Columbia University, received my M.A. in film studies two years ago. Currently I'm working toward my Ph.D. I'm twenty-six years old. An aerobics instructor in my spare time. Five foot four, a hundred and ten pounds. Long auburn hair; long and straight. Eyes, *mmm,* soft blue. My measurements since we're on the subject? Thirty-six, twenty-four, thirty-four." She giggled, pausing. "Oh, and as far as what I read? I'm very much into Gabriel García Márquez and the South Americans. So? Let's talk. My number is—"

Martin flung aside some sheets to grab a pencil. To his distress, the receiver momentarily popped from his ear; he caught it against his arm and hastily drew it back up, barely cupping it in time for the last four digits: 1-0-9-2

He grimaced, jotting these down.

Her voice returned: "Again, my number—"

Martin brightened—ready—pencil poised.

At last: "1-*900* 555-1092."

His expression fell.

"Only *$2.95* a minute," she cooed. "Just a ten minute minimum!"

He sat there, the receiver plastered to his ear.

She went on sprightly: "You're over eighteen, *rii-ight?...*"

11.

"Maaartee-san!" cried Tani's voice over the open speaker. "Maaartee-san!"

"All right, *godamnit!* I'm going up!..."

12.

That night.—

That night in his neighborhood, Jackson Heights, Martin cruised for a parking space. He swept along 78th, past a cement courtyard and park, past the tightly parked cars lining both sides, until spotting a Ford Escort apparently ready to pull out. Easing alongside the car, he motioned to the driver inside. The woman, a stunning Korean with streaked hair, frowned and shook her head, *Nope.*

After stopping for a red light on 37th Avenue, Martin drove for a block-and-a-half until eyeing a Dodge Neon with its signal lights on. Smiling, he pulled up to the striking strawberry blonde inside, but this time before he could even make a gesture, she too resolutely shook her head, no.

Martin rolled on. And on. Twice around the block, he tried to approach yet another driver. This third woman, an attractive mulatta wearing afro-puffs and a red satin choker, tried to ignore him, until he lightly struck his horn. At which point, she too wearily conveyed this night's almost universal message: *No.*

13.

That night, later.—

Bag of chow mein in hand, Martin entered the lobby of his apartment building, stopping at his mailbox. If there was *one* thing he truly dreaded, this was it....

Anything? Hmm.

Bills, bills; then two padded business-size envelopes, each conveying Martin's name and address, in an exact, if all-too-familiar typewritten style.

He knew what they contained without opening them, but opened them anyway.

In the first envelope, along with his returned, badly creased work, was the standard rejection form (dirty and illegible from being copied ad infinitum); in the second he found ... nothing. Not even a small "no thank you" note. *But wait!* What's this?... Martin slowly unfolded the rumpled page in disbelief. Across the face of one of his best poems—was it? *Could it be?*—a smeared *mustard* stain!? He sniffed it:

"*Mutha'-fucks!*"

14.

Once inside his apartment, Martin calmly locked the door, put down his belongings, unbuttoned his jacket.

That done, he sharply tore the rejection note and mustard-stained page in half—along with all the other ruined copies of his work—and, entering the room, flung them— "Join the party!"—onto the mountain of rejection letters building up in the far corner.

Regaining his composure, Martin regarded the newsprint image of Charles Bukowski he had taped on his wall.

"Pop, how did you do it?" he asked aloud. "How did you fuckin' survive?"

Although perhaps Bukowski's pocked and ravaged face offered a clue.

"Us against them! Us against them!... "

With Buk's image giving him strength, Martin-the-martyr sat before his outmoded portable word-processor, printing out another stack of self-addressed envelopes. Preparing for his next assault.

Beyond the empty Chinese food containers, the fresh copies of his poems and stories—done that day at work—rested neatly in an open file folder on his sofa bed. On top was a fat roll of stamps.

The mind-numbing chore of submitting work to small press publications and periodicals involved the necessary inclusion of a self-addressed-stamped envelope with each manuscript. (Not including a SASE, it was said, would only confirm one's ... "amateur" status.)

Of course (sure as a hangover followed a bout of heavy drinking), it would follow that later—much later—it would be these *selfsame* envelopes that would return bearing the obligatory bad news.

And much of the humiliation, as Martin saw it, lay right there: it resulted not just from being rejected, but in having to provide your *own* envelope for it!

At times it was hard to imagine a worse co-dependent relationship.

This time, no different than any other, Martin sealed crisp copies of his work in at least a dozen newly-addressed envelopes, hastily noting the submissions on a scrap record sheet.

Then he lunged for his denim jacket and was out the door.

"Watch it, now!" Slamming and re-slamming the mailbox lid, determined-Martin made sure *this* batch—beyond all others—was securely deposited.

His hope renewed, he next decided to treat himself to an ice-cold one and a copy of that week's *Vox*, his favorite Village tabloid. There was a seedy all-night bodega on the corner of 79th, where drunken derelicts would stumble in to buy cigarette "singles" for a quarter.

15.

Back from his sacred mission, his consecrated destiny, Martin settled on the hardwood floor of his studio apartment.

Newspaper rolled under his head, beside his half-emptied foaming forty-ounce, Martin studied the cracks along the ceiling, listening to the distant sounds of what he imagined was the number 7 train. One association led to another until at last, surfacing through a host of dim recollections, one memory took color and came into view. Growing at once brighter and clearer...

Again, in the distance, he spotted a boy, this time playing on a remote outcrop of rocks: a sandstone formation, near what he recognized as his old parochial school.

Pulsing with energy, pretending to fly—lost in his own timeless world—the boy vaulted over chasms, jagged crevices, leaping carelessly from exposed boulder to rock. On this day, the sun blazed brightly. And, drenched in this light, the boy seemed happy.

Blessed.

That is, till he heard a distant cry—a lonely woman's voice—drifting up, calling him. At which point, abruptly turning, the boy immediately lost his footing and plunged down a deep dark hollow, violently banging his head on the rocks below. Dark blood splattering across the stones.

Vaguely distressed and disoriented, Martin awoke to turn on the TV and open his pullout sofa bed. His beer was nearly gone, and he felt too lazy to go out and buy another one. Plus it was late.

Instead, he ended up watching Wall Street Week in the hope it would serve to put him back to sleep.

But instead of the TV, his bleary eyes focused on a framed photograph on his bookshelf. Through the blue light, he could just barely make out her attractive, dark features.

His own mother—then about Martin's age—looked so much like him it was like peering into a mirror.

"¿Qué quieres de mi ahora, Loca?" He asked her.

The woman remained in the shadows, facing him, her dark eyes begging.

No reply.

16.

The Soft Descent

"Emptiness,"
she said.
"All emptiness
is open to me ..."

The Sky Is Barren.
Dreams Are Useless.
Dissolution Rules.

Long ago, I dreamt
I fell through
the clouds ...
I fell easily and
kept falling.
My arms extended,
my eyes open,
I descended
through the clouds
without a whisper,
without a sound
(as in a flickering
silent picture
show).

How well—
how well
and easily
I kept falling.

How often
since then
have I had this image
in my mind ...
that
of my body
falling

fall-

ing

without a whisper,
without a sound.

Some nights later, Martin was alone again, trying to work out an old poem, when his thoughts strayed to days long past and memories of his departed mother ... *madrecita.*

—What recollections did he have of her?

A petite, fine-featured woman with dark curling hair— again Martin envisioned her in a familiar pose, lingering by the half-open shade of her bedroom window, staring out into the street.

Always this strange and tomb-like solitude: permanently shut away from the sun and the rest of the world.— *Why?...*

Once, while she stood by that window, Martin considered, in fantasy, sneaking up behind her and shoving her out. ("*¡Hala, vaca!*") Were it not for that rusted window guard, she might've fallen too. Dropped down and down, in slow motion, five full stories, arms flailing, legs kicking wildly—her head smacking the sidewalk and splitting open like a ripe watermelon—brains and bitter sadness splattering for yards! Martin looking down at horrified bystanders, timidly waving a hand.

Other memories?

Not due to any sickness he could see, his mother's darkened form unable to get up from bed for days on end, her chest gently falling and rising, rising and falling. His mother sleeping more than anyone in the whole world.

Martin fixing his own breakfast, Martin walking himself to school, Martin pleading with her to take him to the big park, the one with the Indian caves, the quiet winding paths, the giant ballfields.

Rendered nearly powerless in the oppressive dark, his mother sometimes not bothering to answer the door when it rang or even pick up the phone. Stomping his feet, Martin flouncing into the next room to snap on the TV, turning up the volume. At last, she would cry out in a wrecked voice, "*¡Bájalo!*" But he would turn it up, losing himself in silly-happy dialogue and cartoon violence. "*¡Bá-JA-LO!*" With that, the volume went even higher. Way up! In the end, staggering, she would burst into the room, eyes puffy, face incredulous: "*¿Pero qué eres, IDIOTA!?..*"

He recalled another time, years before, the two tranquilly reclined on her wide bed, taking an afternoon nap, facing each other, when Martin, suddenly bored, mischievously reached over and yanked down *hard* on her pajama bottom, his jaw dropping at the sight of her thick, hairy PUSSY!

"*¡Cochino!*"—and WHACK!—his mother slapping his face so hard his ears rang for a full fifteen minutes.

Other times? He remembered his mother without provocation, abruptly swinging—pelting him. Now, crumpled in a corner, open hands held up in surrender. *Thwack!* Martin seeing stars: a hot, tingling sensation on his skin where *mami* hit him. "AAAAAAAAAAAAAAAHHH!.." he bawled, shivering. Then striking him again and again, suddenly ranting, "*¡Si no fuera por ti! ¡Si no fuera por ti!*" And with her bare foot, kicking him. Stubbing her big toe, somehow. "—*¡Ayyy, Dios!…*" And as she did a hopping dance, her face screwed up in pain, Martin breaking into a laugh—a loud laugh—his cheeks still wet with tears.

Then, of course, there were the happy times. Her sadness ebbing, her mood lightened; his mother affectionate with him, suddenly warm and loving.

Together on the sagging bed, her softness against him, her skin milky: pleasant. Martin closed his eyes, floating back through time, feeling her light teasing fingers on the nape of his neck, softly along the back of his head, now stroking his hair gently, gently comforting him.

Her face then pressed against his, her lips kissing him. *Smack!* Affectionately kissing him. *Smack! Smack!* Martin cringing. Her voice laughing; light laughter passing between them, cascading, ringing like bells.

The two embracing, squeezing each other a long time, in a firm hold on life, Martin slipping into a dream. Tight against her bosom, tight; hanging on, her heartbeat in his ear. Hearing her heartbeat then, he could not comprehend, could not imagine how it wouldn't last forever....

Then, recalling how his grandparents would show up to take him away.

(The bastard son.)

As always, Martin at a loss.

In the end, the very end, amid the flashes of light and wide gaps in memory, the fierce bouts of anguish and pain, his grandfather arriving again, muttering—let in with his own key—this time to pack Martin's things: whatever remained. Martin frightened, confused: *"¿Qué haces? ¿Pero dónde está Mami? ¿Dónde está Mami?"*

In return, *nothing*. No response.

A widening silence, a crushing loneliness.

Sirens wailing in the distance, in the night…his mother, *madrecita*, being taken away forever, away from that window, away from that bed, her shattered face receding, fading, amid a swirl of shadows, into memory, now as always. "Amid a swirl of shadows" Martin wrote, "into the lonely night…."

17.

They were at the corner of Second and Avenue A, where a film—*Beyond the Valley of the Dolls*—was being projected across the entire side of a building from the bar across the street.

Nikki asked him for an update.

"With the magazines?"

"With the new ad. Any luck?"

He shrugged.

"Maybe the ads work better for women?"

"There's that distinct possibility." They crossed the avenue, alphabet-bound. "I'm about ready to join one of those stupid dating services."

"I know someone who did that. Some gal from work."

He laughed. "Yeah? How'd it go?"

"Terrible."

Martin cracked up.

"She put up the money," Nikki went on. "And *zilch*."

"Really?" he asked. "Which agency?"

"Can't remember. They advertise on TV, though. Late at night. One of those 'personal introduction' services."

"And she didn't meet anyone? Really?"

"Oh they set her up on a few dates."

"And?"

"Apparently anyone with money can get over on the 'screening process.'"

He laughed again.

"Stick with the personals, Marty," she said. "At least, you have less to lose. And you may still get lucky."

"Lightning strikes when you least expect it, right?"

"*Si, señor.*"

He turned to her, grinning. "And, after all, I met you."

Nikki smiled.

18.

On the far side of Avenue B, they turned left and crossed the street.

Avenue B was considerably more run-down than Avenue A, nocturnal types here and there hawking brand names of ecstasy and heroin, with this particular corner being the most popular. The farther you went into the Alphabet (descending B, C, D ... crumbling into the East River), the shadier the neighborhood became, until parts of it—bombed-looking, rubble-strewn—began to resemble portions of the South Bronx.

Mercifully, at this hour, there were some revelers on the avenue, jetting to and from the performance space, *Collective Unconscious*, across the street or, beside that, the *Gas Station*, a converted Gulf station turned band venue, fenced in by rusting scrap-metal art.

Martin and Nikki safely arrived at the nondescript club entrance where a toothless cretin was outside, strumming a monotonous tune on a homemade, three-string electric guitar. On the sidewalk was a childishly scrawled sign that read:

Show me a man
Whose not confused
And I'll show ~~yew~~ you
A moron.

"Ready?" Martin asked.

Nikki smiled. "Yep."

There was no line to wait on, of course—no velvet rope—so they went right in.

"Hold it," rasped a shadowy figure just inside.

After being patted down for weapons, Martin and Nikki followed a long dark hallway to the admissions window. Then they turned right and stepped through a short passage that led to a wide, dimly lit room, done in a garish Hong Kong motif of bright reds, yellows, and blues (Chinese lanterns hanging from the ceiling), the entire floor surrealistically carpeted in ankle-deep sand.

On the east wall flashed incongruous slide projections, and, as Martin and Nikki stepped deeper into the room, they noticed a lank-haired musician crouched over an electric violin, playing contrapuntally to the house ambience music—music filled with all sorts of warped industrial noises, like someone clanking on metal pipes and sawing wood.

As Martin and Nikki progressed to the back, they saw a booth where a tattooed, bald-headed woman was peddling so-called smart drugs, sold in glitter cups like fancy film containers. Beside these were offered certain "herbal treatments" and stimulants containing ephedrine or ma huang, "legal" drugs.

"Up for any?" Martin asked.

Nikki shrugged, pushing on.

Back upfront, full circle, a performance piece was in progress. A blank-faced blond in pearls and formal gown was doing an ultra-slow-motion dance to the warbling music, while another woman, manipulating a claw-like mirror, refracted shards of colored light in some vague commentary. The flashing slide images were mostly of atrocities: holocaust victims piled lifelessly, like rag dolls.

Nikki tried to interpret it, "Society's indifference to human suffering?"

"Good guess."

Tired of treading sand, they found a couch. Beside them, piled high, were all sorts of gear and outmoded electronic equipment: EKG machines, scopes, TV monitors, emitting frequency waves and static. They tried to talk but the loud dissonant music made conversation difficult, so instead they settled for holding hands and exchanging amused glances.

Nikki, sweet Nikki. She always made him smile.

Was there ever anyone more attractive?

Oh he doubted it.

Here, now, in particular, she looked sweetly angelic…

She had large pale-green eyes, a faint cleft in her chin, and at the corner of her full mouth, on the right, a perfect tiny mole, a beauty mark. What's more, tonight, she looked even more striking, with her dense curling hair untied, dressed in a pair of relaxed, low-slung grape flairs and a cropped guava T. At that moment, as she lounged next to Martin, she appeared completely at home and comfortable, as at ease in her own lithe body as a large exotic cat.

How did she manage that? That looseness? Alcohol-free? Living in this city?

"Whatcha' thinkin' of?" she asked him at one point.

"You're looking comfy," he told her.

"I am," she smiled.

At one point—for no reason other than she appeared to be happy—she impulsively reached over and embraced him. This, of course, led to a return squeeze on Martin's part, then to some playful fondling, finally to some light kissing: her skin smelling faintly of lavender, feeling petal-soft and warm to his lips.

Her body leaning against him, her breath soft in his ear, Nikki teased him a bit, rocking gently, gently in his lap. Doped with affection, he took extra pleasure in supporting her weight, every luscious ounce, and in stroking and kissing her mouth and that faint sweet dot above her lip. It was almost too much; unable to resist, he slid his hands along her firm, slender body to warmly caress her lower back, hips, and thighs. He sighed to himself, considering the innumerable, sensual possibilities.

They necked and petted for what seemed close to an hour, the world around them falling off, until she pulled up and sleepily asked, "Maybe we should see what's downstairs?"

Her warmth a narcotic, drowsily content, he whispered, "Maybe later?"

19.

Emerging from the dream—

When they languidly rose from the couch, still holding hands, they noticed the room had become considerably more crowded.

Near the entrance, a different performance piece was in progress. It featured a towering transvestite in an emerald wig, who Martin finally recognized from the band he'd seen at the *Continental*. "*Useless-Nameless.*"

Naked this time—except for being bound in Saran Wrap—eyebrows shaved, he/she was dreamily reciting poetry into a microphone without background music. "This one's called, 'Sophia's Recollection.'"

He/she began:

/"*Last night*
/ *I dreamt*
/ *that you murdered me,*
/ *that while I slept*
/ *close to you …*
/ *you wedged a knife*
/ *into my chest,*
/ *until its icy-cold tip*
/ *pierced my heart.*

/ "*I dreamt*
/ *that you held me tightly, then*
/ *kissed me, warmly,*
/ *as I coldly bled,*
/ *and all my life,*
/ *with all its dreams*
/ *and wishes,*
/ *poured softly away….*"

In the dim light Martin noticed the absence of genitalia. It dawned on him: he wasn't a transvestite, but a transsexual. *Post op*, at that. The transformation complete, "he" had become a "she."

Interesting….

"Let's go," Nikki urged, tugging at his sleeve.

20.

Downstairs, in what resembled an underground bomb shelter, was the murkily-lit dance floor. The music playing in this cavernous refuge was pulsing house/techno.

After buying some bottled juice from the bar (the place being without a liquor license), Martin and Nikki found a lacquered bench to sit on and take in the slamming crowd. It was a freak scene: queens, kings, club kids, B-list models, downtown trendies, ravers (the more frenzied no doubt already high on X)—all grooving, going crazy. Heads wagging and bobbing, feet stomping, hips shimmying, asses shaking; glowing cigarettes dipping and rising in the dark. Through the yellow and red flashing lights and club smoke, as in a dream, Martin could just barely make out the outline of a few smiling girls dancing together topless. And through his heels, Martin could feel the relentless *boom!-boom!-boom!* of the jacked-up driving bass. Out of nowhere some inflamed queen appeared before them completely bare-assed, shaking his arms and legs in a kind of self-absorbed frenetic dance, then leaping back into the crush, and Martin and Nikki turned to each other and laughed.

Nikki nudged Martin. "Ready to dive in?"

"Let's!"

As always, Martin felt a bit self-conscious at first—and stiff—before being able to surrender completely to the enveloping rhythms: to convince himself that nobody here was watching, judging, nobody gave a shit—*nobody*. It was time to get naked: *let it all hang out!*

Smiling, eyes closed to the world, losing herself in the wailing and swirling sounds, in the here and now, Nikki's own movements and dance steps were easily more relaxed and fluid, freshly sensual. And Martin derived almost as much pleasure from watching her as he did from dancing. Priceless. *Que maravilla*, he thought, waves of excitement rising up his back.

21.

Martin and Nikki danced together virtually nonstop until 3:30 A.M., at which point the floor became too crowded and wild, and the both of them, exhausted but in good spirits, left the club. Enjoying the cool night air, holding hands, they walked up 2nd Street, past all the swarming night people: eccentrics, fashion victims, wild-ass kids (these mixed with assorted mental patients and homeless crack-heads)—until reaching Avenue A, where they hailed a cab.

"West Fourth Street station," Martin announced to the driver, club music still throbbing in his ears.

He fell back into the seat next to Nikki. "So," he grinned. "Have a nice time?"

"Great," she said, eyes sparkling. "I really needed that!"

"You're not the only one!" Martin laughed.

In the next moment, they were affectionately touching, then, leaning against each other, playfully groping and kissing. Martin squeezed her moist body tightly, at one point French-kissing the nape of her neck.

"What are you *doing*?"

"Tasting you," he said.

"Oh *really? Why?*"

"Why *not*," Martin said. "Besides I may never get this opportunity again."

"You're cracked," she laughed.

Martin whispered in her ear, "Are you *sure* you have to go to work tomorrow?"

She smiled. Whispered back, "Yes."

That night, on the cab ride to the subway, he kept hoping to convince her otherwise.

22.

Hola.

I mean, "Hello."

I don't know what your name is, of course, so I'm not sure how I'm supposed to address this letter. I will say though that I just spotted your ad in this week's Vox Personals and, for some reason, felt compelled to respond, send something more than a simple "hello" message, followed by a short laundry list of "interests" and my digits.

The truth is, I love writing letters but don't get much of a chance to do so these days since the few people I try to correspond with seem to take forever to write back—or instead just end up picking up the phone.

Nothing wrong with a phone call, of course. But since variety is the spice of life: why not go the extra distance, now and then, find other ways to express oneself and communicate?

I was introduced to letter writing in high school, when the person I considered my best friend (who I was also in love with)—her name was Sophia—would write me two, sometimes three letters a week and of course each time I felt compelled to write back. This, despite the fact that we saw each other every day, had lunch together, and after school often spent hours on the phone! Pretty funny, huh?

What made it even stranger was that we weren't even boyfriend and girlfriend! She was already involved with someone else when she met me. This may sound a bit dumb, I know—even masochistic on my part—but after a while I just couldn't help it. And, looking back on it these days, I still have to say it was one of the best times of my life. Innocent, somehow. Pure. I felt like a knight in one of *those medieval romances. Until that point in my life I'd never felt so awake with love and so <u>hopeful</u> about the possibilities for the world. Not to go over the top, but that first real intimacy was like being witness to the first glimmer of light at sunrise; it seemed to signal the dawn of my life. Anything seemed possible. God was everywhere!*

Christ, should I start over? See, in letters, I often get carried away.

Hi, again... How are you?

I think I forgot to introduce myself.

The name is Marty. Full name is "Martin Lorenzo Sierra."—Nice to meet you!

A word or two about my ethnicity. I <u>am</u> American. Born and raised here. My mom, on the other hand, was from Spain. I use the past tense "was" because she's no longer around: she's gone— departed, as they say.

Anyway, not to worry; it happened a long time ago. She left me when I was a kid.

I'm 26, now (just since last week).

As for specifics concerning my physical appearance (eye color, weight, height), for what they matter to you (<u>if</u> they matter)—you can refer to the back of the photo booth pic I've enclosed with this letter. It should all be there.

True, I'm short, but I'd like to take this opportunity to remind you that many historical figures were runts. Houdini was 5'1, Jean Paul Sartre was 5'3, Steve McQueen was only 5'6—and a good many assholes were even shorter! HA-HA.

I notice in your ad you say you're "into writing," which is cool, one more thing we have in common. Poetry and short stories are my main focus, even though I also love novels and fully admire the depraved individuals who write them. I also enjoy biographies— especially the beginning parts: the hardscrabble early years before an artist "makes it" or becomes established.

Memoirists are great, too, especially if they have the guts to admit to horribly ~~embarsing~~ embarrassing, if not outright humiliating episodes from their own lives; this is a quality more rare among male writers, I think (since men—as <u>all</u> men—they are raised specifically to be less honest about their thoughts and feelings, their *shortcomings—even to themselves). To admit to <u>failure</u> is to admit to weakness, which is somehow unmasculine, as well as un-American. So, personally, I find myself less interested in being superficially "American" and in love with writers—the unconventional few— who feel that way, too.*

Not to sound self-righteous or smug, but these days I want less to do with bull----. I'm fed up with false advertising.—What I want, in simple terms, is to somehow make art and find myself: discover who I am. The method or the means hardly matters: the point is staying true. And I know I will continue to write, in one form or another, to <u>search</u> until I'm permanently washed up, finished—buried. There hardly seems any other point in life.

Don't you agree?

Can I relate my greatest "failure," so far? Be that naked with a stranger?

Bear with me.

Four years ago—unpublished then as I am now, and tired of waiting on my behind—I decided to do something, take a little gamble, put out a book of my own stuff. My work, so far.

It was a way of taking charge of my life, a way of dealing with all the rejection letters, that merry-go-round of cruelty and abuse.

Not that I would go to any disgusting, rip-off "vanity press"; no—in the best f_ck-it-I'll-do-it-myself punk tradition, right along with all the big fanzines and indie record labels, I would start my own imprint. From scratch. And I went through all the steps: shopping around for the least expensive printer, providing the camera-ready pages, finished cover, obtaining the ISBN and copyright. Etc.

(On the "biz" side: renting a PO Box, obtaining the proper business forms, acquiring a tax I.D. number under the imprint's name. Opening a bank account. And printing and posting flyers. All that.)

—Small potatoes, true—but it was a start! My first little baby being a 114-page book entitled, ironically enough, <u>Idealism and Early Wish-fulfillment</u>.

2000 copies.

... Well. It flopped.

Resoundingly.

It made all the noise of "one hand clapping," as the Zen masters like to say. (It's okay, you can laugh; I already have.)

As a last-ditch effort, I took up selling it right on the street. In the Village, on the weekends. First, along Astor Place (in front of the big parking lot facing "the Cube"), then on St. Marks Place, in front of the old Deutsch Americanische building, site of the old St. Marks bookshop.

After about four months, I finally sold maybe sixty copies. Gave away a ton. Then I called it quits.

In the end, I lost money. The whole experience bruised my ego a bit. But, hey, that's life.

At least, I tried.

So, there you have it....

Okay, you're asking, what's the point?

Well, there is none.

Except, perhaps, that being a book peddler opened another door for me, put me more closely in touch with a certain part of the city than ever before. Strange to say, it was the beginning of my first real infatuation with the Lower East Side

After being on the street a while, I grew familiar with the area; comfortable with other street vendors, many who returned week after week. And, like them, I too became mostly invisible to the parade of humanity passing by—as much a part of the local land-scape as the panhandlers, the pocked sidewalks, the graffiti. The East Village then was different than it is now. Darker. Open to any-thing. For a time, it was like having this secret window to the bottom of the world. And, while I was there, I learned to open my eyes and take a good hard look.

Things have changed, I know. Changed a lot.

But the East Village still represents something to me. It's been the one place where I've never had to feel self-conscious. The one place where it was always perfectly fine to be a misfit (in fact, it's expect-ed!).

Feel out of step with the rest of America? Feel like you haven't lived up to your potential? "Career" not exactly on the fast track? Feeling socially disaffected—or at a loss?

Hey, welcome. Welcome to the club!...

These days when I'm down there I continue to keep my eyes open.

I try to experience all that I can. Take in progressive bookstores, per-
formance art, plays, films—everything.

   Hey, for all the cynics out there—for me, the Village is still hap-
pening. It doesn't embrace you, exactly. Never will. It simply lets you
be.

   Right, sappy digressions aside—and getting back to your ad—
I'd love to pal with someone new, someone to catch offbeat films
with, go dancing, see shows. I don't care if it leads anywhere. I just
want to know more people, meet others I can share life with. Enjoy
it while I'm here.

   Anyway.

   If I haven't bored you stiff—and I probably have—drop me a
line. Write or call. My number is 555-6577....

23.

   Beep! "Hi, Martin. My name is Nikki. You don't know
me. But you answered my personal ad, wrote me a *long*"—
chuckling—"intriguing letter. I'll leave you my phone
number and maybe we can talk?..."

24.

   ¿Y hoy?...

Ravel's "Boléro" crackled from Martin's red Toshiba
clock radio.

He peeked at the clock: *7:20 AM*

Maybe I'll just ... lie here. And, closing his eyes, drifted
back to sleep, the music soon accommodated into the fluid
context of his dreams...

   ... Beyond,
the landscape ... was indistinct ...

   ... Again,
 este día,
 he could taste her lips—

against his own,
feel them wet...
...Back arching
mournfully...
...His arms,
like smooth vines,
like thick,
warm-bellied creepers,
at once
entwined
her lithe,
naked
body...

...Thirsting
fingers,
like tendrils,
apart from him,
reached gently,
sweetly
(knowingly),
between
her parting thighs...

...Then,
from the roiling darkness,
blackest night,
like a fierce wind,
a face:

—MAMA!

A moment later—searing music—his alarm detonated, drilling tooth and bone.

25.

At work, Chaz held up an inter-office memo.

" 'Export Department,' " he read aloud, " 'all staff must report to second floor each day to log in precise time of arrival. If any member of staff is late to report to the second floor, *reason* must be noted in appropriate 'remarks column' on time sheet, form triple A dash nine B ... also submitted on separate office-related form, A dash nine C— copy duplicated for own file—to supervisor for final approval and initialing.' "

"*Shit,*" said Martin.

"Check it: 'Lateness,' it says here 'will immediately be deducted from OVERTIME pay—' "

"What the *fffff!*... That ain't legal!"

Wagging his head, Chaz slapped the sheet on his desk.

"It's the friggin' *new* guy," remarked Martin.

"Shit, bro," he snorted, picking up the memo again and waving it around. "I'll tell ya what this is. It's payback!"

Martin looked at him.

"I'm sayin': payback for the 'big one'—*WWII!*" And with that, Chaz crumpled up the sheet and with one sure hand, shit-canned it.

In the next moment, Chaz entered the warehouse, and Martin couldn't resist the urge to dial a memorized number.

Starting, of course, with "*1-900...*"

He could dial the number with his feet. Eyes closed.

As always, the cheerful recorded message began: "Hello and thank you for calling *The Vox Personals*—"

Martin pushed another digit. "Thank you. Please enter

your four number extension."

He entered it.

"Now your five digit security code."

Martin did so. There followed an agonizingly long pause.

Then from nowhere: "You have," said the recorded operator, "*one* new message!"

Martin straightened up, then pressed the digit that would make the system skip forward.

A young woman's embarrassed voice began: "*Hi*. This is Lola. Just flipping through the paper I saw your ad. Of course I *saw* your ad"—clucking her tongue—"What do I look like? How do I describe myself?"—sighing—"God I hate this. Awright, let's see. I'm Uruguayan-American, if that means anything to you."—quick snort—"Long dark hair with bangs. 'Bout five-three. Some people say, some people say I'm *ugly*—I don't know—no, some people say I'm okay-looking—*I don't know*. Whatever. Fuck 'beauty.' This sucks." She tittered nervously. "I'm into the arts, too, yeah. And the East Village. In fact I live there. With my *mom*, unfortunately. Uh, okay, let's see, I'm looking for someone—a 'decent' guy, I guess—to kinda hang out with, check out live shows. Crap like that." Chuckling again. "I'm a painter actually. I do canvasses. Even going to school for it. *Ooo*, wow, big deal right? I know, I must sound like a real zero, a big loser. Did I say how old I am? Past drinking age? Yeah. Still living at home and taking classes. Well what can I say? I'm being honest. If you still wanna reach me after this—and how could you resist!—I'll give you my number…"

Martin scratched down the digits.

The operator finally returned: "Press 'six' to replay the last message—"

He keyed "6."
"*'Lola. Just flipping through the paper*...."

26.
"So, whatcha' doing tonight?" Martin asked Nikki over the phone. He could hear a Patsy Cline song in the background.
"Sandra T., the one 'into Kathy Acker,' is coming over for a bit. You're welcome to join us, if you like."
Talk about feeling like a third wheel.
"Let me think about it," Martin said. "I'll call ya back...."

He stared at the piece of paper in his hand.
Strange.
Why was he feeling this way? *Conflicted?* Certainly he was entitled to date other people. Didn't Nikki encourage it, always asking for an "update," always digging in, asking if he'd met anyone new? He eyed Lola's number uneasily.
Maybe it was just nerves? A simple case of the heebie-jeebies?
But he was in control.
And he wouldn't cut Nikki out of the loop. That much was certain.
No reason to feel guilty. *Right?*

He glanced up at the newsprint image of Bukowski, who almost looked amused, on the verge of chuckling, as if to say, "Listen, pigfart—don't be a fool!"

The next moment—in a fit of optimism—Martin tried the number.

No answer.

Okay.

He'd try again later.

Martin killed half an hour, ripping apart rejection letters....

Second try: On the third ring, someone picked up.

"Hello, can I speak to Lola?"

"You're from a collection agency?"

"No."

"Then this is Lola."

Nice.

Trying not to sound edgy, he started, "Hey, this is Marty? From, y'know ... the *Vox*?"

"Who?—*Oh*." It finally hit her.

"Hi."

"Yeah"—sounding embarrassed—"*Hi*."

"Do you like, have a minute or two?"

"What," she hesitated. "You mean, to yak?"

Yak?

"Yeah."

"I have a minute. Or two," she conceded.

And so they did. Taking their time. Warily loosening their defenses. Martin commenting on the obvious weirdness of the situation, Lola remarking—"Heh, *yeah*"— how hooking up through the ads was always freaky.

"You never know who you might meet, after all," she said.

"You're telling *me*," said Martin.

"It's a crapshoot."

"'Crapshoot,'" he echoed. "—*Exactly.*"

"A lot of whackos out there," she said.

"I *know*. I mean, I can imagine."

"You're not into dirty feet, are you?"

"What?"

"You know, one of those perverts."

"Huh?—*No.*"

"That's good. The last guy who called wanted to know if he could suck my toes. But only after I stepped in red clay."

Red clay? Martin took a moment.

"He was from an ad?"

"No. A collection agency, I think."

She went on, "I don't mind if you're into feet. As long as they're not dirty ones. And they're mine."

"I'm not."

"But if you were … I mean, I'm not a *square!*"

"Honest," Martin said. "I *don't* want to suck your toes." Trying not to offend her: "Not at this moment."

Okay, now that things were off to a cracking start: Martin tried to recover.

He asked her if she'd ever done this before.

"The personals?" She paused. "Does it matter?"

"No, no. Just curious."

Lola admitted, "I've done it before."

"Yeah?" he asked. "When was that? The last time?"

She paused again, as if trying to remember. "'Bout … *three* weeks ago. Why?"

"Just, y'know, askin'." Pressing on, he muttered, "So what happened?"

"You wanna know?"

Martin laughed. "Yeah."

"*Zip.*"

"Nothing?"

"Nope. And three weeks before *that,* I tried another one."

"Really?" Martin asked. "And how did *that* go?"

"Like crap," she said.

He tried not to laugh.

"You met the person, at least?"

"Yeah, we met. A few times. Had a few 'dates.' Or whatever."

"Just didn't 'click'?"

She sighed. "Nope."

"So—here's an awkward question." He wasn't quite sure how to put it. Tried to soften his voice, set the right tone: "Whatcha' looking for?"

"Huh?"

Martin repeated the question as delicately as he could: "I mean, *you know…*"

"I don't know."

"I mean—why did you answer my ad?"

"Beats me," she said. "Why did you place it?"

Slippery girl. Martin's volley:

"I guess … I'm looking for someone," he answered limply, petering out. Then realized he sounded like an idiot.

"Duh," was her response.

Martin chuckled. Asked, "So, then, how about *you?*"

"What am I looking for?" She hardly had to think about it. "Same thing, I guess. Y'know. Yada yada."

Right. Now that *that* was clear.

He felt safe enough to ask: "You're not seeing anyone?

At the moment?"

"Nope."

"That's kinda interestin'," Martin said.

"Huh? *Why?*"

"I don't know. Being a *goof.*"

"*'Mm-kaay,*" she said.

Easy does it: can't let her slip away.

Martin cut to the chase: "Wanna get together, some-time? Meet?"

"In the East Village, right?"

"Right."

"*Maybe.*" Still considering it. Taking her time. Finally: "Yeah—it's a possibility. As long as it's in a public place."

Martin laughed.

"But let me say now," she said. "I can only hang out for a while. Like an hour. Max. I consider an hour my thresh-old with someone I don't know."

"An hour is fine."

"If we get along after that, we can just, I dunno, take it from there."

"I hear ya."

Lola confided, "There've been times when I got a little too 'invested' over the phone, know-what-I-mean? Only to find later it was totally *flat*—nothing happening. At all. Like we would get so carried away with pouring our hearts out that when we finally met we would have nothing to say."

"No 'love connection,'" Martin sagely agreed.

"What?"

He quietly took his fist and punched himself lightly on the forehead. Twice. *Shut! Up!*

"Sounds familiar," Martin said quickly.

"Happened to you?"

"Huh? Oh yeah. A few times."

Try almost always.

"We shouldn't talk anymore then. We should just hang up."

"Right."

But they were on the line another fifteen minutes. Call it insecurity, call it naked fear. Whatever.

"I get to name the meeting place, right?" she asked finally.

"Sure."

"Okay," she said. She thought about it, then gave it.

"Got it," said Martin. "Meet you there."

Martin hung up the phone, relieved. He felt agitated and sweaty. Again, he eyed the picture of Bukowski whose amused expression seemed to say, "Now that wasn't so hard, was it?"

"Not too bad," Martin said aloud, sighing.

"DAAAMN PUSSY!... "

27.

The following day at work, Martin asked Chaz if he could leave early.

"Why, bro?"

"When was the last time *you* got any?"

"I'm married, kid."

"So?"

"So. Best not to ask that sorry question!" Decent as always, Chaz laughed: "Yo—a *date*? Go for it. I'll cover for ya, no big thing."

"*Muchacho*, I owe ya."

"Don't even mention it, *pendejo*."

28.

In front of *Kim's Video*, the meeting place, Martin checked his watch. *8:09.*

Shifting from one leg to the other, he was just starting to get antsy.

Long dark hair, he thought. Bangs. "'Bout five-*three....*" The night prior she had comically alluded to her look as "'Bummy casual': torn black jeans and a m/c jacket with paint drips on the back. All my clothes have these little drips and drabs of paint on them," she said. "It's *embarrassing.*"

So how did *he* look? He could just make out his own black jeans in the glass door. Indigo shirt, black denim jacket, hair not sticking up too badly. He took a deep breath, tried to stand straight.

A slim, dark-haired woman with a beaded lip ring and faux buckskin jacket suddenly appeared before him, hesitating. Martin froze, eyes widening in anticipation. But then she seemed to recall where she was going and swept past him, into the store.

He stood around, trying to blend in, not look too concerned. Then it was twenty after.

¡Que ostia! he thought. He began to involuntarily rock on the balls of his feet.

Another woman stepped up now, half her head shorn, the other side dyed two shades of violet and aquamarine.

Martin looked at the pavement and sighed.

If she's not here the next time I check my watch, he decided concretely. *I'm outa-here'....*

Just then, from the crowd, a new woman appeared.

Approaching him directly, smiling, this time there was no doubt. She spoke in a loud baby-doll voice, "'MARCUS'?" She wore black leather, but the hair was off. Short and spiked, it was dyed platinum blonde with pink-red highlights. Out of her left cheek sprouted what seemed to be part of a corkscrew: a radical piercing of some kind.

"'Marcus'?" she repeated, this time more softly.

"Huh?" Martin squinted. "No, 'Martin.'"

"'MARTIN!'—That's it!"

Who *was* this gal?

Before he could even raise the question, she informed him: "I'm a friend."

He was even more confused now.

"A friend of Lola's, I mean," she explained. "She asked me to drop by."

"Drop by?"

"To tell you she'd be a little *late*."

Martin looked at her.

"I just came down here to tell you that," she said.

"Right—*late*. I mean, *thanks*." Groping for something else to add, he managed, "Nice. —I mean, *sweet* of you."

She stood there, wearing a girlish smile.

"—To do that," he went on, stammering. "I mean—am I making any sense?"

"No," she grinned.

In fact, studying her face, he realized she was actually quite pretty. Sweet smile. Cheerful eyes. A certain light. (Just jackhammer away all those dark post-punk accoutrements.)

Then, uncharacteristically, he blurted out, "I feel like—I should buy you a *drink* or something."

Wow, just popped out of him: he surprised himself. His

id talking.

She burst out laughing, hardly insulted. "Right," she said. "You have a *date*, remember?"

"I know I know," he said.

"Maybe some other time," she winked, now talking over her shoulder as she tipped away. "Maybe all *three* of us can get together."

"I'd like that."

"Me, too!" she laughed.

Da-amn. Too much!

"All right!" he nodded, waved.

For two seconds he felt like Marcello Mastroianni from *La Dolce Vita*: "Ciao bella!"

"*See ya!*" She turned north on Avenue A.

Martin stood there and smiled. He felt invigorated, like some benevolent spirit had just swept over him.

Stepping out to the sidewalk, he followed her with his eyes until she vanished in the crowd.

Was that a dream, what?

Then Martin dimly recalled a film: *Gregory's Girl*. In a final scene, the shy main character, an ungainly, unpopular adolescent, is to meet up with a girl he's infatuated with. Instead, much to his surprise, another sweet, loving gal appears—almost a projection of the first—who, as if reading his *need*, at once starts to French-kiss him. Startled and shocked at first, the boy just goes with it: surrenders to the impossible, closing his eyes to accept her soft, healing kisses. And just when it seems as though things can't get any more unlikely, any more magical, *that* girl steps away, only to be replaced by *another* kind darling, who also warmly embraces him, starts to kiss him. "That's what girls do. We try to help each other out." It was like some hallucinatory, adolescent wish-fulfillment fantasy with women cast as angels of mercy and understanding. And when Martin saw it in the theater, it was so achingly sweet and innocent, so tender and lovely, it made him cry.

In the next moment, reality kicked in.

A young derelict suddenly emerged from the oncoming pedestrians, got in his face: "Spare some scratch, eh?" He wore patchwork clothes, a rank squatter's smell, and, most impressively, a full-color eagle tattoo down the length of his face.

Talk about the mark of Cain.

Before Martin realized what he was doing, he was digging in his pocket.

"Nice weather we're having," the guy said pleasantly upon receiving the coin.

And Martin had to agree, "Not bad."

The guy floated off, taking his facial tattoo with him, and at that point Martin noticed the chalk drawing on the sidewalk directly beneath him. It was a tribal symbol of some kind, etched in black and gray, in a deliberate primitive style like a cave drawing.

"Pardon me!" emitted a petite goth girl, clutching a bouquet of barbed wire, mincing past.

Martin hadn't realized he was blocking the sidewalk. He wheeled around, back to the store—before nearly bumping into a raggedy-looking man, holding up a boa constrictor, declaring: "For *sale!* For *sale!*"

Turning to watch the snake's forked tongue, Martin felt someone tap him on the shoulder.

He spun around nearly smashing into her.

"Martin?" She wore a leather jacket, torn denims, and

had long black hair cut in bangs across her forehead—eyes dark and intense.

"Yeah?" He felt a pang of excitement.

"I'm Lola," she said, smiling. "Sorry I'm late."

Martin quickly mentioned that her friend had stopped by.

"Oh. She found you. Good."

Starting from the store, they cut right.

Martin found a pack of Juicy Fruit in his pocket and in his uneasiness pulled it out. He saw her looking at it. "Wanna piece?"

"Sure." She thrust out her hand.

Lola offered a simple explanation for her lateness: "I got caught … baby-sitting."

"Baby-sitting?"

"Yeah. Twins.—Mina's, actually. That girl that was just here?"

Martin was chewing a wad of gum. "No kidding?"

"Yeah. She's a stripper in Chelsea. Afternoon shift."

"*Hmm.*" Hiding his surprise. "Must be rough."

"I'll say," said Lola matter-of-factly. "Tipping doesn't really happen till after dark."

They stood before a coffee house/bar.

Martin suggested it. "Cool with this place?"

"We're here," said Lola. "Why not."

The popular hangout had a stylized, homemade sign on top that read, *Babyland.*

29.

Babyland was like the many bars and cafes in the East Village whose décor shared a similar kitsch/retro esthetic, the theme in this case varying slightly in that it also centered on "infantilization." Thus, aside from the insider irony of cheesy cardboard cutouts of beatific nuclear families and wide-eyed freckled-faced boys dreaming of being astronauts, of floating egg creams and malted milk shakes, there was also, throughout the place, a multitude of stuffed animals and Fisher-Price toys and games and, amid other bits of mismatched furniture in the back, four extra-large cribs that diapered patrons could climb into.

The "café" part of the establishment was upfront by the door, and, seizing a window table beside a potted plant cradled in a rickety old-fashioned baby carriage, they soon ordered from the waitress, a young sullen neo-punk who wore a sharkfin mohawk and empty 22. bullet shells through her earlobes.

Then Lola excused herself to use the rest room.

When she returned it was all laid out on the table: a mango smoothie for Martin, licorice tea and black forest cake for her.

"Let me square it," she said, shucking her heavy leather jacket. She removed a folded five-dollar bill from her jeans, slipped it to him.

"Too much," he said, pulling out five singles of his own and passing them back.

"You gave me *five*," she said, counting the bills. She withdrew a single and tossed the rest back.

"Thank you," he said flatly. "And *here's* your change." Sliding the same bills back.

"Hey, what gives here?"

"You wanna start a fist fight?" he countered.

"All right, all right," she said. "I'll get it next time." Then cracking a smile: "But I got my eye on you."

"I'll be careful."

Smiling, she asked, "Not one of those guys that gets weird when a woman pays, are you?"

"Nope. Just the opposite."

"Some guys get weird about it."

"Is that so?"

She nodded. "Their self-esteem's tied up with money."

"Not me," he smiled. "I'd be in trouble."

Martin watched as she picked up her cake with her fingers and took a big, messy bite. He liked this.

"*¿Te gusta?*" he grinned. "Taste awright?"

"*Mmm-hmm!*" she nearly choked, laughing and slowly chewing.

Lola's arms were slender: her shoulders a bit bony, hunched together in a way that suggested she was on edge or full of a kind of nervous energy. Over her tight, small-breasted body, she wore a teal T-shirt with an image of a thorn-crowned Jesus and an inscription that read, "Kill Your Idols."

"Hope your tea isn't cold," he said, distracted.

With her mouth full, she shrugged. She wiped the excess chocolate from her lips with her fingers and brought each finger to her mouth. Then she emptied four packets of sugar into her tea. Then some milk. "I like it sweet," she said.

He laughed. "No foolin'."

"Don't worry," she said, as if trying to read his mind. "I'm not on the needle or anything."

On the needle? *Yeee.*

"That's reassuring."

"I know some people who are, though," she admitted, turning abruptly serious. "I mean, y'know … stone junkies. A pretty sad, pretty pathetic lot, if you ask me."

She sighed and went back to quietly devouring her cake.

Martin had to smile.

Lola's face was narrow but attractive. She wore no make-up aside from simple eyeliner: a single pronounced line running along the edge of each upper eyelid, thinning outwards and up, to a point. Her eyes, beneath those even, neatly brushed bangs, were her most impressive feature. Not only were they large and penetrating, but they were *dark*—each iris nearly the color of the pupil—so that at once they appeared entirely black. Her gaze was starkly compelling.

"So," Martin asked. "You're an artist?"

Lola wiped her lips. "A painter. I hope to be an 'artist' someday. When I'm good enough. Anyway, I still have to get through art school."

"Hard?"

"No, not hard, but mostly a pain in the ass. I'm not a 'school' person."

"Meaning?"

"I hate following instructions. Hate being in a class, doing the same as everybody else. Hate being graded. It's all bullshit. This *herd* mentality. Anyway, I'm almost finished. This is my last semester. Hallelujah."

"Then what? What are you planning to do?"

She shrugged. Feigned a look of helplessness. "Get a job, I guess. I don't know. Paint on the side."

"You've worked before?"

She nodded, leaning forward to take a sip of tea. "Oh sure. Done lots of things. I told you on the phone."

Martin tried to remember: "Oh right. You mentioned working in a pajama factory."

Lola laughed. "That was years ago. In high school. Most

recently I had a job in a body-piercing shop on St. Marks."

He smiled. "Have any piercings yourself?"

"A few."

"How many?"

"None of your business."

Martin was enticed. "Tell me."

"No," she teased.

"C'mon. How many?"

"Five," she finally answered. "Not counting the ears."

"Five? Five separate piercings?"

"Yeah." She shyly took another bite of cake.

"Where?"

She laughed again. "Not telling."

"Why not?"

She shrugged. Took another nibble, looking away a bit flushed.

"I bet I could guess," Martin said.

"Yeah?"

He nodded. "I bet I could."

She grinned. "Fine. Go ahead. Guess."

"No piercings on your face. Except the ears. So I'm guessing the navel?"

"Uh-huh."

"Both breasts?"

"Maybe."

The outline of nipple rings were just barely visible beneath her T-shirt.

"*Hmm*, where else?"

Lola took a long swallow of tea, smiling faintly.

"The tongue?"

"Right."

"And…and," Martin chuckled, "I guess that would leave

one last area."

Eyes down, Lola smiled. "You guessed it."

"No kidding?"

"Yep." She laughed.

Martin teased her a bit. "And that doesn't cause ... any problems?"

She laughed. "Nope. Not usually."

"Not even during sex?"

Lola grinned. "That's ... not up for discussion, right now."

Martin was smiling. "Just curious."

Redirecting the discussion somewhat, Lola related, "Actually, I used to have another piercing. In my left eyebrow."

"Yeah?"

"My body rejected it."

"Huh?"

"Over time, the ring rose to the surface. Then popped out."

"Just fell out? For good?"

She leaned over, showed him the spot. "See? Don't even have a scar from it or anything."

Martin gently touched the corner of her eyebrow and saw it was true. "That's funny."

She laughed. "Wish that would happen with other things in my life!"

Martin smiled. Had to admit: this gal had something going for her. *Pretty damn cute.*

"Why are you grinning?" she asked.

He shrugged. What could he say? That he was enjoying himself?

"I'm entitled," he told her.

30.

Their predetermined "hour" well over, Martin and Lola sauntered up Avenue A.

Along the way, she told him that her parents were divorced and that living at home was "a big mistake." She and her mom fought almost daily. "We hate each other, pretty much," said Lola. "She's a hard person to get along with. 'High strung,' you might say."

"What about you?" he asked.

"I take more after my dad, who's easygoing. But I think as I'm getting older, I'm getting more uptight. Or afraid."

"Happens, I guess."

"Maybe I'm starting to see I've got a real struggle ahead of me. My teachers put me down. They say my paintings are too dark. Too morbid. I say, they're just reflections of what I see, of this side of the world. Am I supposed to close my eyes to everything just because it offends a few people? A few *New Age* twits? What's the point, then? What's the point of making art?"

She turned to him. "Are you at all 'political'?"

"Not really."

Lola took it in stride. "I know I'm not a 'team player' but I feel the need, sometimes, to fuck shit up. Like the riots in Tompkins Park, remember that?"

"'Tompkins Park'?"

"Yeah, back when it was called 'Tent City'? 'Needle Park'?"

He remembered.

"You know about the riots then?"

"Heard about them," he said. It was already part of Village folklore. He'd actually seen a portion of the riots on

TV: part of some reality video show, and had been surprised at the violence of the NYPD. In the days before the Rodney King taping, police were oblivious to the legal threat of video technology.

Lola chimed in: "Five hundred blue coats in riot gear. With their badge numbers taped, full of bloodlust, clubbing the living shit out of anyone in their way. And all for the sake of protecting what?"

Stating the obvious: "Property values?"

"Bingo." She sighed. "If ever there was a class war, *that* was it."

"You were there that night?"

"Yep. By coincidence. I was young, but that didn't spare me from being arrested. Trussed up like some rodeo calf."

Martin tried to imagine it.

Lola scowled: "Those *pigs*. People may want to forget that night, but not me! I won't forget what I saw. No way!" She went on, "It may not do much good to protest, but I do it. I have to. I feel the need. The need to fuck shit up!"

"Ye-ah, rock 'n' roll!"

"Fuck shit up!" She went on: "Even if it means just throwing a bottle at a fucking cop!"

Martin couldn't help but laugh, even had to stop walking a minute.

She continued, "My mother doesn't understand it. She thinks I just want to make *trouble*."

"Nothing wrong with that!"

"Nope," she grinned. "*I* don't think so. Besides, it's fun!"

31.

They rolled to the end of Avenue A on 14 Street, at

which point, not quite done with their conversation, they did an about-face, continuing their walk.

Along the way, heading back in the opposite direction, Lola spoke freely of herself, of her life, spewing quicker and quicker as she frequently became excited, with Martin more than willing to listen, prodding the exchange along, interjecting his own anecdotes and occasional "echoes": "*Uh-huh,*" "*Yeah,*" "*Then what?*"

And *without* faking it: he was genuinely interested, finding her to be lively, spontaneous, and fun. In fact, Martin found himself asking more pointed questions, detailing and matching her interests, getting her to name names, make specific lists.

Call it right-brain pathology.

So what were some of her "telling" obsessions, gleaned from this meandering stroll?

Of those that interested Martin—

Favorite artists: Frida Kahlo, De Chirico, early Salvador Dali.

Books: *House on Mango Street, Our Lady of the Flowers, The Lotus Crew.*

Favorite Poets: Ted Berrigan, "that French asshole—Rimbaud?"

"—And Bukowski?" Martin asked.

"That asshole too," she agreed.

(*Direct hit!*)

Music? She named local favorites—Lunachicks, The Voluptuous Horror of Karen Black, Ramones....

Films? Sid and Nancy, *Los Olividados,* Drugstore Cowboy.

Favorite Booze? wine, non-screw cap, red.

Other favorite things?

It tumbled out of her, by weird association:

Narwhals, penguins, spackle, spray adhesive, crunching ice with her teeth, testing things for poison—"cutting my own hair, swearing never to cut my own hair, cutting my own hair again"—reading, being a freak, writing, reading about freaks, green tea, dancing, blinking, daydreaming, compulsively washing her hands, meditation, social/civil upliftment, abstract thoughts and musings, discordance and dissonance, hyperbole, all that's surreal and magical, right NOW. "The voices in my head—*Ay!*, did I just say that?"

"And that's just the tip of the iceturd," grinned Lola.

She was quite the energetic girl: or was it just the sugar talking?

32.

They arrived at the corner of 13th Street for the third time, the jungle wall murals across the street. "This is my block," said Lola. "A-gain."

"This time I better go," she said. "School and all that."

Martin nodded, gazing blankly at the sidewalk.

"So."

"So."

"An echo, around here?"

Martin laughed.

She said, "So. You'll call?"

What? *Vaya!* Martin was startled, his face brightening. "Yeah."

Next he tipped forward, platonic-like, for a peck on the cheek, and she met him for it. *Smack!* Pasted one right on there: he could feel the moist imprint of her lips on his skin as he pulled away, almost blushing.

"Bye," she smiled. And gave him a final reassuring look.

33.

¿Y ahora?

Next day at home, Martin stared at his phone.

He should tell her, shouldn't he?

He wanted to, really. Finally called her up.

In fact, as always, she seemed nothing if not supportive.

Not the least bit hostile or sarcastic, which might've been the typical reaction.

In the end, he wasn't sure whether to feel gratified or disappointed.

"So," asked Nikki, "*after* the date, what did you do?" Earlier she had cheerfully deconstructed the night's events.

"Went home. Plucked more jive rejection slips out of my mailbox of course. And then—strangest thing—I had this urge to hear her voice. To listen to her message, now that I knew what she looked like."

Martin had sat on the hardwood floor, shredded rejection letters at his side, dialed his *Vox* line, waited for the pre-recording. Then, to his surprise, came this announcement:

"You have ... *three* new messages!"

Wha?

Recovering, he pushed the button to continue.

"Hi. This is Lola. *Just flipping through the paper*...."

"To skip to the next message," said the recorded operator, "press *four*."

After a moment's hesitation, Martin felt compelled to press it.

The new message began:

"Hi, there. I'd like to say I've never done this before. But then, of course, I'd be *lying*." Laughing: "No, let me start over—" Gently clicking off.

The operator returned, "To skip to the next message—" Martin pressed "4."

A somewhat more restrained female voice returned:

"Hi, Martin. That was me just now, being juvenile. Don't know what came over me. All I had to eat today was an avocado, maybe that's it. Anyway, my name is Amaris. Okay, a bit about myself, getting right to it: I'm a part-time English teacher, mother of one. Separated. Due to legal expenses concerning my breakup, I've recently had to move back home. But, yes, I still manage to get out. To the city, I mean." (Martin could hear a young child faintly in the background: "Mommy, *who* is that—*who?*" "Ssshh, eat your ravioli!" "I don't like ravioli!" "Yes, you do." "No, I don't!" "Do." "Don't!") "Okay, back to this: I see myself as being open-minded, someone willing to try new things."—sighing—"I'm also a writer and a poet. Unpublished, but so what. (background: "NO RAVIOLI, HEE-HEE!" "Sssshhhh!" "SSSSSHHH!, YOURSELF MOMMY!, HEE-HEE!" "Okay, you're going to bed!" "NOOO, MOMMY! NOOO!") Okay, back to this: I love to read. I'm into art. Especially pagan and gothic art.

"I don't know what else to add, except: you don't know me yet, but YOU *WILL!*" She burst out cackling.

"—Weird," Nikki chimed in.

Martin laughed. "And she left me her pager number and a short poem. About vampires and white orchids or something."

"Sounds appropriately warped. Call her back yet?"

"It was too late. Plus I was worn-out."

"But you'll get to it?"

"Of course."

"And you'll tell me?"

"Tell you?" Martin said. "Now why wouldn't I?"

34.

It was early on, maybe the third "hangout," that Nikki and Martin met in the back brick-faced room of the popular East Village diner, *Kiev*.

Nikki was talking about her life and choices, being honest, venting: "I don't know," she admitted. "It's funny but I find myself less sure of things the older I get. All the things I thought I knew about? I really don't understand at all. And the biggest mystery isn't even the big wide world— it's yourself. Understanding yourself."

And what exactly did she mean by that, he asked?

"Well, I mean, you may think you want this or that— and spend a helluva' lot of time convincing everyone else, including yourself. When in the end you're not even sure. Deep down, you're not sure. You can never be. That object or whatever it is, may be just a substitute for something else."

Martin nodded as if to say, "I hear ya."

"We can all get sanctimonious and say that most *other* people spend their lives pretending. Living out deceptions. But who's to say we're not all faking it, lying to ourselves, in one way or another?"

"You said it." Martin felt it was true.

Nikki went on, "To be honest, half the time, I'm not even sure if I'm coming or going. Happy or depressed."

"Speaking for myself," Martin said. "If I'm not *totally* depressed, I'm happy."

This made her laugh.

Later, seated with Nikki in the coolness of a theatre (it was The Angelika, the film, "Breaking the Waves"), it was again another opportunity for him to assess his feelings, to marvel at the weird progress of their relationship. Whereas the first time he had met Nikki—especially upon first seeing her—he had felt more than a bit anxious, a tad insecure (thinking to himself, I'm *way* in over my head: she's *way* too ... *way* too ...), he now had to admit he felt (for some unknown reason), an odd closeness: a peculiar ease in being next to her, almost as if he were waking to recall that they'd already known each other for years. Somehow, almost at once it seemed, they'd struck a kind of resonance. Call it chemistry, call it luck, it was the first time he'd been around someone so attractive and complex and not felt an overwhelming desire to hide. Martin went with it, not even having to pretend, to "cover up." In fact, the truth was, it was no effort at all; that was the strange thing. Already he felt he could be himself around her; and more importantly now, around her, he liked who he was.

35.

The next day at work, Martin faced his computer.

```
Japantrack - Air Export Operations
MAIN OPERATIONAL ROUTINES
```

Among the tedious options were: *"Consolidation Manifesting, The Shipper's Export Declaration, Direct Airline/ Masterbill Entry, Shipment Booking Entry, Housebill Entry & Update, Consolidation Pre-Scheduling...."*
Martin felt himself drifting into unconsciousness, his head tipping, tipping forward by degrees until—*SPLAT!*—

crashing against the keyboard.

"Yo, *Bukowski Jr!*"

Martin snapped out of it, turning to Chaz where he sat at his desk.

The man was under a heap of papers. Frowning, he asked, "Do me a solid, bro. Book the consol?"

"You got it," Martin said, blinking his bloodshot eyes, reaching for the last of his bitter morning coffee.

Yes the script was always the same:

MARTIN: Hello, I'd like to book space to Tokyo, please.

AIRLINE AGENT: Number of pieces and weight?

MARTIN: Two thousand pounds.

AGENT: Restricted cargo?

MARTIN: None.

AGENT: Company name?

He gave it.

AGENT: That'll be flight *KZ101*, departing from JFK at *0200* hours. Please have all freight and documentation in on time.

Etcetera, etcetera.

But this time, before Martin had offered the concluding line, his mind was elsewhere—in particular, on phoning Lola.

36.

"So?"

"So."

"So whaddaya' say?"

She sounded subdued. "Can't. Not tonight. School work."

"Tomorrow night then?"

"Project is due at the end of the week."

Was she bluffing him? Playing hard to get?

Or was it an example of the "Principle of Least Interest" tactic?

"What the hell's that?" Martin had asked Nikki, when she once mentioned it to him.

"A guerilla dating tactic," she explained. "'The Principle of Least Interest' implies that in a relationship the person 'least interested' has the most power. Why? Because she *gives the least away*."

He offered a compromise. "How about we set a time limit?"

Lola considered it. "Maybe. I don't know."

"Sure," he craftily suggested. "An hour. Like last time."

"I have a lot of work, though."

"Think about it," Martin said.

"Okay. I will."

"Ring ya, tomorrow? Early?"

"Up to you."

Guerilla dating tactics? *¡Carajo!*...

37.

As it turned out that day, Martin had to stay late at work anyway.

As often happened before, the wait for late shipments dragged on and on. And both Martin and Chaz were stranded with nothing to do but fill out shipping labels and listen to classic rock over the radio. By the time the day's final consolidation to Tokyo was delivered to the airport, it was well past 9:30 PM.

Fucking job.

Once at home, after the maddening drive to find parking, after ripping up his daily clutch of rejection letters and tossing them to the pile, Martin tried ringing the other gal:

"*Hi*," began her message. "This is *Amaris*. You've reached my pager. Following the beep you can key in a phone number or, if you like, leave a brief voice message ..."—and Martin thought about leaving one, but then crapped out and hung the receiver.

He then tried calling Nikki but she wasn't in. And of course he had to frown, *Where was she?*...

"Hey there, wondergal!" started the dopey message he left her. "Hope everything's okay since I spoke to ya last. Talk to you later, *mija!*"

Feeling like a wonder-dork, Martin sat around staring at his TV screen which played a bootleg cassette of the film, *Mishima,* a biopic about the intense, dramatic life of the famed Japanese author/provocateur. Martin had watched the film more than a dozen times because: a) he loved films about writers b) he loved the set design, the soundtrack (by Philip Glass) c) Nikki had given him the tape

He sat back now, zoning out, watching the film's final moments, right before the author's lurid death, thinking, wondering what it was *he* actually wanted out of life—a question Martin had posed to himself a million times before.

To die a noble death, striving for something he believed in—or thought he believed in—or wanted to believe in?

Was it all false hope engendered by a tired romantic ideal?

Or simply to give in, live the compromise, come down from the cross like Christ in that Scorsese movie?

What was it that Nikki had said?

"We can all get sanctimonious and say that most other people spend their lives pretending. Living out deceptions.

But who's to say we're not all faking it, lying to ourselves, in one way or another?"

Martin-san watched onscreen as Mishima, shaking and screaming, applied the knife.

38.

<u>Tears</u>

Sister…
What
might
soothe
those
saddened
cheeks?

Tears,
maybe
tears.

What
might
burn
away
those
parasitic
fears?

Tears,
sister,
maybe

tears.

What
might
fill
those
hollow
days,

those
vacant
weeks?

Tears,
sister,
maybe
tears.

And

what
might
wash
away
those
wasted
years?

Tears,
sister,
maybe
tears.

The
touch
of
tears
might
soothe
those
saddened
cheeks.
And
tears
might
burn
away
those
parasitic
fears.

Tears
might
fill
those
hollow
days,
those
vacant
weeks.

And
tears

tears
might
wash
away
those
wasted
years.

But

o

what

might
dull
the
sharpened
pain?

By 2:00 AM Martin was so headstuffed and drunk he could barely manage to tear up his latest attempts at poetry.

"*Mierda. ¡Pura Mierda!*" he shouted at himself. Then: "Fuck you, Bukowski!"

"Fuck you, too!" Bukowski seemed to say back.

What did he want? Was it all pretense? A mind game of some sort? Always the same questions—along with the same doubts and fears.

And each day, each day he got a little older.

"Fuck it! Fuck it! Fuck it!..."

39.

That night, precisely at 8:30, Lola met Martin at the *No Bar*, and together they grabbed some espresso and *flan* in the back.

The *No Bar* was a café in the tradition of an old European coffee house; a simple place with bare walls, unvarnished wood floors, and antique-looking tables and chairs. By the door, as Martin had entered, an intense chess game was in progress; others sat idly reading the latest *Vox* or another local sheet (this one, anarchist) called *The Shadow*.

"Hardly anyone I know comes here," said Lola. Adding: "That's why I love it."

Lola looked as compelling as she had the first time (if not more so), her dark bangs neatly lined, her large hypnotic eyes made even larger by an expert trace of smudged eye shadow. Again she wore a black m/c jacket, torn and patched jeans, the only difference this time being her loose maroon T (featuring the familiar band logo of an upturned Martini glass) and her silver jewelry. On every finger, thumb included, was at least one burnished ring, the kind sold in rock 'n' roll paraphernalia shops.

Again, seated across from him, her entire body seemed to pulse with a kind of nervous energy.

After starting on a number of inconsequential topics, Martin ventured to ask how things were at home.

She was busy emptying six packets of sugar into her espresso: "'At home'?"

"Yeah. How's your mom been treating you?"

She dropped a spoon into her cup and stirred listlessly.

"Okay, I guess."

"That's good."

"No—actually I'm lying. Terrible. Things are terrible. We fight all the time. From the moment we see each other."

Martin faked a smile. "Oh."

"She's … frustrated, that's all. An old frustrated bag. And lonely. It's how she *entertains* herself—picking fights with me."

"… Really?" He was tasting his flan. Not bad.

"That and watching Spanish soap operas, *novelas*," she nodded.

"What, uh, do you argue about?" He now felt obliged to ask.

"What *don't* we argue about! That's a better question."

She sighed, straightening in her chair. "That witch, she's just pissed off."

"Pissed off—at what?"

"At *life*. For passing her by. At me, for still having mine!" She now leaned back tensely.

"That must get pretty tiring," Martin said.

"What?"

"All that fighting."

"Yeah," said Lola. "*Tiring*. It sure does!"

Martin leaned forward to take a sip of his drink. "So why do you put up with it?"

Her eyes seemed to glaze over.

"—*Uh?*" she said finally.

"Why don't you leave? Move out?"

"'Cause," she said.

"'Cause what?"

"'Cause, I ain't got *this*—" She rubbed her thumb and forefinger together, her dark eyes flashing with anger.

"Oh." Martin nodded.

"Plus," she said, frowning. "She's my mother." She gave up trying to explain: "Kinda complicated."

"I'm sure," Martin said. "I'm sure it is."

"No," she wearily assured him. "I mean, really … it's *complicated*."

A bit confused, Martin looked at her.

At that instant a small haggard-looking woman crept by their table after emerging from the bathroom. At first Martin thought she might try to sell them something, a flower maybe, until she said, "By chance, any of you find it?"

As Lola and Martin now faced her, she went on, "I had twenty dollars—*twenty dollars!*—when I came in here. And now it's *gone!* Any of you find it?"

As both Lola and Martin froze, the woman suddenly burst out sobbing. "Please!" she choked. "Please, I'm poor! I *need* it!"

The crone had deep swaths under her eyes and right then Martin noted the pitted bruises on her arms.

"*Pul-leeze!*" she bawled, her whole body shaking pitifully. "Pul-leeze! I *neeeed* it. I *need* it, *now!*"

At which point the manager appeared. "*Hey!*—Hey you! That's enough!"

"Wha?" She turned around, dismayed.

"I said: That's enough! Get out!"

The old woman dropped the act immediately, straightening up.

"Every night this week," he muttered. Then facing her "—Out!"

Chastised, she finally collected herself and, looking rather proper, shuffled out of the cafe.

"Sorry," he said to Martin and Lola and soon went back

to his post behind the counter. "Every night, *every* night!…"

"*Yeesh*," Martin frowned, lowering his voice. "The fuck was that?"

Lola told him, "Betcha' didn't know it, but that hag used to be—*used to be*—a great poet!"

Martin felt instantly ill.

"Or is it, '*poetess*'?" She shrugged.

"What's wrong with her now?" he finally managed to ask.

"A bad case of the dope flu." She sighed. "Christ, I'll be back."

40.

"Before going on a personal ad date," Nikki once told him in jest. "Always check for a full moon."

Now he knew she wasn't lying.

After Lola returned from the restroom, she edged back into her corner seat, mumbling, "Where were we?"

Slouched in his chair, he lied, "Can't remember."

"Oh yeah," she recalled then. "My *mother*." She raised her cup and took a sip. Replacing it on the saucer, her expression changed. Grew soft. She said quietly, "*Perdóneme*."

"Huh?" He looked up. It was the first time she spoke Spanish to him.

"I mean, I'm not always such a schizoid, awright?" She tried to smile.

"I thought maybe it was just the caffeine," he said, half-seriously.

"That could be," she said, frowning. "I do feel a little sick."

"Or maybe," he went on, trying to smooth things out,

make her feel better. "Maybe, I just ... pushed the wrong button or something?"

"Well, I *am* sorry," she said again, sincerely.

"*Ah* ..." He tried to wave it off.

"Just that," she said, "when it comes to my mom, y'know ... I have this thing. This history."

Martin assured her, "Believe me. *Lots* of people have hang-ups when it comes to their parents."

"I know." She took a moment. "I know, and maybe I shouldn't tell you this. You'll think I'm ..." She whistled, rolling her eyes. "But when I was little and my dad left me—that is, my mom and me—I got this idea, *this funny idea* ..." Trailing off.

"Yeah?" he said, bracing himself. "What kind of idea?"

Lola looked embarrassed. "Well, that my mom wanted to murder me."

"'Murder' you?"

"Seriously," she said.

"Murder you?"

"It was just this *feeling*." Lola nodded. "I don't know what else to call it. This *intuition*."

He put down his cup. "Were you ever abused as a kid?"

She shook her head, no.

"Your mom never beat you or anything?"

Again: no. "But it was just a horrible feeling. That she wanted me *dead*. That she was out to poison me or something."

"So," he looked at her seriously, "what did you do?"

"Well, I pretended *not* to notice."

"Not to notice that your mom wanted to murder you?"

"Yeah." She bobbed her head up and down. "Then, more or less, I just stopped eating. So she couldn't poison me."

He narrowed his eyes. "And, she didn't notice?"

Lola shrugged. "I was careful. Like, if my mom cooked me something—a hotdog, say?—I'd take one tiny bite while she was looking? then, as soon as she turned her back, I'd toss the rest behind the stove or out the window. You can't even imagine the roach problem we had!"

He forced a dry laugh. "And then?"

"This went on and on … on and on," she said, glassy-eyed. "Till … till I felt too tired to go to school in the morning."

"I'll bet!"

"Then," she laughed. "I finally woke up. At St. Vincent's."

"You did?"

She nodded.

Martin sighed. "And what happened after that?"

"Well, once there, at the hospital, they ran all kinds of tests. Searched and searched. Didn't find anything, of course. Finally they recommended a child psychologist, but my mom wouldn't hear of it. 'That's for crazy people! *Locos!*' she said."

"And they sent you home?"

"Well, afterwards. Yeah. They had no choice. And my mom started treating me a little nicer for a while. Because she was scared."

Martin was eyeing her uneasily.

"But let me tell you, once my dad left us, took off? We never trusted each other after that." She shook her head. "I mean, *never.*"

"Wow," Martin said quietly, frowning. "*Heavy.*"

A bit dazed, fumbling in his seat, Martin tipped and

dropped his teaspoon beneath the table.

At that point the manager came by asking if there would be anything else. Martin quietly asked for the check.

Lola looked uneasy. She took a moment to finish her flan. "So," she asked. "What about you?"

"Me?"

"Yeah, *your* mom," she asked, wiping her lips. "Didn't you mention that she passed away?"

"I mentioned that?"

"During our talk," she nodded. "Last time."

"Yeah. Long time ago." He tried to regain his focus. "I was a kid."

"So who raised you?" she asked.

"Grandparents," he said.

"In Queens?"

"Inwood. Manhattan. Up near the Bronx."

"I think I know where that is."

"Can hardly remember it, actually," he said. "Like I remember my parochial school? 'Good Shepherd,' it was called. I remember these white rocks just across the street. Sandstone, I think. And I remember these great parks. This one *huge* park, nearby. With giant ballfields. And Indian caves. Beautiful." Martin leaned back. "I remember this one big rock that had a plaque on it, marking the exact spot where the Dutch supposedly bought Manhattan Island from the Indians. For twenty-four bucks."

"—Yeah right," said Lola. "Very generous of them, those Dutch."

"Well, somebody always gets fucked." Martin went on, "What else do I remember? I remember my mom, always sleeping. Being depressed. Only I didn't know why at the time. Or what it meant. To this day, I'm still trying to figure it out."

She asked, "Were you happy as a kid?"

"Happy?" He thought about it. "Nah."

"Me, neither," she confessed. "I remember wishing the whole world would end. I kept praying for those bombs from Russia."

Martin almost cracked up.

Lola continued, "I kept looking up at the sky at night. And saying, 'Where *are* those warheads already?'" She laughed. "Seemed like such a waste to leave 'em in those silos, gathering cobwebs and dust."

"You were praying for Armageddon?"

"Yup. Now and then, I still do. Still pray for it. For one last mondo-cosmic *ka-boom!*"

"Hey," Martin said, laughing. "I thought you were into social justice and all that? Politics."

"I am," she smiled. "That's what I mean."

"—Like that inscription outside of *7A?*" Martin tossed in, "'*World Politics got you down? Try drinking.*'"

"Yeah. Obliteration—my point exactly."

Martin chuckled, draining his cup.

Lola fixed her dark eyes on him.

"Hey," she suggested. "I have an idea. Why don't we get the fuck out of here? Go up to my place?"

It caught him unexpectedly. "But what about your mom?"

"She's out. Uptown, actually."

"And your school work and everything?"

"*Ah,*" she grinned. "Fuck that."

41.

Lola's place—or the one she shared with her mother—

was on the fifth floor of an old brick walkup on 13th Street. Up the rickety staircase just past the first floor lay a scruffy teenager, eyes rolled back in his head.

"That's just Steve," she said blandly. "He *lives* here."

"What's up with him?"

"Goofed up on *K*, probably."

Martin asked what that was.

"Oh, an animal tranquilizer...."

By the third floor, continuing on the subject of drugs, Lola was telling Martin about her first boyfriend, years ago—some creep by the name of "Maze"—who, after their break-up, had become, as she put it, "a serious drug abuser."

"We were still speaking," she said absently. "Tried to remain friends, but it got hard. The asshole started main-lining about four months after we stopped seeing each other. Till then, it was just some chipping. As a weekend thing." She turned back to him. "Y'know, a little taste, now and then."

Mainlining? Chipping? *Oy.*

"So what'd he do for a living?" Martin asked.

"Not a whole lot," she replied. "He was kinda like, a performance artist."

"He recited dramatic pieces 'n' stuff?"

Lola sighed. "No. More like, he juggled on street corners. And sometimes panhandled."

"Oh."

"He was also in a ska band," she added wearily. "But they never really practiced."

"Uh-huh."

"Anyway, he's in prison now...."

Her apartment was a typical Lower East Side railroad

flat, one ridiculously narrow space linked to the next. In the living room, Lola offered him a spot on the slipcovered couch. "Forgot I needed to pay a call," she said.

"Okay. Sure." He sat down, the plastic crackling beneath him.

"You can check out those dumb art books or whatever." She pointed at the stack by his feet, the kind of hefty hardcovers once sold by well-stocked book peddlers along the main drag of St. Marks. The top volume featured the work of the great English painter Francis Bacon.

When Lola re-entered the room, Martin was still flipping pages, regarding the artwork.

"He had a habit of wearing fishnet stockings and garters under his pants," she casually imparted.

"Who?"

"Him. Francis Bacon. Helped him to relax."

Martin looked at a self-portrait of the painter's broad, wildly distorted face and tried to envision it.

She went on, "I also read somewhere that he would gamble to *lose*. He wanted to lose. To always be in debt."

Martin told her there was a French novelist like that. "Some prolific old guy, what's his name?" Closing his eyes, he tried to remember. It finally came to him: "Balzac."

"Guess when you think about it," Lola said, "not too many artists lead 'healthy' lives."

"Nope."

"Thought about this the other day," she continued, joining him on the couch, "that most artists probably need to maintain a certain level of 'dysfunction,' a certain amount of self-loathing. 'Cause why do it? Why wallow in that much dejection and abuse, purposely?"

"I can see that," Martin said. "See your point, I mean."

Lola persisted, "And what starts out as a simple need to make art becomes this endless cycle of rejection and self-abuse. Self-flagellation to work, rewarded with rejection culminating in self-disgust. Then add public apathy to that and whaddaya got?"

"T'ain't healthy," said Martin. "That's for sure."

Finally he closed the book, put it back. After a moment, looking around the room, he asked her where she managed to paint.

"Where?—Right here." She shrugged, indicating the same space.

Martin looked around. "So where's your easel and all that? Your canvasses?"

"Packed up and put away."

"Any chance I can see some of them?"

"My paintings?"

"Yeah," he grinned. "Your paintings."

Lola appeared undecided, but at last, standing up, said, "Well ... *all right*. Wait here." And uneasily left the room in the direction of the kitchen.

Martin could hear her rustling a beaded curtain, open and close a cupboard. Some cutlery clattered to the floor. "Shit!" he heard her cry.

Lola finally returned clutching a knotted garbage bag in her right hand. In her left hand she was holding a bottle and a corkscrew. Handing him the wine, she insisted, "Before you look, you gotta open this."

"Sounds cool to me," Martin grinned and, accepting the bottle, put it between his knees, applying the corkscrew.

Lola joined him on the couch and unknotted the garbage bag, taking a nervous look inside. "These are *early* ones. But I still like 'em."

"I'm sure they're good," he said, grimacing as he pulled out the cork, then peeled away the remaining pewter wrapping.

Lola lunged for the bottle. "Me first!" Taking a long pull, then passing it back: "*Ahora tú.*"

"*Gracias.*" Obliging her, some wine dribbled from his lip.

"And now the art!" she announced, digging into the sack and yanking them out. Kicking the empty plastic bag away with her foot. "*Tah-dah!*"

His eyes widened in regarding the work: two canvass-es—both portraying, in startling hyper-realistic detail, nightmarish scenes of intense psychopathic violence.

In the first, entitled "Pig Party," several NYPD officers were shown gruesomely dismembered, the amputated limbs of one cop brutally wedged up his own obscenely stretched rectum. In the other, untitled, a white-haired girl in pigtails sat dreamily on a curb, site of a horrific traffic accident, munching human entrails like raw link sausages. In her lap, like a grinning moon, a severed head. Carved on the forehead was a tiny cross and, just above it, the word, "Lolita."

Both canvasses were slathered in blood red from top to bottom.

"These are my least hostile paintings," she informed him.

" 'That right." He took another slug of wine, wrinkling his nose, swallowing.

"So," she nudged, "whaddaya say?—Is *mah' clit showin'* or what?"

Martin continued to regard them with a dazed expression. A minute skirted by. At last, he thought to remark,

"Sure ain't 'new age'—I'll say that!"

42.

Somehow or other Lola and Martin got on the topic of "relationships" and Lola was again talking about her first boyfriend from years ago: "Maze."

"Motherfucker," she said, bitterly recalling him. "What a conniving asshole, fuck-ass liar! Like all of them."

All of whom Martin asked her.

"Stone cold junkies," she said. "I'm so tired of them, I can't tell you."

"You dated a lot of them?" he asked with some concern.

"In the beginning," Lola admitted. "Yeah." And added, "Not for any particular reason. I was *young*."

"'Maze' was a *supreme* asshole," she went on. "But maybe still not as bad as the boyfriend right after that: 'Zed.'— God, what a lowlife!"—she rolled her eyes—"He's away, too. Serving ten to fifteen, at least!"

Martin felt like a boyscout. "You seem to know a lot of people in prison," he remarked.

Lola replied with a shrug, "Whaddaya want? I was young. And I was dumb. Eager for experience, y'know. All that bullshit."

"So, what'd he do?" Martin couldn't help but ask.

"Zed?"

Martin nodded.

"The crown prince of fuck-ups?" she said. "Attempted robbery. This was the day *after* he tried to hang himself from a tree in Tompkins Park and nearly got arrested. For destruction of public property: the branch he tried broke in half and nearly hit him on the head!"

"He attempted robbery? Armed?"

"Sorta."

"Whaddaya mean, 'sorta'?" Martin asked.

"Ah well," Lola confided. "He tried to rob a liquor store with a knife."

"—A 'knife'?"

"It was sharp," she assured him.

"So what happened?"

"Whaddaya think?" Lola frowned. "He barrels into a liquor store, right off whips out this stupid blade, demanding all the money. The guy behind the counter calmly draws a handgun, takes aim, and—*BLAM!—shoots* him!"

Martin tried to suppress a laugh but lastly couldn't.

"H-he wasn't fatally hurt, though?" he finally managed to ask.

Lola shrugged. "Nah. No such luck. He went to Saint Vincent's. Then straight to jail."

"Oh *man*." Martin was chuckling.

It was just too terrible.

"Soon after that, probably the next day," Lola went on. "They had a nickname, a little moniker for him, over at the 9th Precinct. I heard about it later."

"And what name was that?"

"'*King ZERO*....'"

43.

Twenty minutes later, Lola and Martin were both on the carpet, the empty bottle between them.

"Let me ask you another one," he said.

They were side-by-side, flat on their backs by now, waxing philosophical, Lola gamely answering each far-flung, drunken question.

"Did you say you believed in *God*?" he asked. He had a

decent head, surprisingly. Nothing like cheap wine to fuck you up.

"*Who?*"

"You know, in like a 'higher power'?"

She thought about it. "Nah."

"Then, what," he asked. "Fate?"

"Hah?"

"Do you believe in *fate?*"

Again she thought about it, finally shaking her head. "Nuh-uh." She clicked the jewelry in her mouth. "I think things just happen. Without reason. One person is born. Another vanishes. No one knows why. Or has any real say."

"So, lemme get this straight, people have no power?"

"Guess so."

"But can't they, y'know, *initiate* things sometimes?"

"Whaddaya mean?"

He explained, "Well, here I placed a personal ad and you answered it, right?"

"Yeah. *So.*" She absently rubbed a nipple ring through her T.

Martin slid the empty bottle away, moving closer. "So, I'm just saying, it *was* through some *active effort* on our part that things happened. That we connected. At just this time."

Lola was starting to look annoyed. "What are you getting at, exactly?"

"I'm not sure." He said finally, "I guess I was thinking it does seem like a lucky break."

"What does?"

"Our connecting. At just this time."

"Oh sure," said Lola. "I believe in luck."

"And I guess," he went on. "Guess, I'm trying to say"—forcing a laugh—"I'm kinda glad you answered my ad."

"Oh aren't *you* sincere!"

"Huh?"

She snorted, "You guys are all the same!"

"What?"

"Next you'll tell me you're hooked, right?"

"Huh?"

"In *love*."

He forced another laugh. "All I'm saying is, I'm glad we met."

"Oh, all right." She faced away.

He prodded now: "Aren't *you* glad?"

She ignored him. Teasingly.

"Hey, Yoko," lightly tapping her on the shoulder. "Yoo-hoo, *Ms. Francis Bacon*."

She faced him again, smirking. "What?"

"Aren't *you* glad?"

"Um." She took a long moment. "Like … can you repeat the question?"

"Cute," he said.

"Say, I got a riddle for you," she said, giggling. "Why do men have a hole in their penis?"

"Huh? Dunno."

"So oxygen can get to their brains."

"That's kinda hostile," he remarked, half-smiling.

"Hang on," she tittered. "Got another: How many men does it take to screw in a light bulb?"

He squinted, shrugged.

"One." She grinned. "Men will screw anything."

"Damn. I guess you're trying to tell me something, huh?"

"Got another," she said, sniggering. "Why did the man cross the road?"

He sighed. "Why?"

"He heard the chicken was a slut."

Martin propped himself up on his elbow. "I guess it's time for me to go, huh?"

"My mom may be coming home soon," she finally admitted.

"Oh."

"Yeah. I live with my mother, remember?"

"Right."

"She may be coming home soon."

"Gotcha'."

"Sorry. Thems the breaks. Especially on a school night."

"Hard," he teased. "You're hard. I'm totally convinced."

"That's right," she said proudly. "I'd sooner be a bitch than a doormat."

44.

At the door: "One last one," Lola said. "Why don't women blink during foreplay?"

He didn't know the answer.

"They don't have time." She winked.

"Good one," Martin said. "I guess."

He was starting to feel abused.

"C'mon," she said. "What's the rush?"

"Meaning what?"

"Let's take it easy."

"Okay, fine." Then, in the next breath: "What are you doing this weekend?"

"Don't know. Painting, I guess."

"Even *Saturday* night?"

"Actually, Saturday, I'm going to a party."

"Oh?"

"Yeah, with Mina. You met Mina, remember?"

He tried not to appear jealous. "The stripper. Yeah."

"Well, she's not *just* a stripper," said Lola. "She's my friend."

"Okay, yeah." Whatever. He was starting to feel cranky.

"It's just some party," she said consolingly.

"Uh-hmm."

"We can go out some other time."

Martin shrugged, trying to feign indifference. Then countered: "What makes you think *I* want to?"

Lola smiled. "*I* think you want to."

He shrugged again, irritated. She was right, of course. Could she read him *that* easily? Was he *that* transparent?

She reiterated, "We'll go out some other time."

"Yeah," Martin sighed. "*Mm-hmm.*"

"*Mm-hmm,*" she laughed.

"I just said that."

Lola laughed again. Finally Martin cracked a smile.

With that, she leaned forward to offer him a kiss. Her tongue in his mouth, he managed to draw her stud between his front teeth:

"—Promise?"

Startled, she nearly gagged, "*Yeh!*"

He let go.

45.

"Call me 'Martin-MacDaddy,'" he joked with Nikki. To which of course she laughed.

"Never fails," he said. "Offer a gal the choice of a noose and a night of love with yours truly. Nine out of ten will take the rope!"

"C'mon," sniggered Nikki. "Don't be so hard on your-self!"

But Martin was just getting started: "Quasimodo, the hunchback of Notre Dame, had better luck!"

"Stop it!" she said, laughing. "Don't be ridiculous!"

"I'm not," Martin said. "I wish it weren't true," he said. "But there it is."

"So tell me," Nikki asked, her curiosity piqued. "What's the worst date you've ever been on?"

They'd known each other for well over two months and in that time had grown tight.

"I already told you some of 'em."

"No, but I mean, the worst one...."

Martin considered it. "You know, I'd rather forget the more disturbing ones."

"But, okay," Nikki said. "Then how about the most recent."

"Most recent ... okay I'll give you a silly one."

"'Silly' is fine." She smiled.

The waitress had just arrived with their order, a sun-shine burger and a spinach salad. They were seated outside the Yaffa Café, on St. Marks Place. "Like, okay," he began, "six weeks ago, gal leaves me a message. Name is 'Tara,' right? Seems okay, down to earth. I call her, we talk a while. Goes well. Call her a second time—more of the same. Pretty smooth. So finally I say, 'Hey, look, why don't we just get together? Okay, right. So the spot we agree on is Third Avenue, in front of St. Mark's Bookshop. On a Saturday, six o'clock."

"And what."

"The day comes. Six o'clock. No Tara. I'm standing

there like an ass."

"She stood you up?"

"I'm not that lucky," Martin said with a smirk. "Anyway, I wait around."—biting into his burger—"Wait around."—chewing … lastly swallowing—"I had a paperback, some Kerouac novel, so I lean against the store, zoning out, and start reading. Finally, maybe forty, fifty pages later, this strung-out wretch shows up—"

" 'Strung-out'?"

"She looked it, I dunno." Martin shrugged. "I mean, rags falling off her, hair a nest. Y'know, full of those natty multicolored extensions, like cotton snakes, you don't know if they're supposed to be dreadlocks or what?—The type only a cool 'urban' white chick would be caught dead with?"

Nikki laughed.

"So, okay. I'm a little pissed now. But I'm trying to be a good sport, y'know? A gentleman. She croaks, 'Hi, I'm not late, am I?' An *hour* late now, no explanation. 'No,' I say, 'You're early.' She then admits how she just 'fell out of bed.' 'Just now? Just fell out?' I say with faked interest. 'No foolin'?' (Nearly dark out, mind you.) 'Rough night, uh?' I ask. She gives me this look. Right. Okay, so she doesn't want to go anywhere to eat 'cause she says she feels 'woozy,' more than slightly nauseous, like she might puke. I'm thinkin', that makes two of us. Anyway, it's past 7:15 now and we're still standing there, trying to decide where to go, what to do. I suggest a bunch of places, spots to hang out, she nixes every last one, when outta the blue she goes, 'Hey, I know, let's go to a music store.' Okay, there's a bunch on St. Marks. 'No,' she says, 'let's go to Tower!' I'm like, Huh? 'TOWER!' she suddenly screams, like it's her only salvation. I'm all confused, startled too. 'Well, aw-right. If you wanna,' I say. And we start to make our way over—I know the whole thing's stupid, but I just give into it, why not."

Martin takes another bite of his burger, chews, swal-lows. "So," he continues, "over to Broadway then, which is jammed of course, teeming with people. We go inside the store, more of the same. It's a Saturday, don't forget. She makes a beeline for this CD rack. I follow. While she's look-ing at some CD, I pick up some rock magazine from the shelf nearby, start flipping through it. I keep glancing up at her. She's picking up another CD now, studying the back. I go back to looking at my dumb magazine, flipping more pages. I look up at her—still with the CD—go back to my magazine. And so on. Till one minute I look down, the next I look up. And—she's gone!"

"What," Nikki choked.

"—I mean, like POOF!—vanished! I look around, star-tled—y'know, dumbfounded, thinking, 'Wait! Shit!—what just happened?' I look around—not a godamn trace of her! I'm left standing there like a jackass! And that was it. That's it!" He took another bite of his burger. Chewed. "Like a joke without a punch line. Story of my life."

Nikki tipped over, convulsing.

Martin swallowed, grinned. "I looked all over for her. Front of the store. Even went to wait a while by the revolv-ing doors, thinkin', 'Well, shit, maybe she just got lost or something.' Also thinking to myself, 'No one could be that self-centered and cold, *right?*'"

Nikki covered her mouth, trying to contain herself.

"But *ha!* Guess again!" laughed Martin. "Bye-bye taran-tula hairdo! That scamp was *gone!* Chalk up another one for *The Twilight Zone!*"

Nikki was on the verge of losing it again. Finally she asked, "What'd you do? After that?"

"That night? After being ditched?"

She nodded, still giddy.

Martin shrugged. "Hung around for a bit more, propping on some stupid headphones for music I had no intention of buying, like all the other assclowns in the store. Then, when I finally had enough, I left. Tipped to the movies. Blew it off. Happens, there was a Buster Keaton festival over at the Forum. Lucky for my sorry ass."

46.

And what about Nikki?

Did she remain aloof, untouched by the dreariness of the world, untested in her perfection and destined only to laugh down from Mount Olympus at mere mortals, eejits, like Martin?

Wrong.

Much as Martin thought she was without peer or equal, perfect as any swingin' gal could be, Nikki kept trying to offer evidence to the contrary.

When Martin asked her to reveal a few humiliating episodes from her own seemingly charmed life, she didn't hesitate to offer up some choice pathetic, agonizing gems.

THINGS NIKKI TOLD MARTIN ABOUT HERSELF:

Like the time, in the second grade, sitting in the front row of her class, when she loudly sneezed—let loose a real blast—and realized she'd also peed on herself. "Peed," as in "cut loose." And not just a little! An actual *puddle* had formed in her seat that quickly! Nothing she could hide.

Then, for the worst of it, being led out of the room, her bottom soaked—"of all the luck, wearing white cotton that day; yes, how absorbent!"—led away by the teacher like a grim-faced prison guard, to the jeers and guffaws of her fellow classmates, other girls included. Little Nikki, petrified in her humiliation, too numb to think, wanting, wishing to fade away, leave this sorry earth and never return. "Oh, don't worry, sweetie," her mother lied to her once at home. "It's really nothing. You'll get over it, forget it. Your little classmates won't even remember it by next week. Just give it a day or two...."

Another time, fourth grade, during gym class, being led outside to a nearby park, because it was a lovely spring day, allowed to play tag with all the boys and girls. Then running down a hill, slipping and falling. That was all she remembered. Later, back with her classmates, about to reenter the school, someone mewling, "*Eeeewww*, what is that *smell?*" Then, to her horror, turning to see that her new pleated skirt was smeared not only with grass stains, but dog crap, acquired apparently in that brief tumble down the hill. Again, in front of her classmates, being led away by her teacher (another, grim-faced too) to call her mother to pick her up, young Nikki bursting into tears, chest heaving, asking over and over, "Why me? *Why me?...*"

Martin had asked her, "In school, were you popular?"
She shook her head, no.
"Not ever?" Martin asked, disbelieving.
"Nope."
"I was kind of a loner. Always off to the side. Y'know,

sorta invisible."

"No way!" Martin said. "Me? I was always in the back of the room. Mr. Nonentity."

She admitted to being a bookworm, "straight-A class A nerd."

"Me?" Martin grinned. "I was dumb! All my teachers thought I was mildly retarded, I swear!"

She was totally into books: C. S. Lewis, Roald Dahl....

"Me?" said Martin. "Comics. Marvel Comics, like *The Avengers*. I wouldn't even read them, though, I'd only *look at the pictures!*"

Nikki laughed.

"And TV?" asked Martin.

"My mom wouldn't let me watch more than an hour a night," she confessed.

Martin? "Six, seven hours a night! All I could stand, as long as I turned it low, not to disturb my mother who was either asleep or writing."

"I was homely," she stated outright, one day.

"Yeah right," Martin replied, smirking. "Homely as Rachel Welch in the '70s, homely as Brigitte Bardot in the '60s!"

"I'm serious!" she said and, as evidence, produced childhood pictures.

"See?" she pointed out. "Glasses, how dorky I was. Pudgy, even."

Martin's eyes widened in amazement.

"All I did was read books and keep to myself," she said. "I never wanted to participate in any class activities, most of which were dumb anyway. I mean 'status quo generic.'"

Martin had a little trouble believing it.

"I was like that little girl in *Welcome to the Dollhouse*, the Todd Solondz film."

"You *were* not!" he cried. "Not like *Wiener Dog!*"

"Just about," she insisted. "That girl was me. Maybe I was a little better coordinated physically. But, yeah, lost in my own private 'special people club,' all right!"

Martin had to laugh.

Of course, it'd been the same with him. Only he was still that uncoordinated.

Aside from being a lover of Marvel comics, his very typical boyhood obsessions included Japanese monster movies, Planet of the Apes, and the original Star Trek series.

To this day a pair of Spock ears brought him a certain level of comfort.

Days when he felt stressed out, he still daydreamed of watching Scooby-Doo cartoons and wearing a pinwheel hat.

Nikki confessed to a mild Bugs Bunny fetish. "I sometimes used to masturbate with the image of Bugsy in my head, I don't know why. Maybe it was the big soft feet or the tail*."

"I can dig that," Martin said. "The tail, especially."

She also admitted to a mild infatuation with Garfield, the cat.

"I was into Betty Rubble, from *The Flintstones*," Martin divulged. "That Barney was a lucky bastard!"

"When did you lose your virginity?" Martin asked.

"Sophomore year, high school." She frowned. "Horrible!"

"Senior year. College," Martin retorted. "She fell

---

*later able to recall the exact episode triggering the fetish, which involved *spanking*: "Baby Buggy Bunny."

asleep!"

Nikki burst out laughing.

"Is it in, yet? Is it *in?*" Martin cackled. "Just before she passed out!"

Strangely, in high school—even throughout college, more surprisingly—Nikki hardly dated, at all.

"Okay," said Martin. "Now you're just pulling my chain."

She laughed. "I'm not! It's the truth!"

"I hardly dated, either," Martin confessed. "I don't know why. Maybe I was too shy. Or too depressed. I tried to avoid the whole issue, thinking I'd make up for it later, somehow. When I was famous, maybe. A big, famous poet/novelist unlike the kind the world had ever seen!, etc., etc., yada, yada …."

Nikki laughed. "I tried to avoid the whole thing, too. Who wouldn't? I just didn't see myself as a "normal" gal, a future homemaker and soccer mom. I just didn't see it. I never wanted to be married, even. What was the point of being like everybody else? Like in that film *Invasion of the Body Snatchers*, I didn't want to be 'taken over,' welcomed 'into the fold,' made into one of 'them.' I just wanted to think for myself. If that meant living alone as a hermit, being thought of as "queer," so be it. I just wanted to understand life on my own terms. Not be told how things were and given some stupid rule book to follow…."

Martin grew silent, practically swooning, thinking, *This woman, my God!*…

And what was this about her thinking she was "homely"? This was in the past, right? Completely erased from her memory?

"Part of me still feels that way," she admitted.

"You can't be serious," Martin said.

Her gaze was holding his. "It's true."

Homely?! The very thought of it made him laugh.

If this was the case, how she felt, he said, it was the perfect retelling of the ugly duckling story.

"If ever there was a swan!" he told her.

Even though this statement had elicited a visible reaction from Nikki, a gratified laugh, she hardly seemed to swallow it, to believe it.

"Not much for irony, are you, Marty?" she smiled.

"Can't even manage that," he laughed.

He made a small gesture, moving forward, hoping to bring her into his arms, hoping she'd take him up on it. Allow it.

She did.

Martin held her a while, smoothing his hands over her arms, feeling the warmth of her back, catching sight of her closing eyes, her hair on his cheek finally.

His best friend, his *mija*.

Oh Nikki.

Who else could make him feel this way?

47.

"Awright, *Bukowski Jr!* Here goes!"

It was at work, with Chaz atop his desk, offering Martin a rendition of his own rarefied "poetic stylings."

"Ready to take notes, kid?"

"'Ey, get down!" Martin laughed.

"Dig it:

"There was a young sop from Mattoon
Whose farts could be heard on the moon!
When you least would expect 'em,
They'd blow from his rectum,
Like a blast from a double bassoon!"

"Thank you, thank you!" he said, promptly taking his bows. "Just mail the Nobel Prize straight to my house, thanks."

Adding: "Now that's what you call some REAL poetry!" Hopping down from the desk: "*Confessional*, too! Thinkin' you the only poet around—*HA!*"

About his job? It was shit. Or as Martin would say, *mierda*. But now and then, between the two of them, they managed to make it all somehow tolerable.

When it came to amusement, a way to wile away the time between late shipments, if there was something Chaz loved—loved even more than fool limericks—it was music.

The source of this desperate entertainment? A dinosaur 8-track stereo he picked up off the street: "Awright, from the garbage, so what? Shit works, bro!—I'll make it work!"

The reception usually sucked due to the proximity of the airport, but they were able to get several FM stations.

Mornings, they usually listened to WBAI, Pacifica Radio.

Wednesdays hosted the Victoria Starr show, "Ghost in the Machine," Thurdays Delphine Blue's "Shocking Blue": cutting-edge programs each, featuring bands with names like "Barbie Complex," "Dog Mouth," "Craphead." "And that was 'Atomic Bitchwax' from their 'Total Castration'

CD," Starr would announce. "Catch them later this month at the Fierce Pussy Festival, along with 'The Post-Christ Disciples,' 'Screaming Headless Torso,' and 'Shirley McDicklips and the Ass Clamps!'"

When things turned political on the station, they turned to classic rock with Chaz cranking the volume until the walls seemed to bulge and warp—and every unstrapped piece of freight in the warehouse seemed to dance and jitter.

Hendrix, Neil Young, Led Zeppelin ... these weren't quaint "oldies" to Chaz but pulsing artifacts, vital reminders of better times, times when all you needed was a bottle of red, a painted denim jacket, and a portable transistor radio; Chaz supporting the audacious, layered guitar solos with echoes of *"Yeah, get down!"*, *"Play it, brother!"*, *"Amen!"*

Sadly, with non-public radio came the endless commercials.

"Aaah, whaddaya gonna do?" he would grouse, when they seemed to go on and on, ad nauseaum, hammering a listener silly.

"I already told ya," said Martin. "Dig up some funky 8-tracks!"

Chaz had to laugh, scratching his head. "Wish I still had 'em, bro. Suckers are loooong gone. Contributed mine to the Smithsonian." Reminiscing, *"Shit*, big clunky things. You needed a whole separate room to store 'em in, all that godamn plastic and tape! Dig it, had me a friend used 'em to build a doghouse once 'stead of bricks!"

"Get out!"

"Brother, I shit you not!" Chaz grinned. "Mighta' built a whole new extension to his house, too, 'cept he finally ran out!..."

```
Japantrack - Air Export Operations
MAIN OPERATIONAL ROUTINES

(1) Consolidation Manifesting
(2) Shipper's Export Declaration
(3) Direct Airline/Masterbill Entry
(4) Shipment Booking Entry
(5) Housebill Entry & Update
(6) Consolidation Pre-scheduling
```

A brief smile.

Now back to this:

At last, Martin hit (5), the bulk of his daily work.

Facing the stack of invoices on his desk, Martin began with the *Shipper's Address,* then *Company Consigned,* continuing to *Airport of Departure* and *First Carrier.* On and on, down the face of the template.

Hitting *Return* again, a second screen appeared, and Martin hastily filled in the requested information (weight, "airfreight" charge, reference and license numbers, transport and customs fees), completing the form at the bottom, by adding his own name, humble company position ("Export Assistant") and the date.

Finally, he punched "Post & P," and the dot matrix printer behind him began loudly scraping and sputtering, jamming almost immediately.

Realigning the paper, Martin tried again. It lodged and crumpled. He leveled it strategically. And this time, at long last, a completed House Air Waybill emerged (in a twin, multi-layered form) from the crusty, outmoded, mostly unreliable machine.

And, straightening the pile of sixty or so invoices left on his desk, he thought then, *'Makes one down* ... his gaze landing on the sticker over his monitor (placed by some distant, long forgotten export assistant):

"Any Idiot Can Face A Crisis—
It's This Day-to-Day Living
*That Wears You Out."**

48.

"Whatever happened to the second one? The one with the beeper?" Nikki asked. They were on the phone to each other. She was back to his ad dates.

"Amaris?"

"That her name?"

"Paged her yesterday, early. And she rang me back. Left me a message at home."

Replaying it:

"Hi, Martin. Good to hear from you. In case you're wondering, it wasn't too late yesterday when you called, just that I was out and couldn't get back to you right away. You know how it is downtown, sometimes. Can't find a phone when you need one: every one is either taken or jacked. And actually, as far as the hour, just so you know—me being a definite 'nightcrawler'—it's rare that I'm *not* awake at that hour." (She paused and Martin could hear her child: "I don't like apple sauce!" "Shhh, sweetie!" "NO YOU, MOMMY!" "Finish up now, c'mon'!") "Okay back to this: I look forward to our talking real soon, possibly getting together. I like the fact that you write also. That tells me something. Always enjoy meeting up with fellow poets, artists, outcasts—whatever you want to call us. Talk soon. Hang in!"

*Anton Checkov

"Seriously, I never *got* artists who had, y'know—*kids*," Nikki stated.

"Well, she just writes poetry," said Martin.

"Oh, *just?*" she countered.

"You know what I mean," Martin said. "—How it is with some people: they just don't give it much thought, letting things fall where they may. If their sons and daughters grow up to be drug addicts or suicides, that's just more 'material' they can mine someday." It was a dark and cynical thing to say, but, not without reason, Martin felt it was true.

Not one to flinch from dire observations of any kind, Nikki contributed, "I saw this documentary on Nico, in which she recorded her son's heartbeat after an overdose, just so she could use it as a gimmick on a record."

"That's what I mean," said Martin. "Heartless."

"Of course, she was a junkie."

"Little difference."

"Think *we'll* be that way?" she asked. "That selfish?"

"Guess that all depends, doesn't it?"

"Depends on what?"

"*A:* That we're still writing, *B:* That we have enough money."

C: Well, he didn't want to say it....

Written as two separate, but interconnected stories, like strands twisting into a braid, Nikki's first novel told of the journey of two isolated souls, fledgling artists, one a sculptor, one a painter, who in the course of the book suffer through self-delusion, emptiness, and a final spiritual breakdown only to come together, by pure coincidence, in the end.

An echoing theme in the work was how rarely people—even people in love—ever seemed to connect.

The book began:

A *young, clear-eyed woman emerged from the dark.*

"Disappointed? Sad? Need someone to talk to? A person who'll understand?" Her voice was soothing, her manner strangely sincere. "I know how you feel...."

49.
Sophia,

Hi!
Look who just fell out of the sky.
(Me.)

How are you, Sophia? How have you been? How has life been treating you? Since high school?

I came across your contribution to the yearbook the other night. I was just thumbing through the book, blowing dust off it. And there on page 123 was the beautiful piece by Sophia Cordi, with the line above it that read, "Fantasy is the messenger of the unconscious"—Redon.

I can't say why I was even handling the book except that maybe I was feeling a bit down on my birthday with my best pal not around, and I thought that maybe inside—just maybe—I'd find something or someone to touch on, to cheer me up. And I did find that something or someone: that photo collage and the memory of you!

So I thought afterwards, "Why not write this person a letter? Tell her how you feel, right now? Life's too short not to take some risks...."

I can only hope that your parents' address is the same, that they can forward it to you. It's been almost nine years—nine long years—after all!

I'm curious, all of a sudden. What's happened to you since high school? Did you finally attend college? Become a poet? Make a husband out of your boyfriend? Last I heard from you was when you rang me up eight months after graduation and invited me to a party with you and Janet West, remember that? You said you were putting off college for a year. Janet was working in a bookstore. You yourself had a job. Something about a "sandal factory" or was it a shoe store? I'm not so sure, now: it was late in the day and I was already a little crocked when I picked up the phone. I was still living with my grandparents then. Trying school.

Actually, the truth is—I can say it now—I was going through a bit of a rough time. When you called, I guess it was like someone flicking on an emotional switch that sent a jolt straight through me and left me nearly incapacitated. I swear, at the sound of your voice, my heart froze. I sorta fell into shock.

So, anyhow…now you know. As you might've already guessed, I'm more than a bit sorry I turned down your invitation. I really am.

What about these days? What are you up to now?

Me? Not much. Working in the freight industry. Nothing to brag about. But it's stable at least. I keep telling myself, "Be cool. Just put away a few more dollars." I don't know when I'll put in my notice, here, but very shortly I imagine. I'd be surprised if I stay another month! After that, who knows.

So far, I've wasted a few years doing nothing at all. Or close to nothing. Working all the time. Facing each day. (Dreaming, I guess, like most people.) Writing. Trying to keep the creative spirit alive. Planning. Plotting. Playing what some people might call "the waiting game."

I went to college and all that. Did well, actually. Surprisingly.

Remember how lousy a student I was in high school? How I always had my head in the clouds? Well, I turned it around. For what it's worth—and apparently not much—I graduated with honors. Can you believe it? Me? If we were still together—I mean, in touch—I think you might've been proud.

Anyway.

It's funny, Sophia, funny how certain memories and feelings persist.

I mean, I remember little things about our lunch hours together and times we spent on the school terrace that sometimes seem more genuine—more fully real to me—than the reality of the present, even of this very moment as I sit here now writing this letter. And it's as though time has made no difference in the ability of those impressions to affect me, too. They seem as charged with feeling today, as alive, as they did then.

Funny, but in a strange way I keep hoping to meet you as you were then, wishing that you can see me as I am now, a bit more your "age" finally. I have to say, Sophia, that I've gone through many changes. Sometimes I even wonder if you'd recognize me now. I still have my silly moments, believe me, but I've also grown more serious and reflective in recent years. Not wanting to really: it just sort of happened. I think I'm more aware of the general disappointment around me, more aware of the bitter sadness in the world. More than ever, I want to be a writer now, leave behind some small mark of having passed through this world and having experienced it, too. I know that sounds a bit pretentious, even foolish. Who's to say that I have anything unique to express about the world and who's to say that anyone will ever care to read anything I write?

Anyway, now that I've finally begun to get "realistic" about things, come to grips with disappointment, understand that a person has to be willing to live life on life's own terms, I'm ready to begin again.

The point of this letter, Sophia, the reason for this letter—I'd like to go back into my past, if just this once, to make sure I haven't left any loose strings. I want to make sure that there isn't anything that I may've left unfinished or undone. Things need to be helped along, sometimes. That's one thing I've learned. On its own, life so rarely seems to provide an adequate sense of closure.

I'd like to know how you are, of course. How you're feeling these days. If you're doing well. And I can only hope that the world hasn't treated you too roughly in the years since high school. I'm kinda hoping that you'll write to me to let me know. I was afraid of phoning your parents, maybe catching you off guard, which might've been cruel. Writing to you has always been especially gratifying to me, as you know (you started me on the habit!), and easier—but particularly in this case. I mean, I'm not even sure you want to hear from me after all this time. And of course, in a letter, I'm at least guaranteed a say.

The rest is up to you….

50.

"So you talked?" asked Nikki.

"Yeah. Amaris called me back. And we finally spoke a good long time. At first she said she was up to something the next day and couldn't meet me. Then agreed to meet, anyway."

"Where?"

"Nik, she made a *weird* suggestion. You'd *never* guess…."

51.

That day, Martin followed a winding asphalt path to the designated spot. The grounds caretaker had provided him with accurate directions. It was like a scene straight out of a '60s Hammer film.

Was that her?

There was only one figure he could see: a kneeling woman clad in black.

Martin stepped up, feeling more than a bit anxious.

He called out, "Amaris?"

At last she faced him. Stood up. Lustrous, shoulder-length hair with bleached highlights and red tips. Dark, blue-tinged shades. Liver-colored lipstick in contrast to a powdered face.

She removed her sunglasses finally, smiling and squinting in the light. "You showed!"

"I said I would." He extended a hand. Saw for the first time that she was Amerasian.

She grabbed it, shook it. "So, at last we meet," she said.

"Yep. Call it fate, call it persistence."

"I prefer *fate*," she said, and, right then taking a second look at him, blurted, "Hey—you're *shorter* than I expected!"

"What?" Martin blushed.

"Just *kidding*," she said, laughing. "Makes for a nifty ice-breaker, don't it?"

Red-faced, he tried to force a dry chuckle. "Terrific."

Still holding his hand, in one swift motion she then zeroed in and kissed him hard on the mouth.

Again he was caught off-guard.

Startled, but not put-off by her boldness.

Amaris laughed at his reaction—then apologized and gently wiped his lips. "Forgive me. It's just—I like to take care of it ASAP," she said. "You know, that 'first-kiss' business. People put *way* too much importance on it, I think."

"Right." Wiping off the lipstick traces with his fingers.

"Drives me nuts," she said, helping him.

"Uh-huh..."

"Actually," she remarked, "if you don't mind my saying it, you don't look so bad in that color." And removing a slim tube from her box purse, suggested, "Could you use a full application?"

Martin was amused.

"I'll pass. For now. *Thanks*."

Amaris unrolled the lipstick and, without a mirror, deftly reapplied a coat. "Suit yourself." And laughed.

Poised, comfortable with herself. Martin liked her already.

He joked, "Prefer men who primp, is that it?"

"So long as *I'm* with them," she confided, laughing again. Then, putting her glasses back on: "Hope you don't mind."

"What."

"These," she indicated. "My *dayshades*. It's just, with the light.—I hate the sun."

"You do?"

"Affects my skin, my mood," she asserted.

"It does?"

"Well, I much prefer the moon, y'know. Being a creature of the night."

Creature of the night. "I see," he said, chuckling.

She appeared pleased. "A sense of humor," she said. "That's refreshing."

"Whaddaya mean?"

"I don't meet a lot of people who like to laugh," she explained.

The truth was: Martin was finding it hard *not* to be amused.

At last falling silent, his attention was drawn to the location.

Before them lay a twin gravesite with fresh, waxy tulips.

He grew sober. "Come here often?"

"All the time," she confessed. "I love it here. It's so peaceful."

Oh he could see that.

"It's peaceful, all right. Can't get anymore peaceful," he said.

"At least you know you won't be bothered," she added.

"Suppose not," he said.

"Parks are for suburbanites!"

"Yeah. (*YEAH!*)"

The large granite headstone proclaimed GARCIA.

"You're Latina?" Martin asked.

"French and Japanese, mixed."

"Those distant relatives of yours?"

"Not too distant," she said. "They're my parents."

"Your ..." his voice trailed off. He felt uneasy all of a sudden.

Smiling she faced the double grave and said, "*Mommy, Daddy*—meet Marty."

He admitted, "I don't get it. I thought you said you *lived* with your parents?"

"—Say hello, Marty."

"Hello," Martin said.

"—I do. My adopted ones."

"Oh."

"Who are also my aunt and uncle."

"Oh."

Clear enough.

"Thought I told you that on the phone?"

"No," Martin said.

"Can't think of everything, I guess."

Martin agreed.

"Yeah," she went on. "They took over the reins, so to speak, after both my parents were killed. In a car accident. Head-on collision with a *NY Post* truck."

"Damn," Martin said. "*Tragic.*"

Of all the ways to go.

She shrugged. "It happened ages ago."

Martin then explained about his own parents. Or the lack of them. And how he was raised by his grandparents, which, he pointed out, set up an interesting parallel between them.

She asked (slickly picking up where they'd left off in a previous phone conversation), "They live in Queens, you said?"

"No. Spain. Retired."

"See them often?"

He shook his head: nope.

"Not at all?" She seemed surprised. "Don't speak with them?"

Half-ashamed, he shrugged. "A letter, now and then. Christmas cards. That kind of thing."

With her taking the lead, they slowly began walking. Walking away from the sun.

Sticking with the subject, she asked, "You don't get on with them?"

"I guess you can say, we've had a 'falling out,'" he owned up. "A difference in opinion. A disagreement about 'lifestyles.'"

"And, what are they like, your grandparents?" she continued.

"All right. Just regular people. Y'know, aspiring to fit in. That's it."

"My aunt and uncle are like that," she admitted.

"They always wanted me to have a more conventional life," he said. "Y'know, a 'professional' career. That whole bit."

"And you weren't up for that?"

"Shit, no," he said. "I mean, I had other plans. Huge ambitions."

"Which were?"

"Being a *complete* masochist," he explained, "I wanted a life full of perpetual failure and disappointment—"

"Oh yeah?" She laughed.

"Yeah. So I chose the *'art* life!'"

She laughed loudly again, before saying, "Hey, I told you about my writing too, didn't I?"

"Yeah."

"I'm not published, either. Not really. Xeroxed zines don't count."

"Which means?"

"Maybe, you're not so alone?"

"We have a *few* things in common?"

Amaris laughed. "At least."

52.

Who was this Amaris? More importantly, what other interests and enthusiasms did she and Martin share?

It was during their phone conversation the previous evening that she had provided him with substantial clues, direct answers, patiently enduring his geekishly predictable volley of "guy" questions.

At the top of the list were all things "dark."

Movies? *Ed Wood* (yes!), *The City of Lost Children*, Dreyer's *The Passion of Joan of Arc*, Cocteau's *Beauty and the Beast*, *The Hunger* with David Bowie, *The Rocky Horror Picture Show*.

"David Lynch?"

"I liked *Blue Velvet*," she said.

"What about *Eraserhead?*" Martin asked eagerly.

"Hated it."

So maybe it was an acquired taste.

Authors: Bram Stoker, Edgar Allan Poe, Mary Shelley, Marquis De Sade.

"I also like Batgirl comics," she admitted, unabashedly. "Other comics too, like *Dirty Plotte* and *Yummy Fur*."

Favorite poets? the Romantics especially—"I'm into *mood*."—Coleridge, Byron, Baudelaire. Again, Edgar Allan Poe.

"You really dig Poe, huh?"

"Check this out," she said, producing an item from her purse that day in person.

It was a photo of Amaris splayed across Edgar Allan Poe's Baltimore grave.

"That's me. Drunk," she said. "But I swear I had no alcohol that day. His *creative spirit* must've intoxicated my body."

He laughed. "Wow."

She added, "If he were alive today, I'd sit on his face!"

Music? She rattled off a bunch of German names Martin had never heard of until arriving at more pronounceable, old school bands like The Cramps, Bauhaus, Joy Division, Buzzcocks; a few marginal types like Klaus Nomi, and Syd Barrett.

Other random interests and small pleasures?

"Off the top of my head?" she said, pausing to think.

Spewing forth like a ticker tape from her subconscious: "Trip-hop, Psycho-billy, Death Metal, porn, men who can sew, bacon, people watching, people following, eugenics, body modification, French bulldogs, medical oddities, apple and raisin pancakes for breakfast, malt liquor."

Secret ambitions: to learn to play the banjo, eat ice-cream with a fork, walk a tightrope blindfolded, train a see-ing eye dog, eat a tamale in bed with her fingers, fuck a rodeo clown.

"Are the personals a portal to another dimension? Could be...

"What am I looking for? Good question. Salvation? *Nah.*"

"Like-minded cynics, cosmic fools, mushroom hunters, star-gazers, night-geeks, decadent misanthropic peeps blasting through spheres, space-truckin' super-freaks. A lug who won't jock my style. A cute boy to mash with," she answered. "Can you deal?"

Aside from her taste in exotic clothing, mood, and dark make-up what else, in particular, did Martin notice about Amaris, physically?

Her blue eyes. That was unusual on a French/Japanese.

Taller than him by an inch or two (two years older, as well, as she'd told him that day).

What else?

She had beautiful hands. The first time Martin had ever perceived that on a woman. They weren't tiny and delicate, ultra-feminine: in fact, her hands were rather large, but not bony or mannish at all, only ... elegant with long, beauti-fully shaped fingers, smooth soft skin, well-manicured nails (lacquered black, of course).... They caught his attention almost at once, as she used them to accent her conversation, underscore a point. It was her habit to use her hands extensively, like a continental European, touching him lightly as she spoke or gripping his arm dramatically in fully expressing the weight of a disappointment.

And speaking of disappointments.

"Divorce. You mentioned something about it?" Martin asked her.

"We're still in the process. Filling out documents."

"Sounds like a drag."

"It is. Believe me." She paused to remove a pack of Dunhills from her purse, offer him one; he declined. "We've been separated ten months."

"Ten months. And you haven't seen him since? Romantically?"

She lit up, shaking her head. "Nope. It's over. As dead as dead gets."

They walked in silence for a while, then Amaris said, "It's sad. Few nights ago, I was filling out legal papers when my son trotted in, saw what I was writing, and pointed to a couple of words I'd just jotted down." She imitated a child's voice: "'Mommy, what do these words mean?'—I nearly cried."

"Which words?"

"'Constructive abandonment.'"

Martin looked at her blankly.

"—Legalese," she explained.

"Meaning?"

She took another drag. "No sex."

53.

They strolled along the trail, past an impressive array of black tulips, lily-of-the-valley, and yellow irises.

Finally Martin asked, "Is it tough with a kid? I mean, going out and all?"

Amaris shrugged. "I have family to look after him."

"Your aunt and uncle?"

"Uh-hmm. Also grandparents, on my real mother's side. Plus friends."

He asked her if she ever felt guilty, despite that.

"That's why I always carry one of these," she said, indicating her beeper.

"Oh. Right." He turned to her and smiled.

On the subject of family, Amaris told him how her uncle (and father surrogate) was actually a step-uncle and how her aunt had been married *six* times.

"You're kidding?"

She shook her head, no.

"Six times?"

She nodded, "My aunt actually had bad luck, though. Each of her husbands kept dying on her."

"That's tough," he frowned.

"Yeah." Amaris raised her chin, expelling a fine plume of smoke. "What's a poor gal to do?"

Finally they approached a cement bench in the shade and sat down.

It was then, regarding her self-consciously "vampy" attire—a black knit dress with black stockings and boots— that Martin could hardly suppress a reaction.

"Want to let me in on the joke?" she asked.

OK, he came out with it: "That *pentagram* on your hose."

Smiling, she leaned back a bit, extending her legs so that

her boots were raised off the ground. "Like 'em? Bought them on St. Marks. In a pagan shop. Bought two pair, in fact."

"Halloween sale?"

She gave him a wry look. "Ha." Wagging her head. *"Queens' boy."*

With that he asked: "You're not into magic—a 'witch,' by chance?"

"Let me guess," she squinted. "Are you teasing me or being deliberately obnoxious?"

"Just answer the question, *Morticia*."

She knew he was joking.

"Since you're asking," she said. *"No.* No, I'm not a witch." Smiling again: "But I know people who are."

"Really?"

"It's not what you think, though. It's mostly about getting in touch with 'nature.' Fertility rites and all that. A kind of *primitivism*. Totally innocent."

"Oh yeah?"

She nodded, reaching into her purse for another cigarette. "I used to room with someone who was part of a coven, and she used to take off her clothes all the time with her other neo-pagan girlfriends, invoking nature spirits."

"Sounds awright," Martin said.

Eyeing him, Amaris smirked. Then she lit up another smoke, flipping the match.

Then her pager sounded.

Reaching for it, she muttered, *"Christ."*

"Trouble?"

She checked the number. Sighed. "Don't know. But I guess I should get to a phone."

Bummer, he thought, frowning.

Just as he was enjoying himself.

They left the cemetery and crossed the street to the first available pay phone. Martin stood at an awkward distance while she made the call.

Finally she hung up. Approached him.

"Sorry. It's about River. Nothing catastrophic. But, I guess I need to go."

"'River'?"

"My son's name."

"Like the actor?"

The dead actor? he almost said.

"Uh-huh."

They stood awkwardly a moment.

"Well, it was nice," Martin finally said. "Nice *almost* getting to know ya."

Amaris smiled. "We'll do it another time, okay? Soon. Maybe go dancing? Would you like that?"

Would he?

"Shit, yeah."

Amaris again apologized for making it so abrupt.

Martin told her not to worry.

He then leaned forward, intending to give her a friendly peck on the cheek when, unexpectedly, she swooped in, wrapping her hands around his neck.

Her beautiful hands.

"I could choke you about now," she said.

His brilliant reply?

"You could."

"Choke you to death." She looked at him, demonically.

Er, uh...

"Yeah."

Instead, raising her hands to his face, grasping him

tight, she kissed him forcefully on the mouth.

Pulling back: "All right, then!" she laughed.

That was a little scary, he thought afterward, with a shiver.

Pretty hot....

54.

Over the phone, Martin told Nikki: "I tramped all the way back to my car, strapped myself in, when I realized, looking up into the mirror, that I'd been wearing a *fat* coat of lipstick the whole time!"

"So she got you," tittered Nikki.

He laughed. "Yep. Looked like Marilyn Manson's sick cousin."

"Talked since?"

"Not yet." He admitted, "Still recovering." He laughed again. "Anyway, whatcha' up to tomorrow?"

She took a moment to recall. "I'm supposed to meet Mariella around two."

"What about later. At night?"

"Not sure yet."

"Maybe we can hang out? After?"

She thought about it, teased, "Maybe."

Martin laughed. "*Maybe*, yeah. Listen, sugar-cheeks, just *try* to keep it in mind."

55.

The following night, as it turned out, the eatery of choice was *Benny's*, a modest Mexican restaurant on Avenue A.

As Nikki ordered, Martin witnessed—through the plate glass window—a grubby specimen across the street swipe another man's prosthetic arm. (Slapstick, East Village style.)

"And you?" smiled the waitress, turning to him.

"Uh," matter-of-factly, "guess I'll take a whole wheat chicken Bay Burrito; brown rice and pinto beans. Extra guacamole."

Yeah.

Dressed down in a pair of faded Levis and a light blue mohair sweater—no make-up except for eyeliner—Nikki looked as unassumingly attractive, as radiant and sweet as the first day they'd met.

Martin asked how things had gone that afternoon with Mariella.

She mumbled something, and Martin had to ask her to repeat it.

"Okay, I guess," she said.

"The 'reunion' was the main topic of conversation, I take it?"

"What else?" Cutting her veggie burrito.

Martin prodded, "*Psyched* for it then? The big commitment?"

Quietly chewing her food, Nikki took her time. "To be honest?" she said. "I'm tired of hammering it out in my brain."

"What, feeling the pressure?"

She shrugged. Sighed.

"Guess, in the end," he reminded her, "you could always move up the date. If you had to."

Wearing a lopsided smile, Nikki looked away. Martin smiled. "You're not saying anything."

"*Oh*," she said listlessly, "been over this so many times.

I mean, how long has this been going on?"

Martin knew, precisely, but chose not to mention it.

They ate in silence awhile. Nikki was sulking.

Then, shaking her head, she confessed, "It's just—God, sometimes … I hate her. The way she makes me feel."

"Why?"

Nikki sighed again. "I keep telling her, 'This is what we *both* decided on. Our *last* chance to let it hang out. Have some *fun.*'"

"And she says?"

"Well, two days ago she sounded all for it. Said she even *met* someone at a club. Had a blast. This morning I ask her about it and she tells me, 'Oh fuck all that—why can't we just be together?'"

"You said?"

"Marty, I told her the truth." She frowned. "I'm just … not *ready.*"

He reminded her, "Nik, she's a big girl, y'know. She can take care of herself."

"I know."

"She can make up her own mind. To stay involved or walk away."

"I know, I know."

"So," he said, "she's made up *her* mind." He popped a nacho chip into his mouth, crunched. "Now you make up *yours.*"

"Easy for *you* to say," she smiled.

56.

That fateful day, the morning Nikki and Martin first met, they had agreed on the spot outside the Waverly Theatre on Third Street. And when Martin arrived there five minutes early, he discovered a woman already there, facing away, fitting the description she'd given him ("long wavy chestnut hair, about 5'6, slender"). It was late spring and warm, so she wore a breezy floral print dress and a pair of laced, thin-soled sandals. The greater part of her smooth legs, he couldn't help but notice, were exposed in the sunlight, and he somehow noted another detail (gaze drifting down): that above her left foot, and under the entwining straps, was a delicate, daisy-chain anklet tattoo.

She looked like some young, sultry southern gal from a country music video, or a dreamy nymph from a wish-fulfillment beer commercial (in which young, lithe beauties—the embodiment of male longing—always seemed to be just standing around, *waiting*); and at that moment, giving her the once over, Martin felt a weakness in the knees, a catch in his throat, signifying (yes, it was there, too) *lust!*

No way. It *couldn't* be her.

Her thick mane loosely tied into a pony tail, her back to him, she stood calmly eyeing the monitor near the glass entrance, which featured film clips of movies currently showing as well as "coming attractions." Appearing lost in thought, she languidly scratched an elbow, then crossed her slender milk-white arms.

… Nah, that couldn't be her, he told himself again. For one thing, he was used to potentials* showing up grossly late; for another, she just seemed too … well, *beautiful* standing there—too much like out of some damn Hollywood movie (and real life wasn't like that, right?). *Right?*

Martin sidled up to her anyway, ventured a greeting. And when there was no response, he shyly tapped her shoulder:

" 'Nikki'?"

---

*People from the personals

At last she turned. And he saw her pale-green eyes for the first time.

"*Marty?*" She smiled warmly.

Martin was struck dumb, strangely gripped.

Her eyes took on a look of concern. "Your name *is* Marty, isn't it?" she asked.

He wasn't so sure himself now. "I *think* so," he managed.

Right then, Martin could hardly believe his luck.

57.

As it turned out—as she calmly explained that day at the café— it had been a question of "chemistry" or the lack of it: Nikki to this person she had just broken up with, was just tenuously apart from. "The 'spark' was gone," she said. "Or there was none to begin with, I don't know." Hard to say, she reflected, still obviously wrestling with aspects of the issue, certain intangibles. And lately, as she herself phrased it: "There hadn't been any real excitement. Or romance. Just a kind of...desperate hollowness." Nikki sighed, stirring her tea. "I guess the real problem between us was rooted deeper, in deeper feelings." She frowned. "As things were, I just couldn't look forward to a future with this person."

Her candor surprised him. And, almost at once, he felt himself succumb to the pull of some greater intimacy.

"'A kind of desperate hollowness,'" she repeated uneasily, pondering the phrase. "Is that what it always comes down to, in the end?"

"God, I hope not!" Martin laughed. "We all need a reason to *live*."

58.

"All right," she said. "That's enough about me! Not another word!"

They'd just stepped out of Ace Bar on 5th Street, already pleasantly inebriated.

"Don't be silly. *Jesus.* You're with *me*," he cried. "Vent all you want. Open the floodgates!"

"*Sister Midnight*," said Nikki, with a laugh. "*That's* who I want to discuss!"

At the bar, at Nikki's prompting, Martin had related more of his meeting with Amaris, including the final bit with her hands at his throat.

Anything else?

"Turns out she lost her virginity in a graveyard," blurted Martin.

"What!" Nikki turned to him.

He laughed at her expression: a mixture of sudden revulsion and shock.

"Amaris mentioned it the night before," he said. "Over the phone. Just dropped it into the conversation."

"And you still *agreed* to meet her!?" She looked at Martin like he was nuts.

"Hey, there was a certain something about her," he said. "Can't say what."

"God, you'd say that about *anyone!*"—imitating Martin's enthusiasm—"*Squeaky Fromme*: Hey, there was a certain something about her!'*"

Martin laughed. "What's wrong with giving people a chance?"

"Marty, do I have to spell it out for you?" Nikki snapped her fingers in front of his face. "*Yoo-hoo!* Next thing ya know, I'll be reading about you in the *Post*, the subject of

---

*Charles Manson protégé and aspiring Presidential assassin

some human sacrifice or something!"

"But she's not even into *white* magic," he argued.

Nikki gave him a look.

"Anyway," returning to Amaris' initial confession, "she remarked about how *appropriate* it was."

"Oh really?"

"You know what the French call an orgasm?"

"What?"

"*Le petit mort*. Translated means 'little death.'"

Then, at two steps, a strange apparition materialized from behind a parked van.

The shadowy figure crowed "—Get *HAPPY* now!—*SMILE!*"

Nikki took two steps back: "What the hell!"

"I know you!" said Martin, laughing. He'd spotted him just weeks ago inside of Tompkins Park, trying to "blend."

"Tree man!—"

A neighborhood character: he was an old, wiry hobo, who always wore actual tree branches* and twigs projecting from his collar and hair.

"Issa' beau-tiful night!" he slurred to no one in particular, before losing balance, tipping forward, and landing squarely on his face.

Martin observed: "Man has obviously *had a few*."

"Should we call 911?" asked Nikki, with some concern.

He lay there, sprouting greenery, as limp and lifeless as a scarecrow.

Martin smiled, almost ready to join him on the warm pavement. "It's the weight of all that vegetation. He just needs time to recharge."

"Spare lil' change?" he burbled, face still flat against the concrete.

*some extending for several feet

Nikki stepped back again.

"See?" Martin laughed, unsteadily crouching down to cram a tightly rolled dollar bill in his hand, before proceeding forward. "For *fertilizer*," he cheerfully explained.

"Y'know, this is definitely *not* politically correct!" commented Nikki.

"Just follow me," Martin begged.

59.

FULL MOON OVER THE EAST VILLAGE:

On the corner of 4th and Avenue B, a deranged vagrant in a layered body suit fashioned completely of strung garbage bags intoned, over and over:

"*Yea*, though the sky's as dark as night, I have seen the light! *Hallelujah!...*"

Between 2nd and 3rd Avenue, on 14th Street, an elderly grubber with stringy hair and one black eye was on his hands and knees, rooting through curbside trash. "Whatcha' lookin' for, pops?" someone asked him.

"My teeth, godamn it!" he gummed. "I know I left 'em 'ere, somewheres!"

In defiance of the squad car that trailed them, siren in full flare, a line of twenty-seven Hell's Angels, black Harleys glistening, roared down Houston Street, turning north on Avenue A (against the light), then west on 3rd Street to their fabled, shadowy headquarters....

On the corner of 6th Street, ragamuffin skate punks congregated, soliciting funds, while up the block, a high-spirited gal with neon-green hair and yellow day-glo lipstick hawked issues of a revived journal entitled, *Fuck You: A Magazine of the Arts.*

"*Fuck you*, sir?" she cried to impassive pedestrians. "Ma'am?—*Fuck you?*"

Along the way Nikki and Martin amiably chatted.

"What's next on the agenda?" she asked. They'd just come out from yet another nondescript local dive.

"A little movin'? Little groovin'?" His head was spinning.*

"Dancing?"

"Unless you'd suggest something better?"

"*Dancing*," she grinned, reaching for his hand. "*That's* something we haven't done in a short while."

He smiled broadly: "Ain't no time like the present!"

Holding hands, tipping right on Avenue A, Martin and Nikki rolled past the raised gate of the *Pyramid Club*, past the slouching street vendors displaying their usual wares of tattered books, clothes, incense and scented oils. Reaching *Alcatraz* (a head-bangers bar) and the crowded corner of St. Marks Place, they swung left. "We going where I think we're going?" Nikki asked. "Mind?" Nikki rocking hard against him, eyes narrowed in mock intensity: "Oh I *mind*, buddy.—I *mind*...."

Up St. Marks Place, across the cracked and uneven pavement, Martin and Nikki eyed the joint with the bright yellow and blue awning—their favorite drag bar/restaurant—*Stingy Lulu's*, where in the past, they'd met to share meals and lost time together.

Nikki asked, "Remember the time that blond waiter flashed us his new tits?"

"Oh yeah," Martin laughed. "Bugged."

*But in a "good" way

Up they went, passing the many places they'd hung out in together: intimate *Anseo's*, folky *Café Sin-e*. Onwards past the dark doorways and boarded storefront windows brightened with overlaid posters and flyers. Slack West Indie merchants softly chanting: "Smoke, smoke." "Sinse, sin-semilla." "S'up, *mon*—you don't have to buy it, just look-at-it." Voices that were usually annoying but somehow not tonight. Across the way was Moroccan *Café Mogador* and the open-all-hours *Yaffa Café*. On their left, they passed the basement *St. Marks Studio Theatre*, the sidewalk billboard banked with fluttering tiny yellow flyers, declaring tonight's program: *Cannibal Cheerleaders on Crack!*

Martin couldn't recall the last time he felt this good. Was it the booze? the neighborhood? the weather? *Nah*, he thought, tightly holding Nikki's hand as if hanging on for dear life....

Crossing the street, forward up St. Marks, they passed *Theatre 80*, treading over the worn cement foot-and-hand-prints of old actresses: Joan Crawford, Joan Blondell, Gloria Swanson, et al. (When they'd first met, it was a grind house, showing scratchy, often hilariously ruined "Old Hollywood" prints—double features.) Across the street was the casually dilapidated *Holiday Cocktail Lounge* where afterwards they'd go for drinks, Serge Gainsbourg a favorite jukebox pick.

Nikki brought up that morning's telephone conversation with her mom. "We're finally getting there, I think. To that place of tolerance and mutual respect." She faced Martin, eyes widening: "Oh, did I tell you. She's thinking of getting hitched, again?—*Número cinco*, can ya believe it?" "*Damn*," Martin said, trying to wrap his mind around that thought. Nikki laughed. "Marriage number five! And she still wants to *rush* it!" They walked past the iron-wrought gates of the old *Club 57*—once a vital part of the East Village art scene—now, ironically, a mental health institute.

"Checked him out?" Martin asked. Nikki said, "No, not yet. She wants me down there, though. To meet him. In *Miami*." They swept by several cheerless street vendors, whose wares—displayed on ratty blankets—were being impounded by the police, until at last arriving on the busy corner of 2nd.

"So what," Martin said, "you'd be like, the maid of honor at their wedding?" "Hell *no*," laughed Nikki. "I'm not *that* far gone. I'll be there, at the reception, sure. But only as a *guest*. To show my support." Martin said, "Gotcha.'" Nikki joked: "This one should last all of *three weeks!*" They lingered at the light, watching yellow cabs zoom by, bumping and pounding over potholes and heavy iron plates. At this point, looking ahead, the street took on a carnival-like atmosphere, heightened by lights and a palpable nervous energy. Swarms of people moved in all directions, seemingly to no end; the noise level increasing, too, mostly with the din of traffic: screeching brakes, sirens, bleating car horns, thumping woofers of pimped car stereos: *chuga-boom! chuga-boom!, boom!-boom!-boom!, chuga-boom!*...

All around night-trippers laughing, shrieking, arguing. Languages intermingling: English, Spanish, French, Arabic....

"Will you take me along?" Martin asked. "Where?" asked Nikki. "Y'know," he said. "To Miami."

Nikki laughed. "If you want to be *tortured*, I would!"

He had never met her mom or anyone from her family

actually, just as she had never met any relatives of his. It seemed strange: this rootlessness, this disconnectedness and pervasive lack of attachment. As if, at any moment, either of them could just blow away, like spores of a late season dandelion, float off and vanish without a trace. In New York City, this happened every day. It made him suddenly feel melancholy.

Nikki sensed something was up, nudging him:

"What's wrong?"

"Nothing."

"You looked *really sad* for a minute," she said.

Martin squeezed her hand tightly, appreciatively.

"I'm fine."

She leaned closer, holding his gaze, as if trying to confirm the truth of this statement.

Right then her concern tickled him, gratified him.

"Really," he said, chuckling.

She smiled, bumping him with her hip. "*¡Así!*"

Crossing 2nd Avenue, pushing ahead through sidewalk traffic, they took in a dazed soul handing out psychedelic flyers, the corner Gem Spa Newsstand, and then crammed tourist stalls and brightly-lit souvenir shops.

On stoops or lolling on the sidewalk were the occasional congregations of retro-punks, existing almost as postcard images, most in leather jackets embellished with chains, metal studs, and Wite-out, or dressed in layered clothes visibly torn and held together with safety pins; some wore the perfect "hedgehog" or Statue of Liberty cut, or the neatly ironed spectrum-colored Mohawk; others, less fashionably, wore their sheared and dyed scalps cut along the sides with giraffe and leopard skin markings. These retro-punks stood idly shooting the shit and now and then posing sourly and cadging for "y'know, man ... like change?"

Along the way, Martin and Nikki discussed how things down this block *used* to be: "A *drug* center, I swear. That's all it was. And not all these stalls and crap." He squinted at the shops. "Things have sure changed a lot since."

"Not to mention, they even managed to outlaw all the booksellers—"

"Like the street artists from Soho, *god forbid!*"

"Booksellers!" railed Nikki. "Imagine that. These days you couldn't even peddle your own poetry books! It's *against the law!*"

It was the sad truth: a case of shifting priorities, civil apathy, and denial of cultural history in the Village.

"Know yer rights, *mija!*"

"'*Rights,*'" she said, smirking. "*Uh-huh.* They went with the constitution."

In the middle of the block was the Community Center, once home of *The Dom*, a famous bar and dance hall, then site of Andy Warhol's *Exploding Plastic Inevitable*. Now a drug treatment center.

Crossing the street—threading through advancing strangers, swirling shadows—Martin and Nikki finally stepped up to a plain, unmarked steel door. Martin pulled at it—it gave—and they slipped inside and up the long flight of stairs illuminated by blue tube light. Paying the cover, they advanced to the second floor of a space for years known as "BB's" or *Boy's Bar*, tonight hosting the bi-weekly glam revival party dubbed "Blackdoor NYC."

No sooner did they set foot inside the place, than Martin offered, "Buy ya another?"

"Shouldn't, really."

Martin teased, "Oh don't be *coy*."

Batting her eyelashes, like a cartoon southern belle: "*Coy? Coy?*"

"A short one, Scarlett?"

"Awright, then," she yielded. And, together, they swaggered across the murky, scarcely crowded room, a T-Rex ballad warbling over the PA.

Finally at the bar, she turned to him. "Let me get it, this time. You grab us a spot?"

"Sure?"

Squinting: "Wanna throw down?"

"I can deal." And, grinning, Martin swung back across the room, finding a small table by the entrance, where he took a seat against the mirrored wall.

60.

At first glance, the joint resembled any other East Village bar, painted black and illuminated by hazy light. There was an old pool table off to one side, several TV monitors (projecting arcane commercials), and along the walls more mismatched tables and chairs.

What made the place visually exciting, though, was not the room itself nor the minimal décor, but the people who would eventually come to occupy it—the fetishistic, oddly-obsessed and slightly-off-kilter revelers—who would put in an appearance on this night and give it an almost delirious air.

All types showed up, and as Nikki brought up the Red Stripes, she and Martin watched them arrive:

There were rockabilly boys with pompadours and elephant trunk haircuts, short-cuffed vintage clothes, leather and suede creepers. And there were the out-of-wack sixties revivalists and Edie Sedgewick cultists: those with Twiggy-like short hair, false eyelashes, green and blue eye shadow; neo-mod girls sporting the "Cleopatra look" in micro-mini skirts and Op Art go-go boots.

Sixties revivalists also included nuevo-hippies, un-washed art degenerates mostly, wearing the occasional Afghan jacket and other yippy paraphernalia: fruit-colored granny glasses, top hats, and love beads. The occasional high-rise afro wig even made an appearance: as did the sporadic Barbarella-like leather or PVC outfit.

The retro-futurist eighties could be seen: doomsday ethos crossed with gloss punk, *Blade Runner*-inspired arti-fice fused with *Liquid Sky* geometric face paints. Heavy Metal studded wristbands, plastic style, and exploding hair.

But most notably represented and reinterpreted, taking center stage, nearly radioactive in the spot light, was the era of "glam rock." Ambisexuality. Lip liner for men. Glitter eye shadow and blush. Camp projections. There were those glammers—heroin-thin diamond dogs—who vamped around in muddy eye make-up, wearing varia-tions of spandex jumpsuits or flashy rock 'n' roll wear. There were razor cuts: the ever-present tousled rooster or long disheveled shag, like images culled from long-forgot-ten issues of *Creem* magazine. "Glam" style was glittery "show-biz" crossed with a jungle-print trash esthetic: a reveling in the underbelly of sleazy seventies club culture, vaguely illicit, diseased, and junk inspired. The androgyny and dark glamour of Ziggy Stardust, Iggy Pop, and The New York Dolls was most evident.

Neo-seventies dames, on the other hand, were more stereotypically "feminine" and retrogressive, strutting about doll-like and pouty, in tight high-water flares and platforms, satin chokers, and belly-baring baby T's. Flat long straight hair, parted in the middle, was *de rigueur*; tiny primary-colored little girl barrettes were in. Thick upper eyeliner and thinly shaped eyebrows were popular, as were cherry red lipstick and bright rich nail polish. It was a glossy, "harmless" projection of early seventies Playboy bunny/baby femme appeal.

What was most peculiar and disturbing was that with some of the patrons, it was not merely a costume party—these were not just playful role reinterpretations: some actually *believed* that they were living in their own self-chosen, largely re-imagined eras.

As Nikki once remarked: "They all seem kinda lost in their own private little time warps."

So it seemed the dreariness and sadness of the "real world" was just too much to bear for some people.

And it didn't end with music sub-cults: one party regular completely believed he was Barbara Eden from the old TV show *I Dream Of Jeannie* and padded around in harem costume and curled-toed slippers, arms crossed and blinking, "Y-yyes, master!" Another mental defective seemed convinced he was the Soviet spy, Ilya Kuryakin from *The Man From U.N.C.L.E.*

61.

Finishing her drink, Nikki suggested, "Let's go downstairs before it gets too crowded."

"Too late for that!" Martin laughed.

Through the jostling crowd, Martin and Nikki descended a long, brightly-lit staircase to the main floor and another bar. The wall behind the bar displayed textured junk art from the '80s: plastic dolls, piano keys, scrap metal and other debris, permanently soldered to the wall and painted flat black, existing now as a fossilized apocalyptic back-drop. If the upstairs room of *BB's* had seemed dark and forbidding upon arrival, this floor was even more so. Except for sparsely hung Christmas lights and a few blink-ing gel-colored spots on the far end, it was completely dark. The pounding music was a louder, shag-nasty glam alternated with rare punk and funk tunes. And as Martin and Nikki made their way to the opposite end of the room, near a short wooden stage (their eyes adjusting to the light), they soon found a decent spot in which to move.

All around them, the usual partygoers, tripping or drunk, were going wild. The floor was jumping. Hands hovering and waving, arms flailing, heads rolling, bodies churning.

Taking the stage beneath a liquid projection light show, three be-wigged black girls began lip-syncing to a glam tune and dancing in perfect unison like The Supremes; while, behind them on a pedestal, a slender Japanese woman in a gold bikini and platinum wig, worked a hoola-hoop. Off to another side, a near-naked belly dancer was fluidly grinding, a pink day-glo smiley face centered on her very-pregnant belly.

Hips swaying, torsos dipping and rising, occasionally hands touching and locking—Martin and Nikki got loose, getting into the crowd around them and each other.

A young retroid in turquoise feather boa and *007* glass-es teetered by on what must have been foot high, glow-in-the-dark rubber platforms.

An amused Nikki nudged Martin: "See those?—*Flores-*

cent stilts!"

All around them revivalists were performing wicked dance moves or borrowing steps from the past: the Pogo, the Mashed Potato, the Pony, the Jerk. On the sidelines or seated on the embankment surrounding the dark dance floor, others were just crowd-watching or cooling out or nodding, now and then absently raising their sweating cups of beer or fat glowing joints.

There was a good vibe—plenty of handshakes and smiles to go around—and everyone seemed unusually friendly tonight.

The air filled with a kind of sweet promise, Martin and Nikki danced and danced. The music cranking, the floor vibrating under their feet, still slightly buzzed, they were lost in a timeless groove. Under the pulsating lights, they reaffirmed their connection to this time and place. And to each other. And, for a time, Martin and Nikki caught and held on to it.

Finally, at nearly four in the morning, the remaining crowd shagged out and dispersing, they gave in.

"Well, Marty," she said, smiling. "*That* was something."

62.

Martin and Nikki snagged the first available cab to Jackson Heights and drifted up to his studio, where they hung out on his open sofa bed, eating Ben & Jerry's "Chubby Hubby" ice-cream and lazily chatting.

Sometime near sunrise, he offered her a choice: "Drive you home ... or sleep over?"

Nikki seemed unable to decide. Even appearing uncomfortable.

Suddenly uneasy, Martin said, "Nik, don't *talk* yourself into something you don't *feel*."

She appeared relieved at once. "Maybe, I should go then?"

Turning away, Martin was hardly able to conceal his disappointment:

Oh I'm *such* an idiot, he thought.

63.

Upon his return, Martin wearily dumped his car keys on the sofa, finally noticing a blinking red light.

A sign? A second thought? A reconsideration?

Lunging at the machine, he hit "play."

A pause, then an operator's nasal recording:

"There appears to be a receiver off the hook, please hang up...."

64.

That morning, after drifting off to an agitated half-sleep (yes, to the sad, yearnful imaginings of protracted love-making with Nikki, let it be known), Martin dreamt he met his mother for tea in Inwood Park.

In this dream (or half-dream), they were both adults, relatively the same age: so close in fact they could be dating.

His Mom, speaking perfectly modulated English (that she never spoke in real life), said, "It's funny but I find myself less sure of things the older I get. All the things I thought I knew about? I really don't understand at all. And the biggest mystery isn't even the big wide world. It's yourself. Understanding yourself."

Martin frowned. "I think I heard that before."

"I tend to repeat myself," his mother said.

"No, it isn't that," he said, looking around and recognizing the park of his childhood: giant ballfields, Indian caves....

"Take me for instance," she went on. "Me and Nikki. Talk about being on a treadmill."

"What'll it be then, between you?" Martin asked. "Another hiatus?"

"That's what we've decided on," his mother said.

"And if you get back together after that—and it still isn't happening?"

"Then, it's over. Finished," she said. "We'll split up for good."

Martin nodded, falling quiet.

His mother went on, "To be honest, half the time, I'm not even sure if I'm going or coming. Depressed or happy."

"Speaking for myself," Martin said, suddenly feeling oddly uncomfortable.

"Yes?"

"I forgot what I was going to say," said Martin.

"Anyhow," she said, with a shrug. "That's just how it is."

"How what is?"

"Life. The way things are," his mother said decisively. "Nikki may *never* feel about me, the way I feel about her."

"Yeah, I know," Martin said. "I know."

His mother raised her cup to take a sip:

"Love really sucks that way."

Before awakening that morning, Martin had yet another ridiculous dream:

He had risen from a long, half-restless sleep, and was now standing over the open toilet, taking a much needed piss—

when flipping the handle to flush

he glanced down, just in time—

in time to see his dick and balls detach cleanly off (like so much clay), and go—*PLOP!*—straight down into the bowl, twirling around in the cheerful whirlpool of yellowy water, before being sucked down....

Coño! he thought, half-asleep.

There go my cock and balls. Hardly upset, even.

65.

"Hey, dude!" began a casual male voice. "The name is Moses. Moe, my friends call me. And you can, too!

"Obviously I'm *not* the woman you're looking for. And I'm not looking for *you*. I'm just calling to lay a tip on you.

"That's right, I'd like to tell you how *I* meet lots of sweet girly-girls. In a word? *Party Line!* Okay, that's two words. But you know what I mean. Sounds kinda lame, I know. But it works, it really does! If you're interested, snag some pen and paper.

"Dude, these lines don't cost much! Just $2.99 a minute. And obviously it's much cheaper than joining a singles' club. Much cheaper than a night in a singles' bar too. So why not give it a shot!

"Anything beats *personal ad limbo*, right?

"This is Moe, your new *buddy*, watching out for you, saying, 'Happy hunting, dude!' And hold the line for those sweet, sweet girly-girls, you manly-man you!..."

"To skip to the next message," said the prerecorded operator. "Press 'three.'"

Martin hit "3."

"No more messages...."

66.

"So tell me," Martin asked. "How was the party?"

"What party?—Oh, that. *Boring*." It was several nights later. Lola was speaking over the phone.

"Didn't go over too well?"

"Nah," she sighed. "Two of the four people who were supposed to go cancelled. I knew they'd do that. Then, when we finally got there, it was like, totally lame. A real letdown."

"And that was it?"

"Yep. Now, aren't you glad you missed it?"

67.

The next evening, Lola was already in the lobby of the *Anthology Film Archives*, when Martin stumbled in late.

Apologizing, explaining how F train service had been held up, he asked if she'd been waiting long.

"Just got here, myself," she owned up. "But I already grabbed a ticket."

The show they'd decided on earlier was Andy Warhol's *Trash*; and it seemed Martin hardly had time enough to pay his own admission and find a seat with Lola before the lights dimmed.

"Shit, talk about *seedy*," chuckled a nearby audience member. The film was shot in and around the East Village circa 1970, before the closing of the legendary *Filmore East*. Yet what surprised Martin was that it hardly seemed dated: virtually the same cast of marginal types seemed to reside there still.

Trash's loosely structured story centered on "Little Joe," a bedeviled addict, who—along with all the other degenerates in the film—stumbles from one listless adventure to the next, hoping to somehow "score."

Déjà vu? Martin had to wonder.

Lola sniggered through most of the movie, but especially at the wretched closing scene, when a transvestite's brazen, half-baked scam to get on welfare as a pregnant mother blows up in his/her face. All the caseworker demands in exchange for a favorable report is a pair of the transvestite's silver high-heeled sandals, but he wouldn't get them. "No! They're my *only* shoes!" shrieks the transvestite. "Anyway, we're *entitled* .... I'm gonna have a baby ... and you CAN'T HAVE MY *FUCKING SHOES!*" In the end, the vindictive government worker rises in a squinty huff: "You think you're gonna get welfare?—You're not gonna get a *DIME!*"

The audience laughed witlessly at this like it had been collectively pricked in the behind with a happy needle.

"That was so *burlesque!*" said Lola once the film was over and they were headed up 2nd Avenue in the warm night.

"Evil, right?" Martin knew she would dig it.

"Oh yeah," she laughed. "Totally evil. A *sleaze fest!*"

"Kind of like *Polyester.*" He was talking about a John Waters film.

She said, "*Pink Flamingos,* more like."

"The blurb said those were the same characters—the transvestite and 'Little Joe'—that turned up in 'A Walk On the Wild Side,' that dope Lou Reed song."

"Oh *yeah?*" she said with some attitude.

"Just thought I'd mention it."

Lola made a pit stop at a decrepit bodega for some clove cigarettes, then they continued to 11th Street, turning right and rolling to Avenue A, where they picked out a bar next to the popular music venue, *Brownies*.

The *No-Tell Motel* was another East Village nightspot (like *Babyland*, *Max Fish* on Ludlow Street, and others) that shared a kitsch/retro esthetic. The storefront windows displayed drawn Venetian blinds and two signs propped against the glass that read: "*No-Tell Motel*, Bar & Lounge" and "Vacancy: *Yes*."

Inside, past a doorway trimmed with bottle caps, a person swept past old strip posters, a classic jukebox, large soda cap signs, and other assorted trash Americana to join the crush at the dimly lit bar. One old sign by the mirror read, for no apparent reason, "Audrey's Diner," another, "God Bless America!"

In the back was a lounge area comprised of zebra-striped floor, Salvation Army sofas, thrift store lamps, and about a dozen tacky black velvet portraits. Contributing to the self-consciously warped ambience was a suspended TV monitor that flashed loops of Super-8 smut, featuring "erotic" dances by the cheerful '50s pin-up icon, Betty Page.

After buying drinks from the heavily pierced barmaid, Martin and Lola pressed to the rear, past a mounted rabbit's head with antlers, and a passageway tiled with campy, obscure album covers from the '50s and '60s.

A weeknight, they had no problem finding seats.

Lola leaned back on the leatherette couch near Martin, after taking the third or fourth sip of her drink. "… God," she said. "I don't mean to go all 'touchy-feely' on you."

Consciously or not, she was steering the conversation to a more intimate level.

"No, go ahead," he insisted, smiling. "Tell me."

"About my last *real* relationship?"

"Why not."

She appeared embarrassed. "What would you like to know about it?"

Martin took a swallow of his drink. Laughed. "Was it terrible?"

"When it ended. Sure."

"Ended badly?"

"Don't they always?"

"What happened in this case?"

"Y'mean, who dumped who?"

Martin shrugged.

"We dumped each other. Sort of." Lola grew quiet, frowned. "No. Wait. Actually, he dumped *me*."

Her expression changed, grew harder: "Not that I'm keeping a score card. But I've dumped more guys than've dumped me."

"I don't doubt that."

She took another moment, sighed. "We were going out. Treating each other … ah, badly, I guess. Being petty and mean. Stupid. Finally, one bad night, we split without speaking, I called him up, I said, 'Well, what's the story? Is it over, or what?'"

"What'd he say?"

"That's just it," said Lola, frowning. "He wouldn't say *anything*." She stiffened, her face drawn. "I kept asking him, 'Well, what is it? What's the story?' But he wouldn't say anything. I could hear him sucking on a cigarette. Newport, that's that kind he liked, the asshole. I could hear the TV in the background. 'Say something, you fuckhead!' I yelled and nearly burst out crying. I was calling from the street because my *bruja* mother refused to pay the phone bill. Finally he goes, 'I don't think it makes any sense.' ''*Sense'*—what are you talkin' about?' And I had to repeat myself. 'Us,' he goes. 'Being together. It doesn't make any sense.' 'Whatchoo' *mean*?' I ask, waiting for him to go on. Of course he doesn't. He was quiet again, copping a drag, the prick—that silence was killing me. I kept after him. Finally he goes, 'I'll make it real clear, okay: I *don't* want to see you anymore.' 'What?' And I felt my heart beat ninety miles a minute. 'You listenin'?' he goes. 'You listenin' to me?' And repeats himself: '*I don't wanna see you anymore!*' And I choke a little. 'But *why?*' I say. I kept after him. Just wanted him to talk. He wouldn't though. He finally mumbles, 'Look, I'm not in the mood.' 'Awright. Okay,' I say, 'I'll call you next week.' Days pass and I call, and he still wasn't talkin'. Finally I ask, 'You feel the same way?' He goes, 'Yup.' That's all: 'Yup.' I say—'Fine. Fine,' and hang up. Hang right up on his stupid ass."

"You never heard from him after that?"

She swallowed. "Nope." Shook her head: "Nothing. Not even a postcard. Prick. Fuckhead. Like … like I never mattered to him. Never existed. And all that passed between us was like a joke, ha ha…. *Dumped* over the phone. That's so cold, so shitty. I swear I could never do that to anyone in my life!"

"How long ago was this?"

"Last October. The 27th, to be morbidly exact."

"I can see you're over him."

"No, I am." She remained a bit down. "I mean, I ran into him a few weeks ago—we go to the same school. Even though we met through an ad. He was in the cafeteria with his scamp buddies. And, at one point, we just happened to catch each other's eyes. And stare. And I tell you, it was like the purest form of *hate* I ever felt!"

"So you won't ever see him again."

She turned to him, glaring: "What, are you *kidding?*"

Martin finished his drink. And she continued, "I would-n't see him again if he came crawling on bloody knees."

"Excellent," Martin said.

She bridled, "*God*, how I fucking hate him!…"

68.

"He was into all this *weird* stuff," she went on. "'Atrocity memorabilia,' some people call it."

They were on their way to *CBGB*, up 3rd Street, Lola still compulsively rattling on about her ex-boyfriend—some-what to Martin's weary dismay.

"Uh, 'atrocity memorabilia'?"

"All kinds of depraved and macabre shit," she explained. "Crime scene photographs, skull casts, tomb-stone rubbings of famous serial killers, swatches—you name it."

"Swatches?"

"*Swastikas.*"

He sighed. "Oh."

Just then they were tracking past the emblazoned steel door of the New York Hell's Angels H.Q.

"Yeah. He even collected artwork by convicted killers and insane people—the famous ones, of course. Like paint-ings done in prison. He had one by that fat pig, what's his name, the former clown … John Wayne Gacy."

"The child molester?" He turned to her.

She nodded. "Killed over thirty kids and buried them in his basement."

Martin frowned. "And he still appealed to you, this

guy?"

"Okay," she granted. "It was 'unconventional,' maybe. But in a way I could see where it was coming from."

"You *could?*"

Lola nodded again. "It's this ... dark *fantasy* with a lot of guys. '*Staring into the abyss.*' Really—it's just compensating for feeling insecure or invisible or whatever. And I can understand that. I mean, everyone wants to leave his mark, right? But most people can't."

What was he supposed to say to that?

She kept on, "So one way of dealing with it—I read this somewhere—of dealing with this sense of 'powerlessness,' or of feeling insignificant is to *identify* with 'someone or something stronger and more powerful.' "

"Shit, you sound like a sociologist."

She laughed. "Well, it's true. It has to do with *empowerment* or whatever. Like with the Nazi stuff, the *Oi!* skinhead music. Even gangsta rap and all that macho posturing. Where do you think all that crap comes from?"

"Haven't a clue."

"Young boys feeling insecure or impotent. It's so basic! It's way easier to identify with some kick-ass sadist, than to commiserate with a victim. Compassion is more evolved, tricky. Hate and violence? *Easy.*"

Martin was impressed. "That's quite an analysis you got goin' there."

Lola remained pensive.

"Anyway," she finally confessed. "The prick was a lot younger than me."

"Oh yeah. He was?"

"Well, only a *year.* But he seemed way younger."

"Was he from here, originally? The Village?"

She looked suddenly amused. "Texas. Some backwater town."

"So, why's *that* funny?"

She shrugged, grinning. "Just that, in the beginning, when I first met him, he was like this cliché white boy, freezer stocked with TV dinners. Only ate Wonder Bread without the crust and processed chicken." She took a couple of steps. "After a while, boy *that* sure changed!"

Martin remarked, "Downtown morphs everyone. Must be the air down here. Or the drugs."

"Sometimes, it gets to be too much," she said.

"How so?"

She explained, "Well, think about it: everyone turns up in this place to 'reinvent' themselves, y'know? So you have all these people fronting, changing get-ups, changing names. Changing sex. Makes it hard to keep perspective."

Martin chuckled, admitting, "That might get old."

"It gets exhausting. Everything is so fuckin' transitory, you start to wonder if anything or anyone is real." Again she grew reflective: "And, personally, I'm fed up with all the fakers and fuck-ups and users. 'Specially the users."

Martin told her that was one reason he didn't move down here himself—that and the ridiculous rents. "I mean I'm afraid I might grow bored with it all, sick of the Village," he said. "Then, I'd have nothing left, nothing to look forward to."

"Now *that's* pathetic," Lola teased him.

Martin laughed. "Glad you think so!"

If she only knew!

69.

At this time, *CBGB* was part of a strip mall. The *CBGB*

"Pizza Boutique" was to the left, and to the right, was *CB's 313 Gallery.*

The club's primitive exterior was coarse whitewashed cement stucco covered with dense graffiti, encrusted with decades of urban grime and soot, its storefront windows boarded up and textured with a crumbling collage of torn handbills and flyers.

Martin graciously opened the pockmarked wooden door. "After you," he offered.

"Piss on that," she laughed. "—After *you.*"

Finally, nearly knocking heads, they both squeezed in together.

Just inside, flat as a rug, laid the world-weary CBGB mascot, a black-and-white Afghan so fatigued it strained to eat a meal—a wedge of cheese pizza—without so much as raising its head.

"Too many *drugs,*" remarked Lola.

They coughed up the green, had their wrists stamped and walked in.

Seven bands were on the bill. They'd missed all but the last two: *King Missile* and *Tribe 8.*

" 'Tribe 8,' " he asked. "That some riot girl band?"

Lola more accurately defined it: " *'Post-riot-girl-dyke.'* "

CBGB hardly ever changed: that was its strength. A former derelict bar, it maintained a rude, ultra-squalid ambience. Intensely dark, of course, every available spot was covered with old band posters, torn flyers, and dusty stickers.

On the far end (as down a blind tunnel), the main floor was oddly narrow and claustrophobic, walls covered with graffiti or scraped bare of plaster. As always, the place seemed in a state of absolute decay and deconstruction.

No band was on stage, only a soundman setting up gear. And just then Patti Smith's cover of "My Generation" played over the PA.

"This spot won't be a problem for you?" Martin asked. They'd angled themselves to the extreme left of the jutting stage and against the wall, beside a huge monitor.

"It's perfect. Why?"

"Just asking." In years past, it was *here* in this same spot where he would prop himself when he went to the club alone, burnt-out after another thankless day at work, a night of empty wandering—right here where he'd hang back with amusement, catching the self-destructive antics of some raucous post-punk band, members of which (in a desperate attempt at comedy) would sometimes drunkenly hurl themselves off-stage or drive themselves headlong into nearby speaker cabs or even the bare-brick wall in his direction. Splat!

"Oh no!" Lola shrieked, facing the smoky dressing room cubicles and two guys apparently on their way back from the bathroom.

Martin turned to look, squinting in that direction.

Lola burst out laughing. "You'll *die,* I swear! I'll introduce you."

The two seemed engaged in a frivolous argument. As in a slapstick routine, one kept swinging back wildly, trying to swat the other.

As they came up, Lola shouted: "Hey!"

They spun their goonish, closely-cropped heads. And Martin, jaw clenched, had to look down to keep from laughing.

"Thought you guys were in Portland!" she said.

"We was," explained one. "We left. That place is beat."

"Yeah. *Beat*," echoed the other.

"Jeremy. Justin," said Lola, by way of introduction. "This is my uh, friend, Marty."

The strange pair awkwardly nodded hello.

"These are the POLINSKI brothers," she announced to Martin.

"Nice to meet ya," replied Martin, still trying to keep a straight face.

"As you can see," said Lola. "They were hatched from the same *egg!*"

Martin saw it was true. It was almost surreal. About twenty-years old, identical twins—and *both* crossed-eyed!

"Yeah," said Justin (or was it Jeremy?), "we're, uh, practically related."

"I'd sooner be related to a *chimpanzee!*" cracked the other.

Martin almost caved.

"So. Whatcha' here for?" Lola asked, as other patrons irritably pushed by.

"Me?" confessed one. "I'm here to watch a godamn band."

"Yeah," said the other. "*He's* here to watch a godamn band. *I'm* here to mosh!"

" '*Mosh*,'" scoffed the first. "Like *you* know somethin' about '*moshing!*' "

" '*Ey*," countered the other. "I was moshin' before you was born!"

The first wore a look of contempt. "Asscrack, do you even *know* what you're talkin' about?"

"*Hey!*" hollered a voice behind them. "Teedledum, Tweedledee! Quit blockin' the aisle!" Musicians were held up, trying to haul equipment to the stage.

"Now see whatchoo' started?" sneered the first. He eyed his brother menacingly.

"What *I* started?" replied the other.

"Who am I talkin' to, dingus?"

"Ya-*self, maybe!*" squinted his brother.

"Ugly-as-sin putz—just get a move on!"

Poking a thumb at his brother: "Hung like a *tic tac*—and he *still* thinks he can tell me what to do!"

"We'll square this later, bitch!" scowled his brother, assuredly. "Oh we *will!*"

Finally, no sooner had the first complied, turned his back to move forward, than the other soundly cracked him across the back of the head: "—*Eat it,* tosser!"

"*Oi!*" Wheeling abruptly, the first retaliated by going for a classic eye-poke.

Will you two PECKERHEADS just get goin'!" boomed someone else from the blocked passageway.

Pointing at his brother, the first threatened, "Later for you, wingnut!"

"*Oooo-ooo,* I'm shakin' all over!" said the other.

They both moved, unclogging the aisle. And, finally, Lola and Martin turned to each other and laughed.

"Close friends of yours?" Martin said.

"Family," she said, cackling. "Didn't catch the resemblance?"

Should he say anything?

70.

The band *King Missile* took the stage, cranked up, their first song, "Mother had a pickax!" and soon, Martin noticed, the Polinski twins appeared front and center, going at it full tilt, recklessly crashing into each other and those around them in "the pit."

"C'mon *get it up!*" yowled one brother.

"'Dat's right—*yeah!* Time ta get *stoo-pid!*" bawled the other.

"Like you need *practice!*" slinged the first.

"*Eat it, donkey!*"—slammed his brother—"Fuckin' *squash* ya!"—the two stumbling and falling, then completely vanishing into a crowd that appeared to be getting swiftly energized by the bottom-heavy rock onstage and the smoldering, freewheeling anarchic atmosphere—almost as good, Martin thought, as in *the old days!*

Right then Lola announced loudly: "Gotta go downstairs! Use the loo!"

"Hope ya make it back!" Martin joked. The restrooms in this club were notorious. World-famous for their uber-filth and Mugwumps straight out of Burroughs' "Interzone."

"May take a while!" said Lola.

And, eyes lighting up, he saw his chance.

When the Polinski twins next resurfaced in the mosh pit, they discovered they had company.

"Look who came to join us, slingshit!"

"*Who?*" said his brother.

"Him, *ding-a-ling!*" bellowed the first. "That guy!" then banging into Martin—managed instantly to drop him through the bobbing crowd, the two piling directly on top. From the hardwood floor, Martin looked for a way out, but all he could see was a flurry of shifting legs and flying steel-toed boots.

"*Aah,* what's yer name, again?" rasped the closest, heaviest twin. Martin grunted it. "Nice ta meetcha', then," he replied, extending a hand. Martin tried but couldn't manage to shake it. "Yeah, rightwise," groaned the other from somewhere higher up—"nice ta make ya like, acquaintanceship, Pip!" "*Aaaaaaaaaaah,*" creaked his other sweaty half, "dummy up, *porky!*"

Soon all three were helped up, back to their wobbly feet, and Martin, still unhurt, felt an odd twang of nostalgia: yes, it had been a while; he'd forgotten what it was like to share in this kind of boyish camaraderie and excitement!

"*Ball the jack, baby!*" hollered one twin, eyes nearly uncrossed in mad anticipation. "Ain't no tomorrah', just today!"

Before Martin could react—even think to react—he was again being shoved and tossed around, spun through the swelling mob that was already out of control—bucked roughly in one direction, bounced in another. In the center of the pit, meanwhile—hooting and howling—the Polinski twins were back at it, in their element: lurching and bugging one way for a while, then circle slamming the opposite way the next.

"Mother-ass—*Christ almighty!*" screamed Martin, feeling unnerved and helplessly foolish: while he couldn't help *laughing*. Even as a blunt weight—a broad, dense twenty-something body—came crashing down from god-knows-where to take down not only him but three or four mindless others.

Hitting the floor again, this time Martin realized it was soaked with spilt beer.

"Jesus!" cried a young female voice. "It fuckin' *reeks* down here!"

"Smells like somethin' farted and croaked!"

"Hey," shouted someone else. "Just found a stinkin' boot!"

"My friggin' clodhopper!—that's where it went!"

More clasping hands reached down to pull them up. But again, before Martin could regain his balance, he was swept back into the mindless, rolling crowd. "Heads up!" someone shouted from behind him. And a heavy combat boot came flying at him. Just in time, he ducked.

KLOCK!—And Martin saw that the boot had hit some-one directly in front of him. A flurry of hands reached down to give that fellow a lift; the red-faced sport rose slowly, shaking his head, grinning—apparently all right.

"Piss off!" he snarled at those showing excessive con-cern.

Other audience members had begun stage diving, meanwhile. And, as the band continued to loudly thrash it out, the incited mob was literally bouncing off the walls. "Anarchy!-anarchy!-anarchy!" one galoot kept wailing. Amid the chaos, Martin was helping to pass along an anonymous body surfer, when suddenly—surrealisti-cally—this person's entire *leg* came off in his hands while the rest of the body continued to be smoothly passed along to the stage.— *The fuck!* Martin thought; before realizing he was holding a prosthetic limb. "*Gimme that!*" growled a no-neck lummox beside him and, snatching it away while let-ting out a war whoop, swung it loosely around like a giant chicken-wing before slinging it unto the stage where it crashed between the drummer and startled lead guitarist.

Martin had wondered about the twins whereabouts when suddenly one of them appeared tottering high on the edge of the stage, ready to do a full dive. "Here I go, *fook-ers!*" he bellowed. "*Catch me!*" And leapt only to have the teeming crowd widely split apart to watch him fall on his face.

The other twin resurfaced next to Martin, chortling: "Right on the *head!* Pity them floorboards, eh?!"

Then nudging Martin: "*Up* and *at 'em,* Horace!" With a mischievous gleam, the twin extended his clasped hands, palms up: offering him a "boost" over the crowd.

Martin debated it for an instant, before putting a hand on the twin's shoulder and the tip of his boot in his hands, thinking "*Whatthefuck! Whynot!*" Then, like in a dream, *up* he went! *Hoisted,* on his back, over the crammed, heaving audience. Like floating *weightless* on an ocean. Like being sixteen again! In motion, Martin took in the dark moving shapes around him, the rippling laughing faces and flailing arms, absorbing the furious energy, surrendering to it, feeling himself being swept as on a raging tide, time speeding up now—faster and faster—until *boom!* He blacked out.

"Shit," he blinked in a flare of light. "Where am I?"

In the next moment, coming to his senses, Martin realized he was—*yes*—onstage at CBGB, in front of the howling, screaming audience, the band's bass guitarist now glaring down at him. Touching his forehead, Martin felt the start of a big knot: *Great, Great*….

Shaking off his grogginess, he got up and prepared to dive.

"*JUMP! JUMP!*" screamed the blur of grotesques below.

All pumped up, Martin stood poised on the edge of the stage—only to choke, suddenly panic-stricken.

Panic-stricken—

that is, till spotting the bass guitarist charging at him, wielding his instrument like an ax, like he might chop Martin's head off. Adrenaline pumping, witless with fear, Martin leapt, managing a near-somersault. He felt himself fall back, nearly crapping in his pants—arms stretched wide, body tensed—caught by a ready audience, who effortlessly buoyed and passed him back over the throng, until he was finally dropped, after fifteen or twenty heads.

As Martin staggered to his feet, the final blow came from a grinning cro-magnon who cheerfully yanked him up: "Aah, you're awright!"—then plowed into him, knocking him back across the aisle.

After that, he was a little slow in rising.

Miraculously, the helping hand this time belonged to Lola.

"God," she exclaimed. "*There* you are!"

"I was looking all over for you!" he lied. His shirt was torn at the shoulder, his hair wildly disarranged.

Seeing the bump on his forehead, she broke up laughing: "Fuck! Look at you!"

Martin tried to play it off:

"*What?*"

71.

Zipping along—

When the next band, Tribe 8, mounted the stage, the Polinski twins were nowhere to be found—in fact, nearly half the young male audience had mysteriously vanished. When Martin asked Lola for a possible explanation, she replied, "Oh, you'll find out why!"

Amused by the band's compelling lead singer, Martin was taken *Tribe 8* at once. As with most punk-inspired bands, performance and attitude were everything; the point was to be abrasive, rude, reckless. And this front-woman *was*. She wore purple locks, a bandolier with holstered bowie knife around her waist and, sticking out of her shorts, a giant prosthetic penis. (It was the night for prosthetics.)

Although she insisted on no stage diving—and threat-ened to mutilate anyone who would try—she fearlessly dove herself, blasting stilted lyrics while propped on the bobbing heads and shoulders of cooperative fans. Other times, she'd drop to the stage and slither across it, belly-heavy, reptile-like, strangling her words in some kind of hell-bent agony.

Apart from abusing and insulting the agitated crowd, other tasteless antics included mooning the audience, pouring water and beer on them (when she was unable to produce sufficient spit), performing simulated oral and anal sex on female attendant groupies, kicking a sound man who appeared briefly on stage to secure some loose wires and then someone else who tried to help that person off.

But the crowning moment, the *climax* came at the end of the last dissolute song, when, her face glistening with sweat, she peered out into the audience, scowling: "Do I see any *dicks*? Any *dicks* left in the house, tonight?" At which point, she ominously unsheathed the long, glinting bowie knife and, with her other hand, rigidly held out the spit-slathered dong.

"Do it. Do it!" crowed a she-devil from the audience.

The lead singer brought the edge of the blade down near the base of the unsuspecting phallus.

"*Ice* it, girl!" "Slice away!" others shrieked.

Then, grinning maniacally, nearly foaming at the mouth, she began to follow through: to intensely cut—carve and saw, back and forth, with the edge of the knife—until at last the almighty oppressor and all-pervading sym-bol of patriarchal evil was ritualistically *unmanned*, to wild applause and cheers.

"—There ya go!" "*Hoo-hoo*, girl!" "Way ta go!... "

Concluding the show, the front-woman triumphantly held the now pitiful, realistic-looking stub over her head like a matador waving the ear of a bull, dedicating the kill to the avenging feminist spirit of the audience.

"That's all there is!" she snarled. "That's it!"

And, as other band members began to drop their instruments and stalk off stage—one or two of them flipping the bird at the uncontrolled crowd—the lead singer tossed what was left of the sorry prop to the back of the room.

"Good night!" she exclaimed, exhausted and satisfied now. "And, sweet mother*fuckin' dreams!*"

"Well, that sure was *cathartic*," Lola remarked, applauding.

Martin looked at her:

:o(

72.

Outside *CB's*, young women were tossing around the severed penis, playing a friendly game of "catch."

Meanwhile Martin looked for the Polinski twins, wanting to thank them for a fun occasion. But they appeared gone.

Vanished.

"Oh, they'll pop up some other time," Lola assured him. "They always turn up … like fleas. Or crabs."

73.

Walking up the Bowery, ears still ringing, the Empire State Building looming in the distance like a brightly lit syringe, they arrived on the busy corner of St. Marks Place, amid lollygagging ne'er-do-wells and starry-eyed sops.

Then Lola surprised him by saying: "Hey, you don't have to walk me the rest of the way."

Startled, he turned to her. "But I don't mind."

He had *wanted* to walk with her, of course; had even looked forward to it.

"No ... *really*," she insisted, trying to be "diplomatic."

Confused, even somewhat hurt, Martin nevertheless decided not to argue. Instead he stated the obvious: "Pissed at me for 'slam-dancing'?"

—It sounded funny to even *say* the word after so many years.

"Nah," she said, distracted. "Just, I wanna be alone, I think."

He attempted to apologize, finally mumbling, "Guess I messed up, huh?"

"You didn't. *Really*," she told him.

Okay.

Martin offered her a friendly kiss, which she accepted with surprising warmth, gently cupping his jaw with a hand and closing her eyes.

At last she murmured, "Bye."

"See ya later," he said, already facing away.

"—Oh, and Marty?"

He stopped. Turned back.

"Take care of *that*," she said, pointing to the lump on his head.

His eyes rolled up in that direction. "Oh yeah," he said, chuckling. "Right."

74.

"More office forms, bro. Take it or leave it."

Martin was at work the next day with a big band-aid on his head. "Boss man's gone dementoid! It's gettin' *sick!*"

Chaz agreed, but, marshalling the troops, added, "Like it or not, we still gotta do it. Follow up. Shit, I got kids to feed, you got rent to pay, am I right?"

That tired point, again.

"Not to mention," he added after a moment, "lately, Haizu-san's been on my case about you."

This caught him unexpectedly. "*Me?*"

"'At's right," said Chaz, plainly. "And not for nothin', bro, but I'm gettin' a little tired of hearin' it, too."

"Whatcha' talkin' about?" Martin said, almost annoyed.

Chaz turned from his desk. "*Amigo*, you *know* what I'm talkin' about!"

Martin fell silent. Whenever Chaz used "amigo," he knew there was no point in arguing.

"Other day, you away at lunch," he said, "Haizu found more pages on the copier glass. Again, he asked *what the fuck was goin' on?* Took 'em, too. Pages of poetry."

Shit. Martin sighed. Busted. Again.

"Be a little careful, that's all I'm sayin'. And, ease up on the lateness an' that shit. Godamn—*fake* some interest!" Chaz wheeled around, again. "I'm sayin' all this for *your* sake. Old boy's due in from Japan; after that, who knows what changes may be goin' down." He began to split up the invoices on his desk. "Meantime, in this 'transitional period,' we may hafta' put up with a little *bull*-shit."

"Seen plenty of it already, dontcha' think?" said Martin. He couldn't keep his trap shut.

"And, maybe, we ain't seen *nothin'* yet," said Chaz, turning back again. "Keep in mind, bro, keep in mind—things ain't never so bad that they can't get worse!"

75.

After that unsettling, uncharacteristic sermon from Chaz, Manager of Export Operations, Martin vowed he would try to "make an effort."

And, as if to prove it, he stepped out into the warehouse immediately, rolled up his sleeves, and got down to some serious, mind-numbing grunt work: re-taping and labeling cartons, banding and preparing skids for that evening's TYO consolidation, the whole while singing plantation songs....

Some time past one o'clock, Martin heard a knock on the door and went to answer it. As he expected, it was a delivery, and the trucker handed him a slip, asking, "Where de' otha' fellah?"

Martin replied, "*Lunch*." Tugging on his work gloves, he inspected the pro. "All stacked on skids, I hope?"

"I only drive it, ye' know. Don't load it."

Martin pulled the heavy draw-chain to open the warehouse gate. The tractor-trailer was backed in on a perfect line, both wing doors opened and tied back.

"—Shit, no!" Martin felt his legs go numb. From ceiling to floor, as far as he could see, the truck was crammed with tall, bulky cartons. Not a single skid in sight!

Martin burst into the warehouse office, got on the intercom.

"*Moshi-moshi!*" answered Tani, the Japanese secretary.

"Listen, uh, this is Marty, downstairs? I'm alone with a tractor-trailer and a shipment of a hundred and sixty-two *loose* cartons that weigh"—he checked the figure—"*two thousand six hundred and thirty-two pounds!*"

There was a pause while she put him on hold.

Martin tapped his fingers, waiting.

"Marteee," she returned. "Martee-san, everyone away! You must take! Sorry!"

"*I* 'must take,' huh?" And Martin came very close to breaking on her: the words *fuckee you!* right on the tip of his tongue. "Unbelievable!" And slammed the phone.

"Well, hoss," he sighed, turning back to the trucker. "Hope you had your Wheaties this morning. Looks like it's just you and me."

"Weeze' about ta' get fucked, a-gin'?"

All he could muster:

"Pass the *K-Y*...."

76.

And would it end there?

Was life ever that simple? Or kind?

After Chaz returned from lunch, eight more heavy shipments arrived, a third without skids, the last tractor-trailer docking, after various delays and half-assed apologies, at 9:30 PM.

And did Martin complain? Say diddly squat?

Nope.

After all, what else did he have to do with his time, his so-called life other than to dedicate it, wholehearted and selflessly, to the cause and financial enrichment of some monolithic global conglomerate that hardly acknowledged his existence?

Wasn't it true that the value of a man's life was seen in how he dedicated himself to his work?

Wasn't it all about learning humility in this life?

If a man is served a plate of steaming shit, *yea*, shouldn't his only response be: "Can I get a spoon with that?"

Now hitting late-night traffic (due to endless post rush-hour road/repair work) on the Brooklyn-Queens Express-way: *another fifty minutes.*

Now the search for parking: *an additional forty-five minutes.*

It was nearly 11:30 PM—Hallelujah!—by the time Saint Martin-san, bottle of malt liquor under his arm, snatched and tore up his daily rejection letters from his mailbox, trudged up to his studio apartment, singing:

"Oh, *I Got Plenty of Nothin'!...*"

77.

That night at home, almost too exhausted to move, he lay on the open sofa, listening to his latest audio cassette purchase: *Run With The Hunted* by Charles Bukowski and mindlessly sucking his forty-ounce.

Yes, *audio tapes.*

Another vice, another depravity he had succumbed to.

Cheesy, yes. And, yeah, in the past he'd often made fun of those "silly" nuevo-yupsters who purchased such crap unapologetically, their supremely important lives so over-scheduled, so overflowing and full, they didn't have the time to turn pages and "actually read."

Now here he was himself, the sluggard, guzzling an Old English "800*," digging Bukowski. On tape.

Notes from the Underground by Fyodor Dostoevsky (as read by George Guidall)

A Confederacy of Dunces by John Kennedy Toole (as read by Arte Johnson)

Song of Myself by Walt Whitman (as read by Orson

---

*'Cause, as far as malt liquour went, it fucked him up the *most*

Welles)

Ironweed by William Kennedy (as read by Jason Robards)

Visions of Cody by Jack Kerouac (as read by Graham Parker)

These were all "books" that he owned, tucked away in his tiny entrance closet, under some dirty socks. His own perverted little secret. His own sweaty fetish.

His glossy porn mags he kept in the open.

The phone rang. And for a moment Martin considered answering it.

That moment passed.

At last, lowering the volume on his cracked Walkman, he listened:

"Hi, Marty. This is Amaris," began the live voice. "I'm on a broken pay phone right now, so I'll have to make it quick: I was wondering if you'd wanna meet up, tomorrow? Maybe even do a little dancing, like we said last time? There's this little thing happening at the *Pyramid Club*, called 'Necropolis.' A kind of goth theme party. Might be fun. And I was wondering—"*click-click!* She was momentarily disconnected. "—*Please deposit an additional five cents,*" interrupted a recording. "—Anyway," she returned, "page me, let me know what you think!—*Click!*" That ended her message.

He'd call her back later. If he could ever get up.

78.

That night, Martin did page her. But after fifty minutes with no call back and, feeling woozy and bored (book-tape done, forty long ago drained, hour fast approaching 1:30 AM), he decided—*what the fuck!*—to dial the *Vox* Personals.

Any luck?

This *was* Martin Sierra, wasn't it?...

Ever the masochist, he lingered, kept the line, this time to "browse."

"Please choose from the following categories," the pre-recorded operator went on.

If only he had another beer!

" 'One' for 'Men seeking women.' "

" 'Two' for 'Men seeking men.' "

" 'Three' for 'Women seeking men.' "

Dry-mouthed, Martin pressed "3."

Beep! "... Hi, er. This is a straight female looking for a straight male? I don't know—they kinda screwed up my ad in this newspaper? I was kinda hoping they would put 'SF,' y'know, in big bold letters, but they didn't? Uh, anyway, if you're an 'MF' please leave a number? And a name or something? Okay, bye—no *wait!* Did I say 'MF'? I meant 'SM!' Oh, for shit's sake! Now I'll have to do this whole stupid message over!—"*click!*

Martin continued to browse:

Beep! "... Hi. My name is Kim. Just to add a little more to my ad, I have long brown hair with blonde highlights. Blue eyes. I'm about five-*nine*, full-figured .... Absolutely no drugs, no beards, no mustaches. No bald guys or midgets.... And don't forget to leave a name, *first* and *last*, and number with the *area code. And* a business phone!..."

Beep! "... Hello. My name is Dorothy. I'm rather quiet. (long pause) I am a professional woman and would like to meet a professional man. (long pause) I hate sports, I really do. But that's the way it is. I like swimming. Aqua-aerobics. But that's as far as it goes. (another long pause) I've recently been in therapy for nine years because I came from a dysfunctional family—(line cut off)"

Beep! "… Hiiii! You have reached *Vanilla* and *Caramel!* We're so glad you've chosen our ad! So we'll briefly describe ourselves":

Another young female voice: "—*Hi!* I'm *Vanilla!* I'm twenty-four years old, five-*five*, a hundred and twenty pounds, attractive, with long shoulder-length blond hair and a most radiant smile! I like long walks on the beach, great conversation, romantic candlelit dinners, and quiet moments!"

First voice, again: "—And, *Hi!* I'm *Caramel!* I have caramel colored skin with dark brown hair below my shoulders. I'm twenty-five years old, five-*two*, a hundred twenty-five pounds, with beautiful eyes and a dazzling smile! I'm a future Botanist, who likes traveling and visiting museums. I enjoy talking, horseback riding, and love to laugh!"

Both voices (in unison): "—We're beautiful, energetic, and sincere! We're seeking two attractive, physically fit, sweet and honest men, twenty-four to thirty-five years old, who will treat us like ladies! Don't be shy to leave long messages!…"

Beep! Click! (a hang up)

Beep! "… Hello! (a male voice cleared his throat) We're an attractive, middle-aged Asian *couple*. And what we're looking for, basically, is a special gentleman to join us in having a bit of fun …. Give us a physical description of yourself, maybe your penis size, what your preferences and limits are, any kinks you might be into—that kind of *thing*. And we'll give you a jingle. Sound *agreeable?…*"

Beep! "… *Hey there!* I want to meet a big loser who will soak up all my time with his petty drama, someone who has absolutely nothing in common with me and who smells funny…. No, to be honest, I'm just *too tired* to be hip! So if you are a scenester or in a band or something, fuck off. Otherwise, leave a detailed message, yeah?…"

Beep! "… Hi. I'm Liz. My extension number is 3567. Please don't respond to my ad if you SMOKE or do DRUGS or are extremely OVERWEIGHT—or are MAR-RIED. I'm just *not interested* … (sighing wearily) Bye…."

Beep!…

Beep!…

Beep!…

79.

The next night, the *Pyramid Club* spun music that was full of dirge-like incantations, guttural groans, and slow desolate howls of infernal agony. Through faux cobwebs, smoke machines huffed and hissed while masked red and blue gel-colored spots cast the appropriate somber, sepul-chral-like glow.

Amaris was dressed appropriately for the evening, wearing a long inky skirt, mesh top with a black bra, and studded dog collar.

After Martin commented favorably on her top, Amaris moved in close, asking, "Know how a person makes one of these?"

He shook his head.

"It's real easy," she explained. "Take a regular pair of fishnet stockings, cut out the crotch. Then pull it over your head."

"Oh, I get it," he said, taking a closer look. "Then poke out holes for your fingers?"

"Right."

Martin nodded approvingly. "*Tri-cky.*" He glanced up as several black, spectral faces floated by in the darkness.

Then she asked him, "Do you believe in *vampires?*"

What did she say?

"In vampires," she repeated. "Do you believe in them?"

Martin wasn't sure what she was talking about. "You mean, like in the movies?"

"No," she said in all seriousness. "In real life."

He almost laughed, but in keeping with the mood of the evening put forth, "You know, I'm *not sure*...."

This answer seemed to please her.

With a little smile, he asked her, "Why? Do you?"

"Do I?"

"—Believe in vampires?"

Amaris confided, "Well actually ... I do."

"You do?"

She nodded. "In fact, I know one."

"You *know* one?"

Again she nodded. "Sounds a bit strange. But it's true."

Smiling: "You *know* a vampire."

"I *do*," she grinned.

He went along with it: "Okay. So how do you know?"

"She told me."

"She told you," he deadpanned. "That's it. She *told* you?"

"Yeah."

"And you believed her?"

"Well," confessed Amaris. "Actually, she did a little more than that."

He looked at her. "Whaddaya mean?"

"She *showed* me."

Now, he was interested.

"How'd she do that?"

"Well, maybe I shouldn't tell you," said Amaris.

"Why not?"

She shrugged. "You'll make fun of me."

"I promise. I won't." Anything to hear a good story.

"Are you bullshitting me?"

Was he that kind of guy? "No."

It was then she gave in: "It was at a club. The Bank. 'Ward 6.' Over on Houston. I saw her and right away felt a little drawn to her. Didn't know why. She was just *intense*. Something about her. Just this vibe.

"Anyway, at first I saw her at the bar. Then, on the dance floor, in the catacombs downstairs. Our eyes met like we'd recognized each other. Like we were somehow connected, even though we were total strangers. Later, as it turned out, I bumped into her again. In the ladies room. This time, smiling, she took me aside. Whispered a secret. Said, she was feeling a bit low, 'depleted' was how she put it. In need of some 'ruby red,' and asked if I could spare some."

"'Ruby red'?"

"I didn't know what she was talking about, either. I thought she might've meant some drug. I told her I wasn't holding. But then she grabbed my hand gently, held it, shook her head, and led me to a stall."

Martin was into it. "What happened next?"

Amaris went on: "In the stall, pressed up close to me, at first she kissed me, kissed my lips, my neck. Soft, soft. I let her. I almost couldn't resist her. After kissing me a while, she smiled at me and told me what she meant, what she needed. My eyes were on her mouth. And her lips formed the word."

"What word?" He was riveted.

" 'Blood.' "

"Wait a minute," he said, backing up. "Are you serious?"

Amaris nodded.

"Blood," Martin repeated.

Again she nodded. "She asked if I could spare some."

Martin was gripped. "And what did you say?"

"I told her, 'it depends on how much.' And she replied, 'Oh, only a few drops.' "

A beat. His eyes went wide "—So you *gave it* to her?"

"Well I was already a little toasted by then so I said, 'Why not.' "

"—You let her *suck your blood?*" Martin was horrified.

"Just for a little while," she stressed.

"But ... how?" he wanted more details now. "How'd she do it? With fangs? She suck your neck?"

Amaris burst out laughing. "No, nothing like that. We were both in the stall, and she looked up at me with her dark eyes. Then she moved in again, kissing me, touching me until I relaxed. Then she took my finger and pricked it. Used a surgical needle or something. I hardly felt it. She stuck a pin into my finger and brought my finger to her mouth."

"She just sucked on your finger?"

Amaris grinned. "Uh-huh. And every now and then, as she suckled, as her lips grew tight, her eyes kept rolling up at me. Her dark eyes. And I got a little turned on, actually. Because she was really *pretty.*"

Perversely, Martin felt himself getting a little turned on, too. "And that's it? That's all that happened between you?"

"That's all. Afterwards you could say we *bonded.*"

"Really? And do you still see her?"

"Now and then," said Amaris. "At clubs."

"Is she here? Tonight?" he asked. Overly excited.

She scanned the floor. "Don't see her."

"And when you bump into her," he persisted. "Do you let her, *y'know*—"

"*Feed?*"

He felt a shiver go up his spine.

Amaris raised an eyebrow. Laughed, "Not telling."

Nodding, Martin fell quiet, lost in the bizarre, erotic possibilities.

Fuck, he thought. *Fuck me.*

80.

Later, as if through a fog—

Drifting from the back room to the bar, where they both ordered drinks, Amaris and Martin sat half-watching the monitor movie, *Nosferatu*. She had lit a Dunhill.

Martin thought it wise to change the subject. And somehow or other they got on the topic of "jobs"—Martin boring himself with details of his own ridiculous life-wasting occupation.

Her turn to shine. He now recalled an earlier admission:

"You teach school, you said?"

"College" said Amaris, exhaling. "Part time. In the Bronx."

"You don't look older than most of your students, I'll bet."

She grinned. "Got that right. Freaks some people out."

Martin smiled. "The younger students can relate to you, I'm sure."

"Uh-huh," she said, raising her glass. "Some I even hang out with. On a social basis."

This struck him as odd. "Really?"

She nodded, privately amused.

"And this doesn't cause any problems?"

She shrugged, smiling. "I keep a short list."

"Oh really?"

"Very short," she grinned. "Any problems—I make sure to get even."

"What," Martin said, "give 'em failing grades at the end of the semester?"

"Ain't telling that, either," she said.

Was she pulling his leg?

This Amaris: *a true woman of mystery.*

Round two:

"So, I've been meaning to ask you," she said. "How'd you make out with the ad?" She'd lit another cigarette.

Martin put down his bottle.

"Okay, I guess."

"Get many responses?"

He shrugged. "A few."

"Only a few?"

"When it comes to the ads, it's different for men and women."

"It is?"

"Big difference. With a gal there are dozens of replies; for a guy, one or two."

"Is that as many as you got?"

"Just recently."

"And how'd they go?" More curious than threatened.

Again Martin shrugged, not wanting to give much away: appear somehow pathetic *or* obnoxious.

"Too early to tell?"

He replied, nodding. "That's one way to put it."

Amaris took a drag of her Dunhill. "It's not like in the movies, right? Where two people meet—strangers—and everything happens *slam-bang*."

"Nah. It's never that way. Or else—it's over just as quick."

"Yeah." She sighed, exhaling smoke.

He raised his Heineken Dark, took a sip. "What about you? Tried other ads?"

"A few," she admitted.

"Oh yeah?" He tried to sound disinterested. "How'd they go?"

Amaris flicked ash into a nearby tray, frowning. "Mostly? They *sucked*."

He felt somehow relieved. "How's that?"

"Huh?" She turned to him.

"I mean, *why* did they suck?"

"Oh." She sighed again. "I don't know … one guy was too old. Another was too uptight. Another seemed—I don't know—too emotionally unstable." She took another drag, squinting a bit. "Maybe, it's just me. Maybe I'm really not ready to get involved right now. So I keep finding fault. Making excuses."

Martin asked, "Has it been hard, making the adjustment? Not being married?"

She thought about it, saying finally, "The security is gone, that's for sure. Can't tell you the last time I've had a solid night's sleep. At the same time, it's also been liberating." She smiled. "It's a relief not always having to answer to somebody."

"You can do as you please now?"

"Kinda. Except that I have a son to think about."

"Oh yeah. 'River.'"

"Yeah," she smiled proudly. "Little River."

"Not a drag, being a mom?"

"Not really," she said. "You get used to it. Another fact of life." She leaned back a bit. "Come to think of it, without him, I think I'd be pretty lost. I mean, that's what's great about kids. I know it's cliché and all, but it's true. Kids are the antidote to suicide. They give you a purpose. A reason to get up in the morning."

Martin took another sip of his drink. "See," he said. "I wouldn't know anything about that."

81.

She asked him, "Where'd you say you live, again?" They were headed south on Avenue A, after leaving the club.

"The Heights," he told her.

"Brooklyn?"

"Queens," he laughed. "Do I look rich to you?"

"I'm parked just around the corner," she said.

"Oh yeah?" he smiled. Adding: "Would you mind swinging by?"

"'Swinging'?" She grinned. "Of course not."

82.

As her Honda Civic warmed up, Amaris claimed she had something she wanted to give him. "Oh yeah?"

"Here ya go," she said, gently dropping it in his lap. It was in a brown paper bag.

Martin carefully reached inside, removed the item, exclaiming, "You're really *into* this stuff, huh?"

She laughed. "You might say I have a 'closet interest.'"

"Well, thanks," he said politely, turning the book over to scan the back. *"The Best Vampire Compendium Ever!"*—Stephen Rice, author of *Vampire A-Go-Go*

"Wait," Amaris said. "Let me inscribe it." She took back the book, removing an antique fountain pen from her purse.

When she was done, the inside cover read:

To one of the few,
I hope you will regard this volume kindly.
May it prove useful in exploring your own vampire nature.
A kindred soul,

A.

83.

"Excuse the mess and all."

Once in his apartment, the first thing Amaris noticed was the titanic stack of rejection letters piled in the corner.

"What on earth is *that?*"

"Mount Everest—no, just some junk." He shrugged. "Care for another drink?"

She declined.

"Not even a short one? Another white Russian?"

"Well," she wavered. "But go easy on the alcohol, okay?"

"Yeah right." He went to mix it.

84.

As Martin reappeared with the drinks, Amaris stood casually regarding small-framed photographs on his bookcase.

"Who's this?" she asked, indicating the one on the left.

"Actually, my mom." He handed her a glass.

She examined the photo closely. "She looks *young* here. Like a teenager."

"Baby-faced, like me."

"How old was she?"

"In that photo? In her twenties." He took a sip of his own drink.

"And when she?..."

He almost blanked out. "My age."

"How did it happen?"

"Huh?" Eyes wide, he took another swallow.

"I mean..."

Martin shook his head. "Dunno."

"You don't?"

He shook his head again. "One day... she just left."

"'Left'?"

"Vanished."

Amaris paused uncomfortably. "And you never got an explanation?"

"Not really.... Y'know, she was *ill*." He tapped his head. "I mean, up here."

"Oh ... *sorry*," Amaris said.

Martin shook it off.

Allowing a long moment to pass, she then asked of the other photograph.

"Which?"

"Here." She pointed.

In the photo, the woman was dressed in thigh-high boots and a billowy silk top. The occasion was the Halloween parade in the Village. He felt relieved just to be reminded of the image.

Martin said, "That's Nikki. My *mija*. My best friend."

"Your 'best friend'?" She chuckled.

"Yeah." He smiled. "What's so funny?"

She smirked. "That sounds … a bit suspicious."

"'Suspicious'? Why?"

Amaris shrugged, grinning. "I don't know." She turned to the photograph again, appraising it. "She's pretty *hot*, actually."

"Whaddaya mean?" he asked uneasily.

"Just my type," she admitted. And laughed.

85.

Later, both more intoxicated, they sat cross-legged on the hardwood floor, randomly going through bootleg videos, all of which, coincidentally, were Nikki's: *Edie in Ciao Manhattan, Christiane F., Gun Crazy*….

"I really get off on this one," Martin said, picking up *The Attack Of The Fifty-Foot Woman*. "I don't know why. Maybe the idea of a giantess wrapped in a skimpy towel."

Amaris laughed.

"Must be some Freudian thing," Martin said hazily. "Something *Oedipal*."

"You wanna climb inside that big pussy?" said Amaris.

Martin laughed. "Maybe." He thought about it. "Who wouldn't?"

She moved in close to him. "Get all *snugly* in that womb?"

Martin laughed again, but suddenly felt a bit uneasy. He distracted himself by going through more videos. He picked up *Story of O*, a film he wasn't into.

"I guess you really have to be drunk to appreciate some of these," Martin said.

"What about this one?" she asked, picking up *Faster Pussycat! Kill! Kill!*

The cover featured a leather-gloved Xena-type clobbering men.

"Would you be into *that*?"

"Whaddaya mean?" Martin said, getting defensive.

"*You* know what I mean." Her tone held a faint challenge.

Despite the alcohol, he was starting to feel vulnerable. "Can we change the subject?"

She looked darkly amused: "Why?"

He couldn't think of a reply.

"It's okay," she said coolly. "I'm into *all kinds* of things."

"Like, what?"

She shrugged. "I met a guy recently who had an Amazon fetish."

"What's that?"

Amaris looked at him, disbelieving. "Oh, c'mon. You know."

"I don't."

"Femdom," she said.

He looked at her blankly.

"Lots of guys have submissive fantasies," she said. "It's okay."

"What's 'okay'?"

"Being dominated."

Martin had to smile. "Hey, any good-looking gal in a G-string wants to pound me into submission, she's more than welcome." Adding cheerfully, "Provided she sits on my face afterward."

"I'm sure that can be arranged," said Amaris, grinning.

Martin felt his mouth go dry.

Okay.

What was he getting himself into?

Arching an eyebrow, he blurted, "I'm sure that's true." He rose to his feet, unsteadily. "But, as for now, I gotta use the restroom." And started in that direction, legs a bit rubbery.

"Don't masturbate!" Amaris called out.

"Ha-ha," Martin said. "Good one."

But, the truth was, after freeing his pecker, he had a hard time peeing.

86.

When he returned, Fellini's *The Clowns* was playing on his VCR. Amaris was lounging across the hardwood floor like a queen.

"I'm ready for another," Martin said. "How about you?"

"Okay," she chirped, hoisting her empty glass. "*Slave.*"

"Hey, watch that." Martin chuckled, grabbing it. Quite liberal with the alcohol, he soon returned handing her the drink.

"Ran out of ice, Mistress," he said.

"That's okay." She took a sip, making a face. "Whew!"

Martin laughed, raising his. "Down the hatch!" He took a long swallow, feeling the alcohol fumes singe his nose hairs.

Then he dropped beside Amaris, watching the movie.

"Ever see *Satyricon?*" she asked, pushing against him.

"No," he admitted. "But I've read the book by Petronius."

"Like it?"

"Yeah," he admitted. "One of my favorites."

"Name some others," she insisted.

"Other books?" Leaning back, he tried to recall: "*A Fan's Notes* by Frederick Exley, *The Fan Man* by William Kotzwinkle, *Play The Piano Drunk* ... by Bukowski—"

"Oh, I hate that last one," she said.

"Why?"

"That misogynist asshole!"

He looked at her. Was she *loca?*

The next moment had a dreamlike quality.

Martin wasn't sure at what point it happened, but as they sat near each other, suddenly debating personal likes and dislikes ("male" vs. "female" authors), they began to gaze at each other expectantly, drop their defenses, finally to exchange gropes and short, playful kisses.

Yeah it was all a front: fuck literature!

Soon they were French-kissing and laughing in earnest, teasing each other mercilessly, Amaris aggressively unbuckling his pants, as Martin dug under her fishnet top to unlatch her sexy black bra.

"Hurry up, you sexist prick," she told him.

Martin was startled. "Hang on a second," he demanded.

"Second, my *fucking* ass!"

Martin unfolded his sofa, and, fueled by alcohol, they soon proceeded to engage in a kind of heady, rough sex that involved some quasi-wrestling and light bondage, with Amaris taking charge like she was a professional.

Using her mesh top, she insisted on tying his wrists while she got on top and fucked him.

Soon her hands were around his neck. "*O-kay!*" Martin let out, alarmed. "Maybe *not!*"

She informed him: "Hey, pity it's not up to you!"

Her hands were strong! And, while he hated to admit it—*godamnit!*—he was turned on!

Feeling like a weakling, a discredit to his gender, he choked: "Charles Bukowski rules!"

"Fuck Bukowski—that fat drunken prick!" she hissed, inserting him inside her. "Hold still!" Closing her eyes, after an adjustment or two, she then tried to focus on her own amplifying sensations as she slowly undulated, rolling her hips—the straining and contracting of her movements now creating almost unbearable pleasure for him. Martin, for his part, held back. "*Proves zip!*" he assert-ed weakly, straining against his binds, trying hard not to come. "Hold still," she kept insisting, when he began to grind against her. "I like my *bottoms* to hold still," she wickedly told him.

"As long as you don't forget who's boss!" he managed, pathetically.

"If I had another doggy collar," she threatened, "I'd snap it around your neck!"

Red-faced: "Yeah, you wish!"

"I'll turn you out, ponyboy! Make you mine!" Now and then, as she rode him, he would see her grinning down at him, her eyes hard with a kind of fierce determination. "Don't you come!" she implored, squeezing him harder now. "—Don't come." "*I won't*," Martin grimaced, trying to slow his breathing, let his mind drift—away from this sex-ual assault. "Now repeat after me," she said, antagonizing him. "—Edith Wharton, Willa Cather, Jane Austen, Isak Dinesen!" "Isak Dinesen was a *man!*" "Wrong, fucking wrong!" she laughed. "Now repeat: '*Women's literature* rules! *Women's literature…*'" and she was soon redoubling her efforts.

"So tell me, do you—do you—*like* it?" What could he answer? She was persuasive. "—*Yeah.*" "And my tits? Like *'em?*" "*Yeah!*" "Then show me!" And leaning forward, releasing his neck, she brought a jutting breast to within inches of his mouth. And as Martin awkwardly raised his head and proceeded to wetly suck it, she insisted: "*Harder.* So I can feel it. Bite—*bite it!*" And Martin took her hard nipple, slick with his saliva, between his teeth and lightly bit down. "No! *Harder!*" she cried. He did so, clamping down hard. And she finally shrieked.

She reared back, and then Martin felt it—WHAP!—he saw stars, his face stinging—after she had just slapped him.

"Hold on there!" he protested, shocked.

"Shut-up!" she snarled, fucking him harder.

Then—WHAP!—again. More stars.

Martin felt too weak to resist: it was like a carnival ride. Like being in a car spinning out of control: a helpless panic blending into exhilaration. Dang!

Her ferocity was daunting. "You like that, don't you!" Don't you, doggy boy!"

Doggy boy? Wait a minute! Hold on!

Pinning him down with her full body weight, pounding him, fucking him, harder and harder. She was relentless. With each upward and downward stroke, he could feel her pussy clutching his cock. Oh fuck it! Fuck it! Yeah, doggy boy—who cared!

"Who's in charge?" she demanded.

"Huh?"

"Who's in charge!" she barked.

He answered quickly before she slapped him again: "You!" In case she hadn't heard it: "You! You! You!"

"That's *right!* Just remember," she sneered. "I can do

this *any time I want!*"

"Anytime. Won't forget!" he gasped. "Won't!"

"I'll make you my bitch yet!"

"Bitch! Doggy boy! Yeah! Yeah!" He was babbling.

Seeing spots, panting for breath, his cock painfully hard, the room spinning, he could sustain only so much more of this, before he felt a sensation like molten lead build up in his groin, and—rearing—*"Fuck, not yet!"* came, groaning hoarsely: *"Uuuhhh!..."* He felt himself shoot up into her—balls scalding—felt her constrict around him, melting him.

"—Jesus H ... Christ!..."

Amaris held him inside her, still straining to squeeze out a full orgasm but too late: he was already numb, losing it. As she mercifully untied his wrists and slid off, he felt the need to whisper, "Sorry." "That's okay," she said kindly. "It felt good anyway—you *asshole*."

After she untied him, Martin discreetly reached for some tissues, dispensed with the soggy condom. They hugged and kissed a while, Martin finally feeling her skin which was warm and sticky now, her softly protruding belly, and round ass—*full and sexy*—Amaris later nuzzling his chest a long time and lightly biting his neck.

At last, in the early hours of the morning, they fell apart, naked under the sheets, hands touching, and in a haze drifted off to sleep.

Sometime later, he heard her rise to go to the bathroom, heard the water flush. After which he again descended into a deep preternatural sleep.

87.

Sunlight slashing through the shades, Martin awoke

again, turning with a stiff neck to realize he was still alone.

Bleary, yet vaguely concerned, he rose and headed for the bathroom where he flicked on the light and with a jolt realized there was a message across the medicine cabinet mirror written in black lipstick.—*The fuck!*...

Marty,
Had to fly.
It was fun...
See you soon.

A

This was *bizarre*.

Stranger still, in regarding his own reflection, he raised his chin to notice *two* conspicuous marks that weren't present the night before. Of all places—on the side of his throat!

Could they be? Was it—*possible?!*...

His eyes widened, focusing in on the twin marks.

"*Ohhhh—Fuuuuuuuuuuuuuuuuuuck MEEEE!*..."

Wait. He took another look, leaning in—sobered instantly.

Blinked.

—*Aw, no*, he dimly realized. *Just acne.*

88.

Yeah, Untitled

> *Lone, swift dashes of a camelhair,*
> *Deft, white tears of lightning,*
> *Quick, wet strokes of thinned oil-splotch*
> *Strewn carelessly across*

a stiff, bleached canvas
(—strokes easily loosening
the tautness
of a drum skin):

Slick impressions, these are,
spat
clammy-wet
(and with threads)
across
a startled face!

89.

"We got fucked, bro."

Martin remarked, "Oh really."

"That's right," Chaz asserted. "*I* got fucked, *you* got fucked, we *all* got fucked. Reamed right up our muthafuckin' bungholes: *cheated!*"

Martin was, of course, back at work, seated on his side of the warehouse office, when Chaz returned from a meeting with Haizu, the bossman upstairs. The meeting this time concerned budgeting and their former branch head, a man known as "Henry" Tanaka, who under mysterious circumstances had been recalled to Japan and summarily replaced.

"How'd he do it? How'd he fuck us?" Chaz was directly facing Martin. "By skimmin'. Big part of the money meant for us—that is, 'export,' the hump was pocketing. Money for a motorized gate, jumpers, even a new loadin' plate. Money for you and me, bro. We got fucked outta all a' that. When the boy upstairs showed me the budget, the way it was *supposed* to break down, I bugged ..." his voice trailed off as he shook his head.

"This just comes out now? I mean, no one was watching *before?*"

"I'm telling you, bro. Ya got middle management in Japan wearing rose-tinted glasses, not willing to target one of their own. But you wanna hear the *best* part, what the man's punishment amounted to?"

"What."

"A 'window seat.' "

Martin squinted.

"A muthafuckin' *window seat!*" he guffawed. "His punishment! Some dicked position in the company. And this is supposed to make him feel *ashamed—mortally* ashamed, or some shit."

Martin cracked up. "That's pretty good." He thought about it. "Fucking guy must have a fat account in Switzerland by now."

"Wouldn't surprise me none. And who could blame him," laughed Chaz. "—*Shit.*"

"Some assholes just *step in it!*"

"Ain't that right!… "

Chaz laughed heartily with Martin a good while. Then, sitting back and blowing a heavy sigh, he faced the JAL office clock, which already read past noon.

Shifting gears, he asked Martin, "What's the call, bro? Takin' lunch?"

He considered it. "You go first."

Sure enough, no sooner did Chaz exit the door than Martin turned to the phone.

All morning long, despite the usual levity, despite the anesthetizing daze of last night's slapstick encounter, something had been bugging him: preying on his mind. And it was only now—alone in the office with the JAL clock ticking—that Martin began to identify what it was:

Shame?

Nah.

Guilt?

Not quite.

Longing?

Maybe. But what else?

Loneliness?

Coño—if that wasn't it!

There was no other way to describe it: it was a kind of hollowness that left him ailing.

In part, the source of this unease may have been that he was still slightly hung-over from the night before. But he began to suspect another reason, largely sentimental: that he hadn't spoken to a particular someone in days and—*Dios*, he was pathetic!—he missed her, missed his *mija!*

He thought of himself and Amaris. (Her slamming him down, fucking his brains out.)

He thought of himself and Lola. (Her intense black eyes, gritty Spanish allure and sad mystery.)

Then he thought of himself and Nikki.

Nikki.

Her large pale-green eyes, empathetic and intelligent; her dense curling hair untied. Full soft lips, smiling.

Her eyes that looked at Martin from the beginning, not *through him.*

Her eyes that penetrated his anguish.

Her eyes that could see into the heart of him.

Her eyes that, at times, could almost trace his mind.

Amazing:

No matter what, she always remained at the forefront.

Much as he hated to admit it, he suddenly realized: an ad date—his life—didn't seem *real* unless he shared it with her first.

Was he a sentimental fool? A sorry masochist doomed to a life of endless humiliation?

Mierda.

If living his life honestly involved only that, so be it.

Martin phoned her at work, caught her voice mail, quickly thought of an excuse for why he might be calling: "Hey, stranger. *What's up?* Listen, *mija*—I was wondering if we could just get together. Maybe even tonight?" The very thought cheered him. "Grab a drink, a film?—The new Wong Kar-Wai movie playing at The Angelika?"

He paused as if he had more to add—something intimate and heartfelt—but froze, afraid of laying it on too thick. "*Anyway*," he said. "Let me know."

90.

That same evening, before opening his mailbox in the Heights, bag of lo mein in hand, Martin mused on how swiftly his day had gone. Only 6:30 PM and here he was! Every day should be as painless, he thought.

He reached inside the box to withdraw a single envelope.

A bill? Another rejection letter? Notice from the IRS?

Martin opened it. Of all things, it was a personalized advertisement from a cemetery—coincidentally, the same cemetery he passed on the Brooklyn-Queens Expressway each morning, where his attention would linger, amid the carved angels and shaded tombstones ... until he realized he was again at work, already in the parking lot*....

"Above-ground burial at affordable prices," read the cheerful notice. *"**Martin Sierra,** discover the savings and peace of mind available to almost everyone!"*

91.

Later, after supper, Martin was mindlessly sacked out on his couch, pouring himself a Red Stripe, killing time by watching TV.

Taped on the wall near his television were several clippings and author quotes pertaining mostly to the outcast (or "art") life, among them this quote by Bukowski:

> *"I thought the life of a writer would really be the thing, it's simply hell. I'm just a cheap twittering slave."*

Beside that, more prominently, was a recent concept "word poster" he'd made using stencils and the copier machine at work:

𝔜𝔒𝔘
get

𝔒𝔏𝔇𝔈ℜ...

𝔄𝔑𝔇
realize

*eyes closed

You

Just

FEEL

Ridiculous...

At last, he decided to ring Nikki at home since she hadn't returned his call.

But her machine clicked on: "Hi, this is Nikki ..."

"Hey, Nik. *Me*. Just wondering if you were there, if we were on, for tonight. Give me a ring when you get the chance. I'll be here, of course. Like ... hangin' out."

92.

And, for a moment, in his mind, it all seemed
to come together ...

about happiness its
about happiness its
about finding an
anchor a center

stability its about
self-worth seeking peace
and giving love
and love receiving
its acceptance des-
pite fear being
afraid by degrees
the more love
and attention the
better it seems
the more purpose-
ful the less
out of focus
more reasonable
despite facade
expectations favorable
impressions the
less a person has
of what was
there to acquire
without expec-
tations as dictated
by others minus
any variations of
any mode of co-
dependency of
those less reason-
ably inclined and
out of focus their
contentment un-
centered not
his own and in

the end nothing
what is it
about it's…
about…
about….

"*AAAAAAAAAAAAAAAAAAAAAAAAAAAAAAAAAA
AAAAAAAAAAAAAAAAAAAAAAAAAAAAAAAAAAAA
AAAAAAAAAAAAAAAAAAAAAHHHHHHHHHHH-
HHHHHHHHHHHHHHHHHHHHHHH!…*"

He was there, all right. *All* night. What else did he have
to do—except cry out and roll his eyes in boredom?

Five hours—and a full six-pack of Red Stripe—later,
Martin was still in front of his TV. He'd pissed the time
away watching "reality television," then two colossally
dumb sci-fi movies, yes bootlegs: *Invisible Invaders* and *The
Angry Red Planet*.

Yes, yes. His enjoyment of them was supposed to be
purely ironic.

Martin was *supposed* to laugh at the cheesy production
values and clueless direction of *every* scene. Not laugh *out
loud*, of course, but *inwardly*—to himself. How *kitsch!*

Sitting there in his sludgy-morbid drunkenness, he just
felt like an asshole.

At midnight, feeling a dark, creeping lonesomeness, he
dialed Nikki's number again. This time when the recording
began, he simply hung up.

Where was she?…

That night, in bed, for the first time in a long time,
Martin vividly imagined her with Mariella.

Yes, Mariella.

And he was filled with such gripping, painful jealousy

that he could hardly sleep....

93.

The next day at work, Martin called Lola, in part to suggest a retrospective on East Village art happening at *The New Museum*.

She seemed reluctant, as usual, so he had to work on her a while. Finally she came around. Agreeing to meet him, "Well, okay. For an hour."

Then, apropos of nothing, Martin dropped that he might bring along a "sampling" of his work.

"Hah?" was her reaction.

He plainly stated that since he'd enjoyed the opportunity to look at *her* artwork, perhaps she might like to see some of *his*.

She said impatiently, "What are you talking about?"

"You know, like *poems* and stuff," he explained.

"Oh."

"I don't *have* to bring them, of course," he said, finally embarrassed. "Just thought you might wanna take a look. Be interested."

"All right," she said. "So. Bring them."

Martin was already having second thoughts. "Well, okay. Guess I'll meet you there?"

"But, remember," she said again. "Only for an *hour*. This time I *mean it!*"

"Right."

"I have a lot of things to do," she told him.

Martin frowned. "Yeah, okay." *And I guess I don't....*

94.

"Get a load o' this shit!" Martin blurted excitedly, upon

entering the hall.

"Yeah, great," said Lola. "Can you *lower* your voice!"

The retrospective at *The New Museum* entitled, "Punk and No Wave: East Village art of the '80s," centered predictably on three famous artists of the era, all of whom emerged from the local club scene: Keith Haring, Kenny Scharf, and Jean-Michel Basquiat. Fortunately, other lesser known—but equally talented lights—were also featured. As was an "eclectic" variety of art: graffiti, stencils, copy collage, documentary photography, video, and several conceptual installations.

From the start, Lola appeared distracted. Uptight.

Trying to reel her in, Martin asked if she'd ever been here before.

"Huh?" she replied.

He repeated the question. "I mean, to this museum."

She finally grasped what he was saying. "Sure," she answered. "Lots of times. With my ... my—oh, never mind."

"Your 'ex'?"

"Uh, well. Yeah ... also, my mom, believe it or not."

He was surprised. "No shit?" Then, smiling—somewhat inconsequentially—he asked, "How is she, anyway?"

"Who?"

"Y'know: *'madrecita.'*"

"Fine," she answered glumly. "I don't know."

Like talking to a nine year old.

Martin tried his best to roll with it, keep things fluid, lighthearted:

"Look at that one there," he said, pointing to a painting. It had a tuft of pink faux fur rising from it.

"Where?"

"Right in front of you."

Lola blinked at it as if she couldn't see it, then regarded it sourly.

He was forced to address her mood, at last: "Lola—what's up?"

"Huh?—*Why?*" She looked at him narrowly.

"Just, you seem a bit 'on edge,'" he remarked. "I mean, more on edge than usual."

She shrugged sullenly, eyeing another painting or two, but offered no explanation.

"Something on your mind?" he asked.

Again a sulky look, followed by a shrug. But he was still picking up an unmistakably hostile vibe. Martin ventured to guess: resentment, maybe?

"Don't tell me it's your mom?" he persisted.

"Huh?"

"Have another falling out with her?" he asked.

At first she wouldn't answer, but finally managed, "Just leave *Broomhilda* out of it, *m'kay?*"

"What?"

"Leave *the cunt* out of it!" she insisted.

Yikes. Okay. He backed off.

Tentatively, they both entered a partitioned and topped black light installation: the interior, from floor to ceiling, was covered with fluorescent colors and trippy, day-glo cartoons. Bright objects and plastic toys were suspended from the ceiling.

After an uneasy silence, he tried a few weak comments about Kenny Scharf's obsession with plastic dinosaurs and the Jetsons. Then Martin said, "I never asked you, Lola—but, since that guy, your last boyfriend, did you go out after that? See anyone else?"

"What made you bring that up?" She turned to him, startled.

Martin shrugged, moving along.

Again she took a while to reply. Finally saying, "No. Not really."

"No one steady?"

"Nuh-uh." At the moment, she seemed distracted by a particular visual arrangement. "I mean, there was this one guy, but I dunno—he seemed kind of a simp."

"A 'simp'?"

"Just how he talked," she said wearily. "How he'd phrase these *questions*. So annoying."

Turning paranoid, "'Annoying,' how?"

"I dunno," she shrugged. He waited for her to elaborate but she let it hang.

They finally exited the installation, which might've been fun at another time.

Lola continued, "He still writes me, y'know. Sends me cards."

"That guy? Yeah?"

She nodded.

"And you write back?"

"No."

"Why not?"

"He's a *pest* … I figure if I just ignore him long enough, he'll forget about me."

They paused before some other paintings.

"When was the last time he wrote you?"

"The other day."

"And when was the last time you actually *saw* him?"

"Five, six months ago." Lola moved up to a canvas as if to better examine it. "I just tossed his letter in the garbage.

Didn't bother to even open it."

"No?" he had to ask, startled. "Why not?"

"Wasn't up to it, I dunno."

Martin frowned. "Shit, it sounds like he's a little hung up on you!"

Lola narrowed her eyes, stepping away from the painting. "Yeah, well. Some people really need to get a *life*."

The next group featured work by David Wojnarowicz.

Lola seemed attracted to one particular composition, studying it a while. Then, without looking at him, asked Martin: "Did I ever mention to you that my mom was fucking *nuts?*"

"More than a few times."

"No," she said seriously, and suddenly her eyes looked heavy and pained. "Did I ever tell you that she was diagnosed? Diagnosed a schizophrenic?"

He turned to her. "What?—no." He felt a pang of dread. He stared at her, waiting for her to tell him she was kidding, that it was just a bad joke.

She looked back at him wearily, then quickly away.

"It's true." She issued a deprecating little laugh. "Classic textbook case. Last night, she even tried to pull a knife on me."

He looked at her, stunned.

"Don't make a big deal of it," she told him.

"'A big deal'?—You kiddin' me!?"

"Will you *lower* your voice!"

Gathering his senses, but no less intensely, he whispered, "*Shit, Lola—listen to me—*you've *got* to get *out of there!*"

She remained unmoved, silently regarding an earlier painting.

213

"I'm not foolin'!" He took her arm: "Hey—*you listening?*"

She angrily pulled away. "Don't do that!" Bristling: Don't *ever* do that! No one—*no one*—ever touches me that way!"

He felt shaken, confused: "*Fuck*—sorry." He didn't know what to do, or say. Everything was always so complicated!

She continued to observe the artwork as if nothing were wrong, nothing out of the ordinary. "Anyway," she finally said, "it's not as easy as all that." Then, more softly, withdrawing: "You *can't* understand."

He stared at her sadly. "But I do."

The irony was almost unbearable. "Lola, I *do* understand!"

She looked resigned. "Just forget it, please."

"*Forget* it?" Martin forced a laugh.

"Just forget that I brought it up," she insisted. "Let's talk about something else?"

"Like what?" It seemed ludicrous.

"I dunno, *anything*."

Of course, Martin tried to continue the conversation about her mother. He plied her with questions, but she was unwilling, obstinate. Out of a strained politeness, somewhat desperately now, he changed the subject, asking about her work.

"Huh?"

"Your canvases, how are they coming along?"

"Don't ask," she murmured.

"—Huh?"

"*Don't ask.*" Her face crumpling.

Unsettled, Martin fell silent. They proceeded with the

exhibit. The next group of paintings by Martin Wong and Richard Hambleton seemed to drive her into deeper gloom.

Finally, Martin felt drained. Utterly exhausted. Hard-pressed to think of anything to say—and, yes, even painfully saddened.

He suggested getting out of there, maybe going for a drink somewhere:

"Choke this art!" he told her. "Let's go!"

Lola paused, giving it some thought. "Actually," she mumbled. "Would you be upset if I just ... went home?"

"You mean, now?"

She nodded.

"Not feeling well?" Giving her the out.

"Actually ... *no*."

95.

On the corner of Houston, Lola and Martin stood awkwardly facing each other. About to go their separate ways.

Lola reminded him, "Got your poems, right here." She held up the manila envelope.

"Uh-huh." He felt like an idiot. *Poems*. "Can I walk you home?"

She forced a smile. "No. I'd rather be alone. Thanks. Plus, I have a lot to do."

Martin nodded, looking at her helplessly.

"Well," she said. "Take it easy."

"Okay. You, too." He leaned over to give her a kiss on the lips. She hardly responded. "*Ciao!*" Then off she went. He watched her walk away, combat boots scraping the pavement....

Come,

Come away
To permit
Your own
Dank tongue
To remain
A soft-bodied
Portion—
To remain
A retracted
Mollusk,
A tied,
Visceral mass
Nestled slickly
Within
The mantle
Of your mouth.

Take away!
Your thick, wet
(Membranous),
Labial palps

From her own
Clean,
Child-warm
Skin:

She!

don't!

need!

ya.

Martin started in the opposite direction. *'The fuck hap-pened there?*...

96.
Now.
Now what?
From a pay phone down the street, Martin decided to check his cursed answering machine for messages.
No calls. Nothing. *Naturally.*

He felt his mood take a nose-dive. Self-pity began to worm in. And Martin's view of the world could be summarized in one word: *mierda.*

"La vida es una miseria," ("Life is a misery,") his grandfa-ther was fond of saying. And this, of course, filled his mind.

Yes, he walked....

Went
Along.

As always...

And,
As always,
The polluted
Waves,
The cold-gray
Wash
Of sound—

The noise of
Day—
Washed out
(or drowned)
the faint (and fading)
sounds
of
his footsteps....

Martin leafed through his wallet, finally extracting a slip
of paper and dialing.

"*Hi,*" began the message. "This is *Amaris*. You've
reached my pager. Following the beep you can key in a
phone number or, if you like, leave a brief voice message...."

Feeling self-conscious, he began, "Hey! This is Marty.
Just wondering whatcha' up to, Amaris. Kinda hoping to
hook up. If you get this message soon, and you're free, ring
me back, let me know. I'll be checking in with my machine,
tonight. Maybe we can set something up, okay?"

He hooked the receiver, feeling vaguely ridiculous.

All right: *stupid.*

Eyeing his watch he was surprised to find it was still
early.

  "*Emptiness,*"
she said.
  "*All emptiness*
is open to me...."

The remainder of the night, as it turned out, Martin
spent wandering the Village, a vague desperation—all too
familiar—creeping into his bones.

He started with the bookstores: *The Strand, Gandhi's, St. Mark's Bookshop*. Then, in need of more immediate self-medication, progressed to the bars: *Mona's, Max Fish, Ace bar*. A sweating, tall pint (or two) in each....

Long ago, I dreamt
I fell through
the clouds....

From another pay phone, in a somewhat righteous drunken state, he even tried calling Lola with the idea of "straightening her out." After the fourth ring, her machine clicked on: "Hi. This is you-know-who. We're not home right now. But after the last beep, leave your name and number, and we'll get back to you"—a girlish giggle—"*maybe*."

Beep, beep, beep, beep, beep, beep, beep, beep, beep—Beeeep!
He slammed the phone.

How well—
how well
and easily
I kept falling.

Around 10:00 he checked his answering machine for messages a second time. The third and final time he checked it was two.

It was 3:00 AM when he arrived at home; 3:20 by the time he got into bed.

He lay there, wide-awake.

"*Mierda, mierda, mierda, mierda, mierda, mierda, mierda,*

mierda, mierda, mierda, mierda, mierda...."

Anything more frustrating than being shitfaced and sleepless, the next grinding workday just hours away?

At 4:44 AM, Martin sat upright, snapped on the light and sat in silence, hoping he might somehow fall asleep this way.

Fat fucking chance.

At 5:12 AM, in a state of near-exhaustion, he picked up the phone. Blindly dialed a number.

As always, the cheerful recorded message began: "Hello and thank you for calling—"

Martin stabbed another digit and the recording skipped forward: "Thank you. Please enter your four number extension."

He entered it.

"Now your five digit security code."

Martin did so. And there followed the usual, ridiculously long pause, "You have," the recorded operator informed him, "*zero* messages!... To continue or to browse other ads, please press—"

What should he do?

"*Mierda, mierda, mierda, mierda, mierda, mierda, mierda, mierda, mierda, mierda, mierda, mierda....*"

Martin punched a digit.

"Please choose from the following categories," the pre-recorded operator went on.

If only he had another beer!

"'One' for 'Men seeking women.'"

"'Two' for 'Men seeking men.'"

"'Three' for 'Women seeking men.'"

Sighing, Martin pressed "3."

Beep! "... *¡Hola!*"
Martin thought he recognized the voice. Waited.
"*¿Hijo?*"
Jesus Christ! No way. No way. "Ma?!"
He dropped the phone. Staggered to the toilet, where he
puked.

97.

```
Japantrack - Air Export Operations
MAIN OPERATIONAL ROUTINES
```

Numbly gazing at the computer screen, green-gilled, he
tapped (6) *Consolidation Pre-Scheduling*, which brought up
the next screen.

> *And, yea   ~~ thus,*
> > *with the tedium*
> > > *of the very worst*
> > *porny flick,*
> > > *another workday*
> *unspooled...*

"Yo, *Chinaski Jr!*"
Martin snapped out of it, turning to Chaz where he sat
at his desk.
"Do me a solid, genius. Book the consol?..."

98.

In the Heights, Martin cruised, looking for parking. He
drove up 78th Street, past the tightly parked cars lining both
curbs. Red light at 37th Avenue, he stopped. He signaled
left. Waited. On 37th Avenue, he stopped again, another red

light. Waited.

On the north side of 79th Street, Martin pulled alongside a Chevy Celebrity apparently ready to pull out. Martin gestured to the driver: "Leaving?"

The woman, an attractive thirtyish Latina, rolled down her window and shouted: "*No!*"

99.

Martin checked his mailbox. Three rejection letters. Two bills past due.

Upstairs, at last. He went straight to his answering machine. Nope, no messages.

He sat down on the floor near his phone. Lola's number was on a crumpled slip of paper nearby, and he dialed it.

"—*¡Quién es, entonces!*" replied an older woman's hostile voice, not Lola's.

Martin panicked and hung up.

Lying back on the floor, he rationalized: *I'll call later....*

After fixing himself a drink, Martin tried Nikki's number. But again got her machine.

"*¡Mierda!*" he shouted.

Then he tried Lola again.

This time neither she nor her mother answered the phone. After the fourth ring, the machine clicked on: "...after the last beep leave your name and number, and we'll get back to you..."

Martin left her a plain message.

He confessed, "Lola, I just need to *talk*, okay?..."

100.

Martin was in bed, nearly falling out, when his phone rang.

He jumped on it, startled *"—Hello?"*

A voice sounding like Nikki's answered, "Hello?"

"HELLO?" he repeated.

"Marty?" Sounding like she was at a pay phone, outside.

"Yeah?"

"You sounded *different* just now," she said.

At that moment, Martin realized who it was.

"Oh … hi." His voice sank.

"Try not to sound so enthusiastic!" laughed Amaris.

Martin felt vaguely annoyed. "No, it's not that. I just kinda dozed off."

"Whatcha' been up to? What are you doing?" she asked.

"Right now, y'mean—nothing. What about you?"

"Where am I? Is that what you're asking?"

It wasn't, but he rolled with it: "Yeah. Where are you?"

"I'm in the Village," she admitted. "St. Marks."

"Oh yeah? By yourself?"

"Yeah, by myself." She paused to let some traffic noise go by. "Wanna come down? Meet me?"

"Right now, y'mean?—Tonight?"

"If you're up for it."

Anything to get out of his dismal studio. "Shit, just name the place!"

101.

They met at *Dojo,* an inexpensive, laid-back health food restaurant on St. Marks Place, where after a short wait, they were quietly seated in the back.

Amaris was dressed in her usual goth finery and was a little drunk. In T-shirt and jeans, Martin felt embarrassingly self-conscious and sober.

To their mutual dismay—until their food arrived—there was a disorienting awkwardness between them. Evidently, the fact that they'd slept together (well, grappled drunkenly) made them no less strangers. Even over candlelight.

Groping for something to talk about, Martin asked, "Well, then, how goes the teaching life?"

Amaris played along, finally smiling.

"All right, I guess. Frustrating, of course. But that's to be expected."

He asked about her students. "Still hanging out with them?"

She laughed. "I told you I was doing that?"

Martin nodded, taking a bite of his shrimp tempura.

"It's true." She grinned. "Now and then we even go dancing."

"You mentioned that to me."

She chuckled, admitting, "Recently, I even had a student develop a crush on me."

"Oh yeah?"

"Yeah. His name is Martin. Like you. Not very bright, though." She awkwardly bit into a Chinese noodle. "One evening … a few weeks ago, we were together … late at night. We were inside a playground, dropping a little *e*," she paused to swallow, "when one thing led to another and…" she made a gesture with her head.

"And what," Martin said.

"We … y'know…"

"Y'know—what?"

"Did it."

"'Did it'?"

Smirking: "*That.*"

He stared at her blankly. "That a fact."

She nodded, blushing through her powdered face. "Right there in the sandbox. Of all places. After we were through, I looked back and saw I left a perfect imprint of my ass. Cheeks like twin basketballs pressed in the sand."

She conveyed these last earthy details with a kind of relish.

Trying to conceal his surprise and mild embarrassment, he said, "*Jesus*, Amaris."

"*What.*"

"Lucky you weren't caught."

"You're telling me," she laughed. "The police kept driving by. Right in the middle, we kept seeing these swirling lights—or at least I *think* it was the police. Maybe it was just the drugs."

He blinked. "No, I mean … you being his teacher and all."

She assured Martin, "He's 'legal.'"

"—I know. But…"

Amaris admitted, "We've been together *lots* of times."

Martin was taken aback. "Have you?"

"Why not?" she maintained, holding his gaze.

He remained stunned.

"It wasn't *in* the classroom, for Christ's sake." She put down her glass, looking up righteously. "S'matter of fact, it's happened *a lot.*"

Martin said, "*How's that?*"

"*Wha.*" She laughed lewdly.

He asked, "How do you mean, 'a lot'?"

Shrugging her shoulders, she finally confessed, "I've

gotten together with more than one of my students."

His eyes wide: "You have?"

And, so, *why* was she telling him this?

She stared back at him. "What, it isn't like *incest*, y'know."

His morbid curiosity flaring, he finally asked, "How do you manage that? I mean, 'it'?"

"What do you mean?"

"I mean, where do you go?"

"Anywhere. Where does *anyone* manage to do it?"

"How many?" he couldn't help but ask. "How many students have you slept with?"

She took a moment before answering him. "You want a 'body count'?"

He felt embarrassed. "Never mind. That was fucked— *intrusive*. None of my business, I know."

She took another sip of her drink, "It's okay. Ask any- thing you like." She laughed. "I may not *tell you*—but *ask* anything."

Martin managed to laugh finally.

"There were a few others. Five or six."

Martin stopped laughing.

She grew more sober. "But, actually, all this is pretty recent."

"Is that so?"

She nodded.

He thought about it, reaching for his glass of water. "Since when?"

"Since ... nine, ten months ago?"

He took a sip. "Since your separation, y'mean?"

"Uh-hmm," she took a tiny bite of food. "Before all this ... I have to admit I lived like a nun."

"Meaning?"

"No sex."

"So then," he quietly suggested, "you're kinda ... making up for it? Making up for lost time or something?"

She laughed painfully. "Maybe." She grew pensive. "—Yeah." Putting down her fork: "See, up till that point, my separation, I thought ... there was something wrong with *me*."

"How's that?"

"I mean—" She'd lowered her voice, glancing sideways. "Sexually."

Martin asked her to explain.

"I married young. And for most of my married life—in fact, nearly all of it—I hardly ever ... felt much."

"That might be a common complaint," Martin joked.

"No. I mean, well ... there was this real lack of passion in our sex life."

"Oh."

"I just couldn't understand it." She went on, "Then, one day, about ten months ago I made a surprise discovery. One afternoon, I came home early to find ..." her voice trailed off.

"*What*."

She paused, forced a laugh "—It's such a cliché!"

"Go on."

She took a breath, starting up again: "One afternoon I came home early to find ... my husband *wasn't* alone."

"—You caught him cheating on you?"

"Getting fucked, straight up."

"Damn!"

"And that's not all." She forced a grin. "It was with my best friend."

"Oh *shit*."

"—My best friend since high school."

"No!"

"Yeah!"

"Oh!—*too much!* You must've been devastated!"

"And how. Especially since my best friend is a guy."

"Come again."

"That's right. A *guy*."

Silence.

"So, as it turned out, y'see, 'our' problem had less to do with me, than with Alex. My husband."

"He was *gay*," Martin understood. "*Is* gay, I mean."

"Anyway," she nodded, "holding another man's cock, he caved. Started sobbing. Told me everything. What he'd been hiding. And he'd be hiding *a lot!*"

"Well," Martin said, "life is sure full of surprises!"

"I'll say," Amaris continued. "Aside from the shock, I was so angry. I mean, to live with this man all those years and have him *conceal* it from me. And worse, to have me feel all along that it was somehow *my* fault. That maybe I just wasn't physically attractive enough. I felt so ... cheated. So angry!"

Martin asked, "How long were you married?"

"A long time!" Her eyes flashed with emotion.

"And you never suspected?"

"I'm telling you." She sighed. "Later ... I felt so *dumb*."

Martin looked at her and frowned.

Amaris reached for her mixed drink. "Actually—if you want to know the truth—Alex was the one who first took up the ads. Right after our separation. Told me later."

Of course, Martin couldn't resist asking: "And how'd it go with him? How'd he make out?"

"He met someone, fell in love—and got *dumped* right away!" Amaris burst out laughing. "That's *life*. Anyway, that's how I got into them. I thought, let's see what these ads are about." She paused again. "For a while I even tried to meet other women."

"Really?"

Amaris nodded, smiling. "I began to experiment. Like my ex. I wanted to see where *I* was at sexually."

"So, what did you discover?"

She shrugged. "That I'm basically 'straight.' That some days I like being a 'top,' other days a 'bottom.' That I like a little 'kink,' now and then." She smirked. "At this point, you might even say, I've tried it all. Men, women. Threesomes."

"And," Martin asked, still trying hard not to seem surprised, "all in all, what was it like?"

She shrugged. "*Fun.*"

Right then, Amaris's pager sounded. Casually pressing a button, she glanced at the number, then ignored it.

Placing his bunched-up napkin beside his plate, leaning back, Martin let a long moment go by.

Then he said, "You know, my best friend Nikki is *bi*."

Amaris thought for a moment. "Is she the one—the 'looker'—you showed me a picture of in your apartment?"

He smiled, nodding.

"She's 'bi'?"

Again he nodded.

Amaris looked at him curiously. "So you've seen each other, then? Romantically, I mean?"

Uh... Great.

Martin hesitated, unsure of what to admit to. He ended up saying, "We're good friends, y'know."

"Oh, I know," said Amaris. "She's your *best friend*, isn't she?"

"That's right."

Amaris looked amused. "Lovers can't start out as *friends?* Is that what you're saying?"

He paused. "I'm not saying that at all."

"Okay. So what about this Nikki?" she pressed, grinning archly.

He admitted, smiling, "*Of course*, I'm attracted to her."

"Yes, *and?*"

"And—*what?*"

"So, nothing's ever come of it? No physical intimacy?"

"Oh—don't know if I should say it—I mean, there have been … certain episodes. 'Slip-ups,' you might call them."

"Yeah?" She grinned, interested.

"One occasion that went down recently."

Leaning in, she seemed eager to hear about it.

He smiled remembering it. Took his time in recounting it: "Well, most recently it happened after we'd been out together. Dancing. At a little club on Avenue B," he explained. "We'd left the place, just got into the back of a cab, all warm and cozy. When halfway on our ride to the station, we started playing around, touching a bit. We do care for each other, after all."

She helped the story along: "You started to touch *and?*"

"We started to touch. To caress each other a little bit. And gradually our touching became a little more than just 'affectionate.'" Martin was smiling. "Before long, before we both even knew it, we were kissing. Really *kissing*. Not at all as 'friends' at this point, but something more. And I gotta tell you, it was nice. I mean, *innocent. Sweet.* At one point, I think, I'd kissed the back of her neck. 'What are you *doing?'* she asked. 'Tasting you,' I said."

"*Yeah yeah"*—rushed Amaris—"the clothes come off?"

"We were in the back of a taxi, for Chrissake. No, first thing I did was ask the driver to take us both to Jackson Heights. But Nikki insisted we go to her place."

"What happened when you got there?"

"I'm getting to that part. Once there, we paid the driver and went in. We hardly made it past the door. I can't tell you what was going through my mind then. It was like this overwhelming *rush*. But I tried to hold back, go slow. Then, the next thing I knew, there I was. All over her. My hands were excitedly lifting her top. She pulled off my shirt, then my belt. After a moment, it was her satin bra—helping to slip off the smooth straps, her body, her face, her eyes glowing in the half-light. Exposed and beautiful." He looked up: "*God.*"

"What happened then?" Amaris was riveted.

He smiled. "Don't know if I should tell you the rest."

Amaris playfully reached for an appetizer fork, raising it: "I'll stab!"

"It gets kinda … *intimate.*"

"But you *did it?*" She wanted to know.

"What do you think?"

Starved for graphic details, Amaris looked disappointed. "How was it, at least? Tell me that."

"Speaking for myself?" he said, a bit flushed. "Like … a dream."

"And then?"

"And then. We woke up." He heaved a sigh. "The phone rang. It was her girlfriend."

"And that was it?"

"Just about. I knew Nikki felt badly, like she usually did.

Right then, we both knew it wasn't right. Because she was still 'involved,' after all."

"So after the call what happened?"

Martin shrugged. "Nikki looked a bit melancholy after she hung up. When she came back, I just handed her her clothes, slipped my own shirt back on. We both knew I couldn't sleep over that night. I ended up calling another cab," he softly smiled. "But we still ended up holding each other a bit. I mean, it was still nice, being together—if just for that moment."

Amaris said, "That's … sweet, your relationship with her."

"The truth is, I realize now, we kinda *need* each other—corny and old-fashioned as it sounds." He blurted: "*Really* … I don't know what I'd *do* if she ever went away for good."

Amaris looked at him intensely. Suddenly Martin felt self-conscious. He forced a smile. "Maybe I've said too much."

"Well, I *asked*."

"And I blabbed." He frowned. "I really shot my mouth."

"Don't sweat it," said Amaris. " 'The heart wants what the heart wants.'" Clearing her throat. "And other clichés…."

At this point, they ran out of things to say. And, once again, suddenly embarrassed, both sat quietly finishing their meal.

Mercifully, the waitress appeared asking if there would be anything else. Amaris looked to Martin. He shook his head. Nope: nothing more for him. "Nothing more for me, either," said Amaris. "I've had enough."

Martin stiffened a bit.

Absently removing a lipstick from her purse, Amaris happened to glance at the time:

"God, it's getting late!"

Martin eyed his own watch; it read, *2:13 AM*

Snapping back to reality, he thought, *Christ! And work tomorrow....*

102.

Once again dragging ass, Martin inserted the key into the office door cylinder.

As usual, the key jammed in the lock.

¡Coño!

—Late again?

This *was* Martin Sierra.

The red light on his phone was already blinking. He pressed the button, the Japanese secretary, Tani, crying out: "Maartee-san?"

"Yes?"

"Boss want to see you! Upstairs!"

Sighing and closing his eyes, Martin leaned back in his chair.

"Tell him," he replied. "Tell him, I'll be up. In a while."

Instead, alone with the phone, he tried ringing a particular somebody at work. Again, got her voice mail.

Again, he hung up.

Stared straight into space in wide-eyed panic.

The red light blinked with Tani crying out: "Maartee-san?"

He ignored it. Put a finger in his other ear.

Compulsively picking up the receiver, he dialed.

"—Hello and thank you for calling..."

He poked a digit, skipping ahead.

"Thank you," continued the message. "Please enter..."
He entered it.
"Now your..."
Martin did so. Waited. Was about to hang up:
"You have," the recorded operator informed him, "*zero* messages!..."
"*Zero* messages!..."
"*Zero* messages!..."

The Sky Is Barren.
  Dreams Are Useless.

103.
He was expecting *this*, maybe?
Beep! "Hi, Martin. My name is Nikki. You don't know me. But you answered my personal ad ... I'll leave you my phone number and maybe we can talk?..."

104.
So, one could ask: who was she? Who was Nikki, really?
And could her intelligence, her kindness, her warmth, her fragility, any part of her, be summed up or implied by a geekish list of likes and dislikes?
Hardly.

But he kept trying. Martin kept trying to keep the thought of her from fading into the abstract, kept wanting to tether certain aspects of her to concrete details. And, yes, sometimes this entailed keeping inventory of her favorite things.
And the more desperate he became, the more he wanted to clutch and collect those things that preserved her

memory for him, or any hint of their time spent together, which even now seemed open and vulnerable to erosion.

How else could one preserve "feelings," except in things? Without form, memories seemed to change every hour of every day; and the past, insubstantial as smoke, often faded.

Yet, now, any attempt at cataloging seemed insufficient, even pathetic:

Her favorite flavor of ice cream? peach. Favorite flower scent? carnation. Favorite tropical fruit? mango. Favorite tree blossom? cherry. Favorite season? spring?—or was it the fall? Already he was starting to forget.

Favorite '60s film? *Barbarella*

Favorite '60s rock star? *Donovan*. '70s rock star? *T-Rex*.

Favorite snack cake: *Snow Balls* ("More for the texture.")

Favorite movie candy: *Strawberry Twizzlers*

And knowing this amounted to what?

Never mind.

Keep going:

Some more of Nikki's favorite things, stemming from childhood?

a) the first page of a new book

b) afternoon naps when it's raining outside

c) listening to music in her pjs

d) the moment the lights dim before a movie

e) when the plastic, nearly empty ketchup bottle makes "that noise"

Other particulars? Other secrets?

Named after the poet Nikki Giovanni, she avoided the

form her entire life, choosing to deny predestination.

Once met the poet on tour, giving her a dozen yellow roses.

More?

She disliked high heels. Disliked that her second toe was slightly longer than her big toe.

Liked cats but was allergic. Liked the sound of tires on wet pavement. Loved the blush of sunrise on an ocean.

Loved the smell of coconut oil.

Nikki laughed and drooled in her sleep, mostly slept on her stomach. Had a soft spot for thick wool socks and feather pillows.

Once as a girl, ate a cocoon because she wondered what it would taste like.

It would be many months, almost a full year, into their friendship that Nikki would reveal her greatest and "saddest" secret.

It was at her apartment. They were watching an Eric Rohmer film, Martin couldn't tell which one but very talky, when she casually imparted a significant detail that in some ways may have shaped her personality and honed her character.

"I have a birth defect," she confessed.

"Really?" said Martin, not quite believing her. "Where?"

She indicated her right breast.

"I don't see it," Martin said.

She told him then, "It's not real."

Upon closer inspection, Martin could see that she wasn't lying. In fact, he'd noted a slight irregularity before, but thought nothing of it.

She placed a hand over her breast. "I mean, this is ... fake. A 'cutlet,'" she told him.

"Really?" Martin was suddenly curious, begged her to go on, tell him more.

Stopping the video, Nikki calmly squared to face him, sitting Indian style, and quite seriously went on to explain how she was born with a physical defect, a benign tumor that had been removed in early infancy and which left, in its absence, a very visible scar extending from one side of her chest to below her armpit.

Resulting from the initial operation and its effect to the surrounding muscles and tissue, Nikki required a series of corrective operations as a child and one, later, as a teen.

On the plus side, the operations were mostly successful, restoring substantial muscle development and full arm mobility. On the negative side were scars that no plastic surgery could erase. Scars that only seemed more pronounced with puberty, discolored and stretching across that side of her upper body "like burn marks." Furthermore, only one breast had developed normally.

Martin was startled to hear all this.

Nikki went on to tell him how, in her late teens, she had undergone cosmetic surgery to repair the defect. "A boob job, so to speak." Only instead of helping matters, things got worse when, years later, her implant, made of saline and silicone, ruptured in her chest, grew infected, and had to be removed in an emergency operation.

"It *burst?*" he asked, quite amazed.

"That's what no one tells you—no one wants you to know," she informed him. "Most boob jobs are *temporary.*"

Martin fell quiet.

"So," she softly stated. "That's right, I only have one. The other isn't there, not really. It's mostly foam rubber: a 'falsie.'"

Martin was gripped by this admission, captivated rather than being put off, and wanted to see it, see the bare flesh and visible scars.

She grew visibly uneasy, nervous. "Maybe one day," she said, trying to smile. "When I'm drunk enough."

"Can't I see it, now?" he asked quietly.

Nikki shook her head. "Not ready."

Didn't she know that *nothing* could change his mind about her? Affect how he felt about her? Not any scar tissue, any simple birth defect?

It wasn't as simple as that. How could he tell her, let her know?

As gently as possible, Martin tried to reassure her, stating the harsh fact that, "Lots—lots of women have mastectomies. *Both* breasts removed. It's happened to probably millions of women. Through no fault of their own."

"At least, they once *had* breasts. Normal ones, I mean. They can say that."

Oh, Nikki.

"Not all," Martin said. "Not all."

"Well, I don't know." She sighed.

He wanted to tell her how perfect she was, how beautiful she was, how truly sexy, truly smart, everything, everything ... but couldn't find a way somehow. Somehow the exact words eluded him, escaping like ghosts into the clouds.

"Still think I'm 'perfect'?" she smiled bittersweetly.

Martin was speechless, felt a catch in his throat.

Perfect? That didn't begin to describe it.

Then, he somehow managed to say it, very quietly: "You're a swan."

He smiled, reached over and kissed her hand tenderly. He closed his eyes, brushing her knuckles along his closely shaven cheek.

When he looked back up at her she was crying.

Sweet Nikki, dear girl….

Much later, she went on to say how the birth defect, this early turn of bad luck, had affected her childhood, her growing up. "Secretly, I always thought I was a freak," she said. "For a long time, I couldn't even take my top off in the girls' locker room. Couldn't shower in front of anyone else. Couldn't bear to have people see me."

"But you always seemed perfectly comfortable with *me*," he almost whispered. "I mean with your clothes on, but physically." He smiled, "We must've hugged a thousand times."

In fact, there were times, in girlish jest, when she couldn't seem to keep her hands off him, fondling and teasing.

"Yeah," she admitted, growing cheerful. "I don't know why. I don't know why I'm comfortable with you that way."

Did *he* know why?

Dare he say it?

105.

9:07 PM

His workday over, vehicle parked, Martin'd just finished locking his front door, torn daily rejection letters under his arm, when the phone rang—and of course he thought of only one person.

Damn finally!

Cracking loudly: "*Mija!*—'Bout time!"

Silence.

"—Hello?"

"*Hi.*"

For a moment he was uncertain.

"Is this Marty?" said the voice. Female. Not Nikki's.

Finally it registered: *Lola.*

"Oh," Martin was startled. "*¡Que pasa!*"

"Whatcha' up to?" she mumbled.

Dumping his ripped mail on the sofa, Martin said, "Nothin'."

"Am I ... interrupting?"

"No," he admitted, "but, y'know, I'm kinda surprised to hear from you."

"You are?"

He laughed. "Yeah."

"Why?"

"Dunno."

Wasn't it *he* who'd left the last message? she asked.

He thought about it. "Guess I did."

She was quiet. He could hear the faint click of jewelry in her mouth.

"So," Martin said. "What's this about? About getting together or something?"

She sounded uneasy. "Um.... Not exactly."

"Oh?"

She shifted gears, sounding nervous, "I, uh, looked over your poems and stuff. Read them."

"Yeah?" He perked up. "Whadja' think?"

She said earnestly, "Did you say there were people who *didn't* like the way you write?"

Taking a seat on the floor, Martin put it bluntly:
"Lots."

She said, "I find that hard to believe. I mean, you write *well*. So focused and clear."

"Yeah?" He chuckled, sure she was blowing smoke. "Tell it to the editors!"

"You're really good," she insisted.

"Thanks!" he laughed. Of course he didn't believe a word of it—though just hearing it left him lightheaded.

A moment later, she added awkwardly, "But, your writing, um … is not why I called."

Still a bit giddy: "No?"

"Nuh-uh." She paused. "There's something more. Something that's been on my chest. That's been bugging me."

"Is it about your mom?"

"No. Not about that cow. Let's not even go there."

"Okay."

"Well … uh, remember that party I went to that time?"

He drew a blank

"With Mina? That weekend party, remember?"

"Okay." He leaned back with the receiver against his ear.

"I told you about it, mostly?"

"Yeah."

"Um, I think I left out an important detail."

"'Kay." Martin waited to hear what it was.

"Well, that night, when we were both leaving the party, Mina and me." She took a moment, adjusting her mouthpiece. "We, uh, were leaving … going downstairs, when, of all things, all people, I happened to bump into … *him*."

"Who."

"'Dre.'"

"Who's that?"

"My ex-boyfriend. Yeah, that's his new name. Used to be 'James.'"

"Oh."

"Yeah, I kinda bumped into him," she said weakly.

"—And?"

Lola mumbled, "Well, I bumped into him. We fell to talking a little. A *lot*."—correcting herself. "Coupla' days later, he called my house." She cleared her throat, buying time. "Anyway, to make it short, we decided ... we decided to hook up again. Y'know, give it another try."

Martin went blank. It was a moment before he was able to bring it all together, gather his thoughts, and then they came roiling in like storm clouds. "But *wait*—" Martin remembered, "This the *same* guy you told me about? The guy you *wouldn't* go out with again, if he came 'crawling on bloody knees'?"

She took a moment. "Yeah."

Then it all came back to him: everything she'd said, every typical, deceptive, self-serving line. And suddenly, unexpectedly, Martin felt himself getting heated: "So, y'know, what's the deal?"

"'Bout what?"

"'Bout what. About the change of heart?"

She simply stated, "I feel differently now."

"*Well*"—he nearly shouted—"did you feel differently *then*?" And the level of his own anger surprised him. He wasn't even sure what he was so upset about.

"I don't know," she muttered.

"You don't *know*?"

She hesitated. "No."

A protracted silence followed. And Martin thought, cynically—all the years he'd wasted suddenly accumulating with force—: *this is it. In a nutshell. Truly.* Personal ads. Blind matches. The whole shit. *Nothing but deceits and lies. Empty talk. False hope. Countless dead ends.* Nothing but shit. *Pure* shit.

And this—*yes, this*—finally, was why people got married, had babies, performed self-lobotomies: to avoid all this. Because *anything* was better than this!

Lola finally urged, "Say something."

"What am I supposed to say?" He was seething.

Lola tried, "Really, I meant to tell you before. I mean, at the museum. But ... I dunno, I guess I chickened out."

By now he was so agitated he could hardly hear a word she said. Suddenly he was just so tired—*so tired!*—of *twits!* So *worn out* from all the time wasted on perennial *children!*

In a daze, he recapped: "So, the two of you just 'bumped' into each other? And now you're getting back together? Just like that?"

"Uh ... yeah."

"What a *coincidence*," he said sarcastically. "The two of you! Just 'meeting!' Bumping into each other like that!"

Hey, what was a little dishonesty? A few bald lies? In NYC especially, no one owed anyone anything.

Just spores in the wind.

Lola let out a guilty sigh on her end. "Listen, Marty, you have to understand ... this has nothing to do with you."

And now came the clichés. Of course. So predictable.

He forced a dry laugh. Responded mechanically, in turn: "Oh, I think it has a *little* to do with me."

Ha-ha ...

"You know what I mean."

Oh he knew. Had been through this, it seemed, a thousand and one times.

"So," Martin ventured, mouthing the last tired line. "That's it then, right?"

"I don't know. I guess."

She "guessed"? Aha-ha.

"We were just killin' a little time," he said outright. "Killin' a little time, 'cause we just had nothing better to do!"

Bewildered, Lola fell silent.

"Yeah. And why the fuck not!" he added, vehemently.

Another extended gap followed, during which they both uneasily held the line.

"Hey," she offered. "For what it's worth. You seemed pretty decent. A good guy."

A good guy. Pretty decent.

They just kept on coming. Lie. Cliché. One, two.

Growing impatient: "Let's just wrap it up!"

"What else can I say?" Her voice growing faint.

"How about 'good night!'"

"What?"

He was dying to get off the line, saw no point in making any pretense. "How about, 'enough of this *crap!*' And, '*so long!*'"

Lola hesitated, sighed. "So long." Hung up.

Martin remained motionless, listening to the silence on his end and his own solitary breathing, then the dial tone, his eyes tracing the cracks across the ceiling.

Then a recorded message came on, which sounded familiar enough: "*There appears to be a receiver off the hook, please hang up....*"

106.

Right then, he wanted one person, one person, one person only.

After allowing himself a moment to calm down, Martin sat up and dialed her number.

Her phone rang, rang, rang….

"Hi, this is Nikki. I'm not in right now…."

Martin slammed the receiver, picked up the receiver, slammed it down again. Picked it up, slammed it down.

Finally he erupted: "FUUUUUUUUUUUUUUUUUUU-UUUUUUUUUUUUUUUUUUUUUUUUUUUUUUUUUUUU-UUUUUUUUUUUUUUUUUUUUUUUUUUUUUUUUUUUU-UUUUUUUUUUUUCCCCCCCCCCCCCCCCCCCCCCCK-KKKKKKKKKKKKKKKKKKKKKKKKKKKKKKKKKKKK KKKKKKKKKKKKKKKKKKKKIIIIIIIIIIIIIIIIIIIIIIIIIIIIIIIIIIIIIII-IIIIIIIIIIIIIIIIIIIIIIIIIIIIIIIIIIIIIIIIIIIIIIIIIIIIIIIIIIIIIIIIIIIIIIIII-IIIIIIIIIIIIIIIIITTTTTTTTTTTTTTTTTTTTTTTTTTTTTTTTT!!!!…"

107.

Inamorata

You smile softly
at me;

Your kisses burst
like blown leaves.

* * * *

In your eyes is
the fragile promise
of spring flowers….

2:30 AM, sitting on the edge of his sofa, shitfaced,

Martin was reading some of his work and thinking—no, *laughing*:

¡Mierda! What fucking mierda! All of it!…

"Meaningless! Meaningless!"

And, suddenly, madly, he was seized by the over-whelming desire to *purge*—gut his studio apartment.

Draining his last forty, he stuffed three thirty-gallon garbage bags full of torn, twisted paper.

Martin started with the mountain of rejection letters and torn envelopes in the far corner, ripping and tearing them into smaller and smaller pieces. From there, in a disgusted rage, he proceeded to attack his own unmarked work, removing original writing and fresh copies from his knapsack, then all the work from his drawers, the milk-crate he kept nearly full beside the bookcase, and shredding those pages, too.

It took a while. But Martin had the diligence of an obsessive.

Every story, every poem, everything he had ever written till then, every scrap of paper he could get his hands on.

Everything! *¡Todo! ¡Todo la mierda!…*

In the end, he managed to destroy everything he could find, even old letters, those to Nikki! Everything! And, tying off the tops of the garbage bags, he felt, much to his surprise, an almost unbearable sense of satisfaction and relief.

He was done!

Fuck it!-Fuck it!-Fuck it all!…

¡Al diablo!…

108.

The next day at work, depressed and hung-over, Martin

rested his head on his folded arms.

"So she dumped you, bro?"

He had confided in Chaz, giving him the lowdown on his most recent dates, not leaving out any embarrassing details.

"—Bro, she dumped you? That it?"

Of course, he didn't mention Nikki.

"Yeah, sure looks that way." He frowned, feeling sick. "She dumped me."

"Awright, but what about that second one?"

"Whaddaya mean?"

"The vampire gal," he said. "Contestant number two?"

"Amaris?"

"Yeah."

"Y'mean," raising his head and turning around, "after all I told you about her, you *still* think I should ring 'er?"

"*Fuck*, bro, every man needs a distraction! I say, *go for it!*"

109.

It was true.

What Martin needed was a distraction. Someone to get his mind off of Nikki, his *mija*.

Mija, confidant, lover, best friend…

Nikki, the only one who'd ever meant anything to him: *La unica, la unica mujer.*

Martin tried paging Amaris all that day at work, and as it happened, just before quitting time, she finally rang him back. They spoke briefly, if somewhat awkwardly, hastily arranging a get-together that evening. "Dinner," he offered. "Some dancing or whatever. We'll have ourselves a *night!*"

"*Uh-huh,*" she replied.

"What's wrong?"

Sounding slightly put off, she mumbled, "I don't know. I guess, I'd rather not get into it."

"Well, tell me about it tonight."

"Sure," she said remotely. "*Tonight.*"

110.

He felt like an imbecile.

Somewhat overdressed for the occasion, Martin waited for Amaris at *Stingy Lulu's,* a favorite restaurant and drag bar of Nikki's. Amid its quasi-50s layout, he sat distracted at a formica-topped table for two, when a towering transsexual waitress appeared before him.

Martin had only to glance up once to recognize who it was: the front person of the band *Useless-Nameless,* this day looking abysmally depressed.

"We ready to order, sir?" She tried to sound peppy, but it came off flat.

Martin forced a smile. "Uh, no. Actually, I'm waiting for someone."

She nodded, avoiding eye contact. "Get you anything to drink?"

"I'm gonna try and stay sober, I think."

Twenty-two minutes later, studying his paper placemat, which illustrated, in vibrant color, "*How To Mix Party Drinks, Hey!*"—*Gin Ricky, Manhattan, Pink Lady, Singapore Sling*—Martin was starting to feel a bit on edge.

"Are we about ready to order, now?" asked the waitress.

"*Uh* ... not yet."

Eighteen minutes later:

"—Your friend still hasn't shown?"

Struggling to maintain his composure, Martin grinned and shook his head.

"Believe me," said the transsexual, leaning in. "*I* know the feeling."

At last:

His table littered with appetizer plates, empty glasses, Martin finished another drink, looking a bit disheveled.

His waitress:

"Bring ya another *screwdriver?...*"

111.

After squaring the tab at *Stingy Lulu's*, Martin numbly staggered along Avenue A, looking for an available payphone. Outside the *Pyramid Club*, he stopped before a graffiti-splattered mini-booth housing two.

Picking up the receiver on the right, Martin loaded one nickel and two dimes, punched his home number, and immediately got—*zip*. Nothing. In a burst of static, he lost the connection, along with his change.

That was the problem with public phones in this area: they were the target of desperate junkies who jacked them with umbrella spokes*.

Martin hung up and tried again, first listening for an adequate dial tone. Again after depositing the coins another burst of static followed, then *click-click*—nothing. No call; no returned money.

"*¡Mierda!*" He angrily slammed the phone.

And now he also realized he was out of change:

Lovely!...

---

*inserted and twisted through the coin return slot, this would loosen a cluster of coins

249

At the bodega across the street, Martin was obliged to buy a bag of *Cheez Doodles* to break a dollar.

Back again, moments later, the phone on the left was occupied. Sighing, Martin stepped to the right, beside the rolled gate (... under the high-posted graffiti flyers that read, *Whipping Boy COST, Who Killed REVS!*), to wait.

The guy on the phone was a crusty, dread-locked boho-type who held a battered instrument case between his legs while he spoke. Quietly crunching his bag of *Doodles*, feeling as if he might at any moment puke, Martin tried not to eavesdrop but of course heard every miserable word:

"... *No*, that's *not* what I fuckin' said!... No, that was *you*. You and your *cunty* friends!... Yeah? When?... No, that was *you*. Uh-huh.... Yeah?—Fine wit *me*, babe!... Yeah? Oh yeah?—That's how you wannit'? You wannit' that way?—*Fine*. Fuck *you*, then!... Naaaw, FUCK *YOU!*"

The dude slammed the phone, abruptly scooping up his case and stalking away. "Fuckin' *bitch*," he muttered.

At least Martin knew the phone was working.

Wiping his orange fingers, he deposited the coins, punching his home number for messages: an apology from Amaris, an explanation—something. He waited while his phone rang once, twice, three times—there it was—*zip! No messages*.

His heart sank as he hooked the receiver.

After a moment Martin found her number in his wallet and dialed.

"*Hi*," began her message. "This is *Amaris*. You've reached my pager. Following the beep you can key in a phone number or, if you like, leave a brief voice message...."

Beep! Forcing a chuckle, he started, "Hey, Amaris! Just

wondering, *heh*, what happened. Can't imagine ya *meant* to stand me up or anything!" Narrowing his eyes, he looked at the scratched number on the dial. "Listen, I'm at a pay phone. *555-2588*. I'll hang here another five minutes or so. Buzz me back at least! Let me know what's happenin'."

He stood by the booth and waited.

Fifteen minutes, no call back. Still like a dunce he waited.

A stoked salesman type with unnaturally white, unnaturally straight teeth finally stepped up, asking to use the phone. Martin pointed to the other one, trying to be sly.

"That one's always broken," said the suit, not wasting his smile.

Finally Martin stepped back. The jackass made his call, bragging for six or seven minutes about a recent "all-expenses-paid" trip to Montego Bay, some new dicked account, and his flash, black Volvo "with all the extras," before abruptly turning in Martin's direction, sneering, and walking away without even hanging up.

Asshole, Martin thought.

Just as Martin hung up the receiver and went back to waiting, the phone rang!

He anxiously picked it up: "H-hello?"

The recorded operator's voice came on: *"Please deposit another thirty-five cents!..."*

112.

So it went:

Back at his piteous studio apartment—

Martin again checked his answering machine. Was the machine working? Yes.

Any calls? No.

Fine. Fine.

Then, not knowing what else to do, wanting to page her again, picking up the phone—he thought wearily, Oh, *hell. Fuck it*....

Hooking the receiver, Martin strode to the bathroom, took a long piss, washed his hands, his face—grabbed some loose change, his car keys, and rushed out the door.

Should've done it earlier!

¡Coño!...

Did he *need* any more distractions? No.

Forfeiting his treasured, hard-to-find parking spot just near the building, Martin warmed up his Horizon—and, in the next moment, gently steered the clunker toward the expressway.

113.

Bayside: Northeastern Queens.

Springfield Blvd:

Nikki's apartment was located on the second floor of a semi-attached home, and after Martin rang her doorbell a few times and got no response, he began to knock on the door.

Just then her downstairs neighbor appeared—an elderly widow whom Martin had met before—"Oh, your friend isn't in."

"She isn't?"

The neighbor shook her head.

He tried to smile: "Any idea where she might be?"

"I saw her leave with a suitcase and some things."

Martin was startled. "Was this, today? This afternoon, maybe?"

"No, dear. Three or four days ago."

As Martin stood there, dazed, evidently dissatisfied, the neighbor quietly reiterated: "She just *left*...."

114.

At the first available pay phone, Martin thought to do the unmentionable: call the "other woman."

Mariella's number was on an old slip of paper marked "emergency only" which he quickly tore from his wallet.

He punched the digits. A pause, then: "Beep-*beep-BEEP!*"—in ascending tones. A recorded message followed: "The number you have reached, *555-0113,* has been *disconnected....*"

"Aw—*fuck me!*" he cried.

Hoping he misdialed, he tried the number again. But got the same result.

He couldn't believe it. "*Mutha'-fuck!*" he shouted and slammed the phone—his hands shaking.

Martin remained motionless for nearly five minutes.

Then, numbly, he retrieved the quarter from the slot.

What now?... What was left?...

His gaze drifting upward along a telephone pole, Martin noticed a parks department's sign posted with an arrow.

With that, he took off, heading in the general direction of a retreat he knew not far away.

115.

This retreat was "Oakland Lake." And Oakland Lake, of course, was the "secret place," the sanctuary where he and Nikki had often met. It was also the refuge he would escape to alone, in his pre-Nikki school days.

It had been years since he'd approached the park from

the north end. Now, instead of the wide tear in the chain-link fence he remembered, there was an actual entrance with stairs in the center of the block.

He crossed into the park, mindful of each tied-edged, broadly placed step.

Inside, the sloping hills surrounding the lake were shadowed with grass and vegetation. The pin oaks loomed dark and full. Tonight the sky was cloudless and surprisingly clear, filled with a spread of stars and a huge, luminous moon.

At this hour, the park appeared completely deserted. In the ghostly light, Martin followed the asphalt path surrounding the water.

What were his thoughts? His associations, as he strolled around the lake?

In passing, he thought of his only remaining family by blood, his grandparents. Imagined them in Spain, on a night like this. Wondered how they were, if they were finally happier, now that they had their own lives away from the twin disappointments of Anna, their daughter, and Martin, their grandson. He had to wonder if they were any more content to finally be free of what their anarchic, "disrespectful" daughter had once called "the slave-driving, soul-crushing squeeze of America."

He thought of other things:

Friends. Those apart from Nikki.

He sighed... it wasn't that he *never had friends*.

Simply that those that he had had somehow drifted away.

Those from college? Gone.

Gone for years.

As those people, other "creative writing" majors were

predictably absorbed into the workforce after school, Martin felt himself more and more alone as the sole hold-out. It was something that right away he'd had in common with Nikki, this outsider status, this unwillingness to belong.

He hated running into old friends, former college bud-dies, who (themselves having long given up the "pretense" of the artistic life) would sharply ask him questions about his "writing career." And as the years went by, it grew more painful. "How were things?" "Lousy!" he wanted to tell them, but of course couldn't. "Published yet?" That was often the killer.

What could he say? What excuse could he give that wouldn't reflect badly on him?

Wasn't it easier to simply avoid the conversation, avoid seeing these people? Conveniently forget to return phone calls?

In part, of course, his alienation was due to his own pride, or shame. He could no longer tell which. But, mostly, he had long ago run out of excuses—things to tell these people.

And, as his former "artist friends" openly pursued *success*, launched yes *careers*, got married, started families, purchased their first real estate, he had even less reason to stay in contact with them. Martin was left behind, left to feel like some kind of adolescent relic, a renegade or a fool. Mostly, by virtue of his poverty and general powerless-ness, the truth was he felt as helpless and pitiful as a waif.

Those were often the times he'd wanted to give in, sur-render his soul. Or simply jump in front of the F train.

But then, very rarely, it happened that he might meet a kindred spirit, a fellow outsider, someone with enough conviction and inner strength—who agreed with his views, agreed with his notions of what was truly important in this life, someone who in effect managed to confirm the validity of his existence.

Someone like Nikki.

Nikki. Who he almost couldn't bear to think of now.

It was all so difficult!

He wanted to agree with his grandfather: "*La vida es una miseria!…*"

Leaving the trail at one point and taking to the trees (over crackling weeds), Martin eventually made his way up the hill to the quiet, half-buried rocks and tree stumps he'd sought out during his college years, often to rest and contemplate his future.

Of course, the familiarity of the location brought back all those memories: the cloistered world of books and literature. He thought of Hemingway, for some reason. Fitzgerald. Gertrude Stein. Ezra Pound. Paris of the '20s—all those bracing fantasies. He thought of Henry Miller, the outcast, the beggar; he thought of Charles Bukowski, the drunkard, the bum. Holy Kerouac, holy Burroughs, holy Ginsberg!

Fools. Saints. Sinners.

In the eyes of America: losers—one and all.

His imaginary family, those gathered around him when his own family was absent in spirit.

He thought of his early college years, and how he felt he possessed a secret, a gift that lay dormant, a talent that would one day burst forth, manifesting itself as dramatically as a pair of angel wings—wings that would take Martin to unimagined heights.

Seated for a while, gazing at the still lake, his view partly obscured by the trees, yes he dwelled again on those days, the high hopes he'd had for himself. From that vantage point, that vantage point in his life—anything seemed possible; the world seemed an open horizon, a wedding banquet freshly lain—he'd seen no reason he couldn't succeed in it—romantically, artistically.

"*Idiotez. Fantasías,*" his grandfather would grouse, reproving his impractical ambitions. And although Martin would insist of his work, his writing: "*¡Es muy importante!*"—precisely how it was important in the "real" world, he was unable to articulate, then as now.

Of course, the "real" world could be called into question itself.

"A *waste* of time!" his grandfather would argue. "*Vas a tirar la vida*—you'll throw away your life—for *what?*"

Martin rolled his eyes, annoyed that the old man could be so mundane.

How could he ever explain? Explain what was *inside* him?

To his grandfather, the world was a serious place. But wasn't art serious? More serious than commerce? More serious than SUVs? More serious than wide screen television sets? More serious than breast implants? Than liposuction? More serious than artificial tans and capped teeth?

His grandfather's ideal, of course, involved traditional values—abysmally *conventional* values. Based on the superficial, the material. Shortsighted and earthbound. Working selflessly to maintain a family unit, a "stable" life, respectability. *Not* to be a loner, a drifter. Strength came from adhering to the group, being a team player, not an individual, not in separating yourself from the pack. Above all was "*decencia.*"

But Martin had turned his back on all that, turned his

back on his family, too—what family he had left. In fact, he'd long ago considered them a detriment to his existence, to his artistic and spiritual growth.

As far as he was still concerned? *fuck materialism, fuck having a family, fuck a "stable" life*, and fuck *"security."* There was only art—and art only! His own mother would've understood that!

"*¡Vas a tirar la vida!*" his grandfather would protest. "You'll throw away your life. *Just like your mother!*"

Martin's face pressed against hers, his lips kissing her. *Smack!* Affectionately kissing her. *Smack! Smack!* Anna, *madrecita*, cringing. His voice laughing; light laughter passing between them, cascading, ringing like bells....

   "Emptiness,"
she said.
   "All emptiness
is open to me..."

  The Sky Is Barren.
   Dreams Are Useless.
Dissolution Rules.

116.

Martin remained on that slope, lost in a tangle of charged memories and daydreams until midnight, at which point, with some reluctance, he rose stiffly from his spot and carefully descended, clinging to deep-rooted weeds and tree branches on the way down. Once again, on the asphalt trail surrounding the lake, Martin decided to walk around the park, and did. Taking his time.

Past a raging chorus of crickets back at the north end
entrance, Martin wearily ascended the wide stairs in the
dark and straggled back to his parked Horizon.

After cranking the old bomb—these days it took a full
five minutes to warm up—Martin made a broken U-turn
on the block and drove up the street, slowing to a near
crawl outside of Nikki's place.

Nothing: the lights were out—there was no sign of her.
Martin felt sick at heart.

117.

That night, morbidly depressed, Martin tossed and
turned in bed, shifting from one awkward position to the
next.

Demons and dark thoughts tortured him until day-
break. In one half-dream, he saw his body being buried in
a mass grave at Potter's Field, in another he was naked and
smeared with shit outside of Barnes and Noble on Astor
Place, utterly invisible to pedestrians. Even to a passing
nun—who as it turned out bore the face of his kindly first-
grade teacher, Sister Rita Marie.

"Can't you see me, Sister!" Martin shouted.

No sound would leave his mouth.

The world would go on without him, like he'd never existed.

"Things just happen. Without reason. One person is
born. Another vanishes. No one knows why. Or has any
real say...."

At around 6:00 AM—harsh morning sun slicing through
his blinds—Martin gave up the pretense of trying to sleep

and readied himself for work. On autopilot, he showered, shaved and made lunch. With what he had left in his refrigerator, he fixed a semi-decent breakfast. Maybe after work he'd go grocery shopping.

At least, I still have a job, he thought. And, what's more, for once he'd be early!

118.

Oddly enough, that morning at work, Martin almost felt content.

He snatched the ringing phone: "'Ey, Marty here— Japan World! Howarya'?"

"*Aah,*" rasped the dispatcher, "no sense in complainin', y'know!"

At that Martin had to laugh. "Yeah. Yeah, I hear ya." Then shifting gears: "Got any freight for me?"

"Yep."

Martin noticed the blinking red light on his telephone. "Hang on," he said, hitting "hold," then the flashing button.

"Martin-san!" his boss said. "Come up to my office, please."

Martin replied, "I'm busy, now. Is it like, *really* important?"

"*Eh? Yes, 'important!' Come up, okay?"—Click!*

119.

Up in the main office the mood had dimmed. Suddenly, there was a pall in the air.

"Kim-san," the new temp, whom Martin was told avoided work at any cost, now had his head buried in an old ledger. Others were somberly pouring over files and

standard import documents, as if these papers had suddenly taken on an inordinate importance. Even Tani, the
Japanese woman who ran the office, remained absorbed in
what appeared to be yesterday's mail. Everyone seemed
preoccupied, too preoccupied to even look up and take
notice of his presence.

Martin joked aloud, "What, we having a *funeral* this
morning?"

No reply.

120.

Martin took a seat in the carpeted office.

The room was tastefully decorated, walls newly painted
ivory, hung with museum posters. The obligatory golf
clubs were propped in a corner. On the man's desk was a
framed portrait of his family: wife, three smiling children.
Also a signed baseball and a globe of the world with the
names in Japanese.

Haizu sat behind the desk, wearing an uneasy smile,
dressed in a tailored pinstripe suit with a silk maroon tie.

Martin? Basically he wore the same things he wore yesterday—and the day before that. A ratty T-shirt and a pair
of old jeans.

"Your eyes are red," was the first thing Haizu said to
him, trying to break the ice.

Martin shrugged. "Guess I didn't get much sleep last
night."

"Out late?"

"No. Just one of those nights, y'know. Couldn't sleep."

"Bad dreams?"

"You said it."

An uncomfortable pause followed. Nodding feebly,

eyes averted, Haizu seemed unsure of how to proceed. He heaved a weary sigh.

Martin had a sinking feeling: he could tell that this was not going to be just another empty discussion on employee/customer relations.

Opting for the sympathy angle, Haizu quietly began by mentioning his difficult position as the new head of the "troubled" New York branch. In a roundabout way, he enumerated the many problems he currently faced, the challenging decisions he was forced to make, and at length expounded on the unfortunate losses of company revenue in recent years. (Delicately skirting any mention of Tanaka and his now infamous role in it.) Next, came his long-winded explanation of the obvious necessity for the company at this point in its illustrious history of having to cut it losses, yes trim its roster, or—to use the more difficult American term—of having to "downsize." (The word pronounced with absolute, practiced clarity.)

Martin's gaze fell to the plush beige carpeting, newly installed—he felt his insides softening. Felt himself float away: out of body, out of mind.

"So you see," Haizu was saying. "Facing these difficult circumstances, the company can no longer *afford*—"

Losing patience, Martin cut in, "You saying I'm *fired?*— That it?"

Eyes wide, Haizu looked startled—as if Martin had kicked the chair from under him. Recovering, still a bit flushed, he painfully admitted, "Yes."

Martin nodded curtly. "That's all I wanna know." He took a deep breath, a final glance at the surrounding walls.

Then, without saying another word, without looking at his former boss, without hardly feeling his own legs beneath him, Martin moved with deliberate grace to the door, opened it, and walked from the room.

Passing through the wider office, all eyes now trained on him, Martin's final word was to the point:

"*Sayonara.*"

121.

Downstairs in the warehouse office—as he immediately set out to empty his desk—what was it he was feeling? Anger? Hostility? Bitterness?

No. Strangely, he felt none of that.

At this point, it seemed he felt ... nothing. He was oddly detached from it all. It was as if the whole scene had happened to someone else, some other unfortunate, and he was just another disinterested bystander.

"Bro, it wasn't *my* idea—you know that." Chaz stood nearby watching him pack his things.

Martin was sorting through folders he'd had in a bottom drawer.

"I tried to talk to him," insisted Chaz. "Tried to get him to change his mind."

Martin found an old *Beck* tape single. Held it up. "This yours or mine?"

Chaz squinted. "Must be yours." He went on, "Like I said, I tried to talk to him. Over and over. Man wouldn't listen."

In short order Martin blankly began to cop office supplies—openly toss them into his knapsack: a few new pencils, some BiC pens, several "stick it" pads.

Chaz said quietly, "What can I say, bro? This company's *fucked.*"

Martin continued to load his bag. "So you knew for a while?"

Chaz frowned. Stood awkward.

"Yeah, well." Martin zipped up his knapsack. He could tell Chaz felt awful about it. Guilty. "Fuck it, y'know. Just ... fuck it."

"Bro..."

Martin sighed, closing the drawers. "Nothing, man—don't even say it."

Chaz was still frowning. "I don't know *what* to say. All these years a' workin' together...."

Chaz had reached into his own desk for something. A dusky-green bottle. "Guess I been savin' this." It was cognac: *Remy-Martin*. "No time like the present, right?" He cracked the seal.

Setting up plastic cups on the copier machine, he poured out two generous shots. "Take home what's left, bro. For tonight."

For the first time since getting fired, Martin felt a real sadness. He was afraid if he thought about it too long he might lose it.

Chaz raised his cup. "Here's to"—he looked at the flag a moment: no—he scanned the rest of the office: nothing there worth toasting to. Finally: "Here's to gettin' drunk!"

They drank.

122.
And that was that....

Incredible how quickly things turned. All this time, it seemed, Martin had just been mindlessly adrift, never considering how things might change—or how to change them—and just like that his life was turned on its head, just like that he was out of his job.

Even more tragic? This could've happened six months ago, or six years into the future. In the end, it hardly seemed to matter.

"Like a joke without a punch line...."

Chaz stood in the open dock as Martin finished warming up his car.

He called out, "Bro, if you ever need anything!..."

Martin had no hard feelings. The truth was, the man had covered for him long enough. And if he hadn't considered it before, he thought it now: Chaz was a decent guy; there was no denying it.

Right there—*that* was the last image he had of him: the man standing tall, framed in the opened dock—Chaz, like a sentinel from another era, his hair flecked white, a vague look of regret on his face.

Just before Martin fully backed out of the lot, Chaz raised a hand—a final good-bye.

Martin faintly waved back.

"And that's that...."

123.

At long last, back at home in Jackson Heights, Martin remained in a stupor for hours.

No one to talk to, no one to call—what else could he do to fill the yawning emptiness but absently watch TV and take the occasional pull of *Remy-Martin,* while replaying the day's events in his mind? In large part, he marveled at the frightful speed of it all:

Again he saw himself in Haizu's office, then emptying his desk. Then waving good-bye to Chaz.

That quick. That final.

Flicking from channel to channel, one talk show seemed like the next. The host appeared deeply concerned with the "important" issue at hand, until cheering up right before announcing another commercial break.

At last, putting down the cognac, Martin flicked off the tube, rose and stood in the room. Not quite sure what to think, or do with himself.

Pausing before his bookcase, he blankly pulled out two Bukowski books: *Love Is A Dog From Hell, You Get So Alone at Times*—then eyed the framed photograph of Nikki.

Nearby was the picture of his mother.

Disregarding the books, he scooped up the frame now, examining the old photo in the light:

His mother: *the poetess....*

Not a bad looking woman, he thought objectively. *I'd date her.* This was the period in her life when she had cut her hair short. She had Martin's features—or he had hers—except that her face was rounder, softer. Her nose was more delicate than his, too—*pretty*—and her lips fuller, frowning slightly in the shot. What else could the photograph tell him?—what meaning could be extracted? *Speak up, loca. Don't just look at me.* Then he saw it. Right then, looking carefully into her eyes, Martin believed he could recognize her disillusionment and pain.

Allowing his mind to drift, he thought of his mother, then: thought of them both together, cherishing what faint memories he had of her....

Like once, being called to the kitchen table and a word-less dinner of *bacalao* and potatoes, a meal he truly hated—his mother intensely scribbling some corrections on a recent poem, her fist crinkling the top of the page. Bored, Martin repeatedly asking aloud if he could take a ride down the dumbwaiter, afterward—the dumbwaiter which he realized had long been sealed and painted over because of the roaches, yet which remained (for all its imagined potential for adventure) a source of endless boyish curiosity for him.

Not hearing his request the second time because of her impenetrable gloom, he repeated it yet again, this time screaming it!

"*¡Pero que!*" his mother hollered back. "*¡Eres idiota!?*"

He recalled how five minutes later, unable to bear the silence any longer, he then impishly picked up his *bacalao* and with a look of disdain casually winged it across the room where it fell—*flop!*—behind the refrigerator and stayed: roach food. To his chagrin his mother not even noticing!

"*¡Estoy ABU-RRIDO! (—I'm bo-red!)*" he moaned aloud. With his fork then, launching bits of boiled potato at his mom as she continued to write and ignore him.

"*¡Pero, que te pasa, hoy! (—What's wrong with you, today!)*" she scowled, at one point springing from her end of the table to chase him, Martin cackling and calling her "*cabra,*" a goat—and snatching her loose, precious pages of poetry! "*¡Mierda!*"—his mom shrieking, tearing after him, "*¡Demonio! (—Devil!) ¡Cuando te coja! (—When I catch you!)*"

In all honesty, Martin preferring a spanking, a sound *thrashing* to being treated like a nonentity, to being invisible and perpetually ignored....

Now Martin reached to the top shelf of his bookcase, moving some papers, locating a ragged manila envelope. Taking it across the room, he leaned back against the windowsill.

Suddenly he had a yearning to look at more photographs.

There weren't many in his possession, maybe a dozen. Reaching into the envelope, he pulled them out, started through them:

First photo—showed Martin as a toddler before a pink frosted birthday cake with two candles. On each side of him (present in body but not in mind) his well-meaning, dutiful grandparents.

Second—a Polaroid. Showed preschooler-Martin, seated on a faded faux-Persian carpet, blankly facing the camera. A skinny silver Christmas tree behind him. Again in the background, like unsmiling ghosts, his grandparents.

Third—Martin, wearing a clip-on tie, standing stiffly in front of his parochial school. Shading his eyes from the bleaching sunlight, next to his tired grandfather.

Fourth—a large, creased school picture. Third grade. Small for his age, Martin front left, in wrinkled shirt and tie, shoulders slumped, eyes down.

Fifth—age nine, Martin beside a slim Spanish woman. (Of the few pictures taken together, this would be their last.) Wearing a floral print dress and cork platform shoes, his mother, Anna, is crouched near him, almost smiling.

This photograph, dog-eared and cracked.

There were more, but he couldn't go on.

He tucked them away finally, sat unmoving, felt the sun on his neck. Closed his eyes a moment.

What next?

Feeling a need to weep without any tears rising to the surface, Martin could no longer resist the urge to try Nikki's number again, so he dropped to the floor and dialed.

On the fourth ring, her machine clicked on.

There was *no point*.

Martin hung up the phone.

With that, he spiritlessly got to his feet, put the manila envelope back in its place, and went quietly to his open sofa to take a nap.

God, he was tired.

124.

He dreamt he was lost in a deep, circuitous East Village dive, like a long sewer. No matter which way he turned, he encountered the same dank, mist-shrouded passageways.

Open-mouthed, Martin felt himself suddenly stumbling. Trying to escape. Heart tight in his chest, he was swaying, breathing heavily—almost about to fall—when he heard a distant alarm: *ringing, ringing....*

Martin had no idea what time it was.

He was in total darkness, uncradling the phone:

"Hello?"

The voice said, "Hi!"

Martin snapped on the nearby clip-light.

"Marty? Are you there?"

He remained silent for nearly a minute.

"I'm here."

"I just got in," Nikki informed him.

Was he still dreaming?

"From where?" he asked.

"Florida," she told him. "*Miami.*"

Still trying to get his bearings, he rubbed his eyes: "*Where?*"

"'*Mom's house,*" she finally explained.

"*Nik,*" he spoke up, "you just leave without telling me?"

"Don't be angry." She let out a sigh. "I just, y'know, needed to take a break."

He sat up stiffly. "You just leave for a whole week *without* telling me?"

"Marty, it was *four* days."

"'Four'?" He paused to think. Was it possible?

"I left Monday and today is Friday," she pointed out.

Martin thought about it another moment, vaguely counting the days on his fingers, suddenly embarrassed.

"I guess I wasn't thinking straight," she said. "You know that desperate feeling, that feeling of wanting to lose yourself, sometimes?"

His spirits were starting to lift finally. "I know that feeling."

"Well, it was like that—everything had taken a bizarre turn."

"I know," he said, almost laughing. "Believe me, I know the feeling."

He was almost afraid to ask the next question.

"Nik, what about ... *you know?*—"

"The 'reunion'?" she finished his sentence. "Postponed, Marty."

"—How's that?"

"Postponed," she repeated. "Postponed *indefinitely.*"

Martin was startled. Asking finally: "Meaning?"

"Off. *Over*, Marty." She said it like it was old news.

"So." He sat up all the way. Shook his head. "—Simple as that, that's it, then?"

"Yep."

Martin still had trouble believing it.

Nikki explained, "She's gone. Had enough. Packed off to San Diego with a friend."

"She went *west* and you went *south*," Martin said.

"Something like that."

Martin asked, "So—what brought this on?"

"Listen, Marty. Wasn't gonna bring this up. Thought maybe it was corny or something. But I want to, now...." She took a deep breath. "I had this *dream*. About you. About us. *Don't laugh*." She settled into it: "It started where we were both in this jungle. Both floating on giant lily pads. On a huge river, I don't know where. At first we were enjoying it, just drifting along, taking it as it came. Laughing, side by side. But, then, things changed. The current began to pick up, get rougher and faster—more wild. And at one point you were dragged away. It made me *so sad*. Because I couldn't reach you. And soon it got so I couldn't even *see* you anymore. And soon you were gone. Forever." She confessed, "I actually woke up crying..."

Martin felt a tightness in his chest.

They both let a long moment pass.

"Marty?"

"Yeah?"

She laughed on her end.

"What?" Martin whispered.

"Can't we talk about it?"

At last he had to smile. "Right now, y'mean?—Tonight?"

She took another breath. *"Why not?"*

Glossary of Spanish Terms and Phrases
(as they appear in the book)

p. 2 - *pendejo!* = idiot, dolt, lowlife!

p. 5 - *cabrón!* = creep! (literally: "he-goat!")

p. 5 - *¿Es todo?* = That all?

p. 7 - *¡Malparido!* = (Ill born) Bastard!

p. 9 - *Que tonto* = How stupid (What a dope; dunce)

p. 9 - *chicas* = gals (chicks)

p. 12 - *borracho* = drunk

p. 16 - *¡Mierda!* = Shit!

p. 29 - *¡Coño!* = Devil's ass!

p. 36 - *¿Qué quieres de mi ahora, Loca?* = Whatcha' want from me now, Mad-woman?

p. 38 - *madrecita* = (lil') mother (as in "mommy")

p. 38 - *¡Hala, vaca!* = There, cow!

p. 39 - *¡Bájalo!* = Turn it down! (Lower it!)

p. 39 - *¿Pero qué eres, IDIOTA!?* = (But) what are you, an IDIOT!?

p. 39 - *¡Cochino!* = Pig! (in the more depraved human sense)

p. 39 - *¡Si no fuera por ti!* = If it weren't for you!

p. 40 - *¿Qué haces? ¿Pero dónde está Mami?* = Whatcha' doing? (But) where is Mommy?

p. 48 - *Que maravilla* = How marvelous (sweet)

p. 53 - *¿Y hoy?* = And today?

p. 53 - *este día* = this day

p. 62 - *Muchacho* = Kid; Lad

p. 63 - *¡Que ostia!* = What a bugger! (This blows!) Also, *Hostia*: (religious) host (used sacrilegiously)

p. 76 - *Vaya!* = Well! (Whoa!) Indeed!

p. 77 - *¿Y ahora?* = And now?

p. 82 - *¡Carajo!* = (Fucking) Hell!

p. 83 - *mija* = (affectionate term) dear, sweety, sweetheart, love

p. 87 - *¡Pura Mierda!* = Pure shit!

p. 91 - *Perdóneme* = Forgive me (Pardon me)

p. 99 - *Ahora tú* = Now you

p. 146 - *¡Así!* = All right! (Like that!)

p. 160 - *bruja* = witch

p. 204 - *Dios* = God

p. 240 - *¡Que pasa!* = What's up! (What's happening!)

p. 247 - *¡Al diablo!* = To the devil; Devil take it!

p. 248 - *La unica, la unica mujer* = The (one and) only, the only (as in "unique") woman

p. 257 - *Idiotez. Fantasías.* = Idiocy. Fantasies.

p. 267 - *bacalao* = codfish (sold in dried, salted sheets)

p. 267 - *¡Pero que!* = But what!

p. 267 - *¡Eres idiota!* = (Are) you an idiot!

Author Interview

Jun Da: *In the cut and dry—sometimes, very "dry"—world of publishing, it's all about genre and category. Where would you say The Losers' Club fits in? How would you categorize the book?*

Richard Perez: *The novel is comic—by that, I mean a comedy—in the classic sense. It has a happy ending, which of course is a big no-no in "serious" writing. I think it was Ernest Hemingway who said, "Every true story ends in death." But he was just trying to sound like a modernist when he said that. Anyway, I guess that makes me a less-than-serious author.*

JD: *So the category?*

RP: *You might say it falls under both romance and comedy, although I didn't intentionally set out to write a "genre" book; the story evolved—then evolved, again—and took its own shape. It diminishes the book to some extent to toss it under a simple category. To say "romance," or even "lad lit." I hate all those terms; they're just fake marketing terms.*

JD: *The first question that comes to mind about the novel, of course, is the title. What did you mean by it? Everyone asks this.*

RP: *Well, there are some obvious clues about its meaning (pages 52 and 257 of the book). But, aside from that, it just seemed appropriate to the material. It's also a play on the culture and time depicted in the book: the pre-9/11 era, the looser, more playful 1990s. (Remember the popular Beck tune from that time?). Also, the story, as most everyone knows, is about an unpublished writer who is addicted to the personals. So he's what you might tongue-in-cheek* *call a loser on various counts: he's a "failure" professionally (which is not uncommon among writers, poets, painters, et al.), a "loser" in love, since he can't seem to maintain a meaningful, long-term relationship (again, not uncommon with artists: a side-effect of the calling), and he's in effect spiritually lost. The main character of The Losers' Club is essentially looking for an emotional and spiritual connection, like so many of us—and not just with his lost family, although that's obviously part of it—but a connection with the world at large. As I see it, his predicament, his loneliness arises because of (a) his calling (which keeps him in a personal and financial hole), (b) his disassociation with a "supply and demand" culture, the American culture of materialism. He feels he knows what he should be doing, "following his bliss" (to quote Joseph Campbell), being true to himself, being creative—writing—and yet the wider culture conspires against this and, for it, treats him like, well, a loser. Now if he found a way to make big money doing the same thing—that would be different. Success is a measuring stick in abnormal psychology—as it is in our culture at large. What determines if you're crazy or not—boils down to this: whether you make money doing it, whether you can "move product."*

JD: *On a personal level what is the book about?*

RP: *He's searching not only for love—through the personals—but searching for who he is: his roots, you might say. Culturally and spiritually. He lost his culture (his heritage) and family at an early age, which left a deep emotional and psychic hole in his life. Is he his mother's son? He still hasn't totally come to grips with who she was—and with what happened to her, which remains purposefully obscure. He's almost re-treading her fatal steps—taking a deliberate path to permanent obscurity, her path—in an attempt to connect with her. As a boy he hates poetry because his*

mother wrote poetry, but as an adult he finds himself not only writing it, but in effect sacrificing his life for it. I find that theme end-
lessly fascinating: what lengths a person will go to connect with a
disassociated part of themselves, what lengths a person will go to
please an "internalized" parent, if you will.

JD: While being lively and funny, the book also has an odd,
dreamy—some might say, fatalistic view of life.

RP: Well, the main character, I guess, is a little bit of a fatalist
and a romantic and, yes, even a masochist—which frankly, as I mention elsewhere in the book (page 97) are qualities of most creative
people. Artists are not people who treat themselves very well. But in
Martin's case, he's still in mourning for his absent family, and he has
virtually no friends, except Nikki. This hole—this alienation he
feels—is a need he tries to fill by immersing himself in the cultural
life of the East Village, the club and bar scene, and surrounding himself with other "misfits" and, of course, indulging in the downtown
personal ads, which takes him deeper into those lively, noisy, and
dark recesses.

JD: What's your obsession with the East Village, anyway?

RP: I can't tell you. Like the character in the book, I've actually
sold my own collected poetry on St. Marks Place. I've been to the
clubs and bars while they were around, been involved in a lot of
craziness with a lot of odd people, had my heart broken, etc. But,
ultimately, the East Village represents some kind of fantasy world for
me, which I've recreated in the novel. A place of reinvention—physically and psychologically. In some ways, a dream world. The East
Village depicted in The Losers' Club is not the East Village of real
life—it's the East Village of my mind.

JD: *Like Ferlinghetti's "Coney Island of the Mind" from the Henry Miller quote?*

RP: *That's it: the East Village is my Coney Island, it's what Alice—in her need to belong—finds down the rabbit hole, which is what's inside her own psyche. And speaking of Henry Miller—he's a major influence on me, too. Not stylistically, but spiritually. He's kinda like my spiritual creative writing teacher.*

JD: *What precisely have you learned from Henry Miller?*

RP: *Just that, it's okay to be passionate about life. I see Henry Miller as being in the Transcendentalist tradition—utterly "trusting" and open to experience.*

JD: *What other authors do you admire?*

RP: *As far as inspiration? Bukowski on one end and Nabokov on the other.*

JD: *Talk about polar opposites.*

RP: *Yet both authors are outsiders.*

JD: *It's surprising to hear you mention Nabokov.*

RP: *Is it? Lolita remains probably my favorite novel. I love the first part of the book, in particular. And I make references to it in this novel. When Nikki first kisses Martin (page 26), it's on the ear, just as Lolita first kisses Humbert (page 133, Lolita [Vintage International publishers]). And there are echoes of Lolita all* *throughout The Losers' Club: like, Oh Nikki: Oh Lolita; in my mind I saw the parallels of a kind of doomed romance. These parallels though have been sort of scrambled in my subconscious and, in some cases, not even deliberate.*

JD: *Now Bukowski was a big influence on you, obviously. He's sort of the fatherly "ghost" or mentoring spirit of the book.*

RP: *Shades of Obi-Wan. It's a great conceit, a bit theatrical: rather than have the character talk to himself, which quickly gets dull, why not have him talking to a projection of his own psyche? I like that idea; it's always fun. William Kennedy also does it quite a bit in Ironweed.*

About Bukowski—he was—and is—even now, a big spiritual influence on me. Whenever I lose confidence in myself, feel like, "what's the point?" I turn to Bukowski and find solace. Bukowski addresses isolation, disappointment—and, of course, rejection. And he's not intimidating like some authors are. Reading Bukowski makes you want to write. In some ways you think, "if this fucking drunk can do it, so can this fucking drunk (me)." (Laughing.) "I love playful writers—talented authors, who—because of their great sense of humor—make me feel at ease. I've already mentioned Henry Miller. His Paris books are important: Tropic of Cancer, Capricorn and Black Spring. Other books I love are Fear and Loathing in Las Vegas by Hunter S. Thompson and The Fan Man by William Kotzwinkle. Goofball books that take a leap of faith—that have energy and are funny. Humor is really important to me. And I don't find a whole lot of humor in most recent books of "serious" literary merit. I used to despair and force myself to read all sorts of things that were considered "important"—that The New York Times Book Review called "essential reading." But now I only read books that I want to read—and I stopped reading The New York Times! Don't let anyone tell you what you should be reading—or let anyone define your culture!

JD: *Getting back to Bukowski—why do you think he's so reviled—or simply ignored—in Academia?*

RP: *'Cause he's blunt. He refuses to be "formal" or "genteel"; he's a vulgarian. He shows up at your tie-and-jacket affair wearing a soiled T-shirt and dirty underwear. He doesn't give a fuck. And not giving a fuck—not caring "what others think"—is really important to an artist: it liberates you creatively. And until you cross that psychological line, you won't accomplish much. Because you can't be self-conscious; you need to create a safe place to play and lose yourself in the moment. I mean, Bukowski is very punk. And he inspires me the way punk rockers of their era inspired musicians who didn't feel secure enough to make noise because they weren't technically "proficient." Bukowski gives you honesty and he gives you shit. You pick and choose. You join in and want to fuck around. Bukowski is important because, for me, he challenged the status quo, he redefined what a writer is "supposed to be." A writer doesn't need to be from New England, or a refined white southerner. Or need an MFA from NYU. A writer can be anyone. Any bum can stake a claim to it; stand up and howl.*

JD: *Is it for more obvious "technical reasons" that Bukowski is dismissed?*

RP: *You can't apply the same criteria to Bukowski as you would say, Nabokov. It's like comparing a folk artist to a fine-art painter. Folk art falls under the province of "outsider art," which is definitely where Bukowski belongs, while fine-art falls under the most* *established rules of academia. One artist (Bukowski) was self-taught, spottily educated, while the other (Nabokov) was highly trained and hyper-cultured, a university lecturer and professor. There's a snobbishness that runs both ways: on the part of the more genteel, academic-based side, (fans of magazines like The New Yorker or Atlantic Monthly) to denigrate or ignore the marginalized work of outsider artists, like Bukowski or Fante or Hubert Selby Jr. The other side of it is people who love Bukowski—and denigrate all "serious" literature in the same way that punk rockers spit at classically trained musicians. Another consideration is that Bukowski represents a lost strain in American literature: the proletariat tradition. In many ways he's writing for the underclass just as writers in the 1930s did, authors like Tom Kromer (Waiting for Nothing), Meridel Le Sueur (The Girl)—these weren't exactly "polished" writers, either. It's a point of view that needs to be appreciated. And we need to make room in the American "literary canon" for outsider, disfranchised artists like these, if it's to be truly representative. "Outsider authors" should be part of every college curriculum—and I wouldn't be surprised if most middle-class or lower middle-class students would relate more to these artists.*

JD: *Any other author influences, apart from Nabokov and Bukowski?*

RP: *Sartre, believe it or not. Mentioned directly by Nikki when she's teasing Martin.*

JD: *Early in the book (chapter 6, page 21).*

RP: *Sartre's novel, Nausea, somehow lodged itself in my mind many years ago. In fact, right at the beginning of Nausea (page 2, Nausea, [New Directions publishers]), there's a part where the pro-*

tagonist mentions watching children playing with "ducks and drakes," and wanting, like them, "to throw a stone into the sea." In my version the protagonist tries to skip a stone; in Sartre's version, the protagonist doesn't even risk it: he just drops the rock, walks away—to the ridicule and laughter of the kids playing there. Another part that stuck with me, a line that I remember is, "I don't know how to take advantage of the occasion. I walk at random, calm and empty, under the wasted sky." (page 70, Nausea) A kind of Prufrock/T.S. Eliot thing. Another line from Nausea I recall is "Every existing thing is born without reason, prolongs itself out of weakness and dies by chance." (page 133, Nausea) There are echoes of that line in The Losers' Club, particularly when Lola is talking to Martin (page 102)—and at the end of the book .... Elsewhere I read that Paul Schrader reread Nausea, too, right before working on Taxi Driver—and it shows. Schrader read Sartre and Thomas Wolfe. "God's Lonely Man" is actually a quote of Wolfe's. (Check out The Hills Beyond.) In my novel, the phrase becomes "God's Lonely Woe-man." Taxi Driver was an important early inspiration for The Losers' Club, because (a) the film is about loneliness—particularly loneliness in New York City, (b) the film was actually shot in the East Village, the location where my book mostly takes place (on 13th Street primarily, where the character of Lola resides). And, of course, Schrader also wrote and directed Mishima, another one of my all-time favorite films, which I also directly allude to in the book.

JD: We're running out of space, here. Any closing words? Any advice to authors out there?

RP: Not really. Read what you want, write what you want, make up your own rules. Stay alive. And don't forget to laugh. Laughter is more important than sex!

Book Discussion Topics

1. What is the significance of the title, *The Losers' Club*? And—taking into account certain specific clues (found on pages 52 and 257)—how does the author seem to define the peculiarly American concept of *"the loser"*?

2. In what ways might the main character be perceived as a *"loser"*?

3. Discuss the themes of loss in the novel, specifically as it pertains to Martin's immediate family, his friends.

4. To what extent have Martin's deliberate life choices shaped his outlook on life and limited his present opportunities?

5. Discuss the ways in which the main character's expectations for his life now clash with the stark reality he finds himself living.

6. Discuss the one (or two) ghost character(s) in the book that may be central to Martin's life and his personal history.

7. Discuss what effect Martin's mother may have had on his life: (a) her influence in shaping his interest in writing, (b) his personal and romantic instability.

8. Discuss the concepts of abandonment and regret and how they relate to The Losers' Club. How may certain abandonment issues be central to the main character's life and outlook?

9. How important are the main character's ethnic roots to him? How does it seem to contribute to (or detract from) his social world and how he perceives it? How does it contribute to his isolationism?

10. How important are dreams in the book (pages 17, 35, 53, 220, 260, 270)—both in getting to know the character and—technically—in advancing the narrative?

11. *How does Martin view the process of trying to become a published author? How has the market so far reacted to his work?*

12. *How does Nikki's presence contribute to Martin's life? How may they be seen as equals?*

13. *Discuss the notion of "romantic outcasts"—and how it may play into the mythology of bohemian life.*

14. *Discuss other books that cast artists as romantic heroes—and those relevant to The Losers' Club.*

Related Reading:

A Moveable Feast by Ernest Hemingway

Howl by Allen Ginsberg

Tropic Of Cancer by Henry Miller

On The Road by Jack Kerouac

A Working Stiff's Manifesto by Iain Levison

"Inside the Whale" an essay by George Orwell

The Happiest Man Alive: A Biography Of Henry Miller
by Mary V. Dearborn

Play The Piano Drunk ... by Charles Bukowski

A Fan's Notes by Frederick Exley

Revolutionary Road by Richard Yates

[East Village street art attributed to Richard Hambleton]

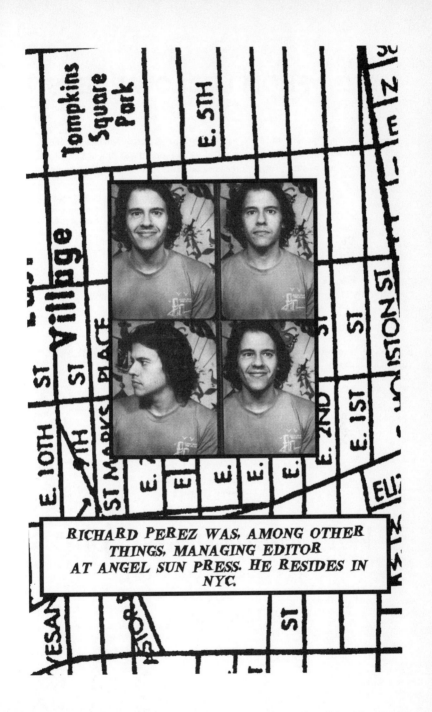

RICHARD PEREZ WAS, AMONG OTHER
THINGS, MANAGING EDITOR
AT ANGEL SUN PRESS. HE RESIDES IN
NYC.

ALSO **FROM LUDLOW PRESS!**

"Funny, hip, sad, and very, very smart, this superbly written novel
tells a story with which all of us can identify in this age
of computers and information overload. This is truly an 'epic quest,'
an often hilarious, sometimes heartbreaking
search for peace and solace and ordinary human happiness."
—**Tim O'Brien**

"Tom Grimes is a unique and enthralling novelist, and one of the best
writers of dialogue we have.
WILL@epicqwest.com reads like Pynchon's Crying of Lot 49
told by Holden Caufield. A brilliant, funny, and ultimately moving book."
—**Thom Jones**

"I'm happy to report that Tom Grimes has written another terrific book."
—**Denis Johnson**

"This book is stupid funny, intravenously hilarious."
—**Dagoberto Gilb**

"*WILL@epicqwest.com* is a work of golden wit and narrative drive. The best
futurism and folkism together."
—**Barry Hannah**

*WILL@epicqwest.com**
(a medicated memoir)
by
Tom Grimes

*It's not only a book but a website!

WILL@epicqwest.com

(a medicated memoir)

Tom Grimes

PRAISE **FOR TOM GRIMES!**

"At times meditative, at times funny and action-packed, Grimes's prose curves in an arc that traverses the distance from clear to piercing."
—**Ann Beattie**

"A remarkably substantial writer."
—**Tom McGuane**

"Awfully good. Smart. Fast. Sensational, in fact."
—**Joy Williams**

"Tom Grimes ... calls to mind the writing of many of the bad boys of contemporary American literature—Kurt Vonnegut, Thomas Pynchon, Ishmael Reed and T. C. Boyle."
—**Reginal McKnight**

"Funny, smart, dreamy ... brilliant, exact and surreal."
—**Charles D'Ambrosio**

"Eerie and brilliant ... Tom Grimes is our new visionary."
—**Chris Offutt**

"Grimes's voice speaks to the spirit and his vision stretches the mind."
—**Boston Globe**

"Transcendent in its own right for its breathtaking set pieces, its dissection of media marketing run brilliantly amok, its elegiac depiction of the sad, last fruits of class warfare. Grimes's deft probing of philosophy is leavened by a talent for quick, biting humor ... [and] his talent for the breathtaking phrase, the arresting word, brings exhilaration to page after page."
—**Philadelphia Inquirer**

"Grimes is a natural ... renders the afflictions of adolescence in both unique and universal terms."
—**The New York Times Book Review**

"Grimes shows an eye for evoking ... a tormented family on the short end of the American dream ... while making believable a capacity for compassion and forgiveness."
—**The Chicago Tribune**

"Pungent with the lunatic language of consumer-driven tabloid America ... Grimes makes a quantum leap into Delillo land."
—**Kirkus Reviews**

"[His work] ... is so well written that you want there to be more: more pages, more unexpected allusions, more pleasing insights.... One can only hope that there is more Tom Grimes in the offing."
—**West Coast Review of Books**

Tom Grimes is the author of the novels *A Stone of The Heart, Season's End*, and *City of God*, the plays *Spec* and *New World*, and the fiction anthology, *The Workshop: Seven Decades From The Iowa Writers Workshop*. His work has been named a *New York Times Notable Book of the Year,* a *New & Noteworthy Paperback*, and an *Editor's Choice pick;* it has won three *Los Angeles Dramalogue Awards*, been awarded a *James Michener Fellowship,* and has been selected for the *Barnes & Noble Discover* series. He now directs the MFA Program in Creative Writing at Southwest Texas State University.

WINNER OF THE 2004 ULYSSES AWARD!

WILL@epicqwest.com

ISBN: 0-9713415-7-5

Distributed by Biblio

To *order:*
Phone (*toll free*):1-800-462-6420

Ludlow Press Books

Distributed by
Biblio
(a division of NBN)
To order books:
Phone (toll free): 1-800-462-6420
FAX (toll free): 1-800-338-4550
Email: custserv@nbnbooks.com

....

The Losers' Club
"Complete Restored Edition!"
ISBN-10: 0-9713415-5-9
ISBN-13: 978-0-9713415-5-5
Korean translation available from
Humandom
Turkish translation available from
Say Yayinlari

WILL@epicqwest.com
ISBN 0-9713415-7-5

....

Order Now!
Amazon.com / B&N.com / Powells.com